Rachel
Beloved of God

By Agnus Scott Kent

Joyce Nolt
Manheim, Pa.

Rachel
Beloved of God

Cover art and illustrations
By Lucille Good

From an old source - 1938
Revised 2008
Printed in USA

For more copies:
Joyce E. Nolt
1593 Lancaster Rd.
Manheim, Pennsylvania 17545

ISBN: 978-0-9790983-2-1

Prologue

Rachel

Beloved of God

The question has frequently been asked, "Is this story true?" The answer is, "Yes and no." The "Rachel of this story is a fictitious composite of three actual Jewish women. Max has his prototype in an actual Jewish husband.

Another composite picture is that of Violet Hamilton - the Gentile missionary to the Jews. She is a blending in her character and experiences of three other missionaries.

The incident at the Hebrew Hospital of Santa X is identical with the experience of a young Jewess, who openly confessed Christ.

For many Jews, to become a christian means suffering. Sometimes suffering to an extent that others may not realize. In some instances Jewish confession of the Lord Jesus Christ involves the loss of everything life holds most dear. But like "Rachel" some Jews today are counting all things but loss for the excellency of Christ Jesus their Lord.

Table of Content

Chapter I	*A Jewish Wedding*	11
Chapter II	*A Mother in Israel*	22
Chapter III	*Eden Amid the Ghetto*	32
Chapter IV	*Eden Invaded*	50
Chapter V	*Eden Disquieted*	66
Chapter VI	*Eden Desolated*	82
Chapter VII	*Light Amid the Darkness*	102
Chapter VIII	*For His Dear Name's Sake*	121
Chapter IX	*False Shepherd's of Israel*	147
Chapter X	*True Shepherd's of Israel*	166
Chapter XI	*The Underneath Peace*	183
Chapter XII	*Eden Restored*	204

Chapter I.

A Jewish Wedding

"What therefore God hath joined together,
let not man put asunder."—Matthew 19:6.

It was five o'clock of a Sunday evening—the last day in December. Twilight was deepening. Through a swirling snow-flurry the lighted street cars and the headlights of a rushing stream of motors gleamed dazzlingly. The holiday spirit of the Christmas week was in the very breeze, and had penetrated everywhere. Even in several of the little Jewish shops the windows were gay with holly wreaths and festoons of Christmas greens.

In the heart of the great Ghetto of New York City, on Upper Clinton Street, an excited crowd was gathering before the closed doors of a synagogue. Impatiently the men on the upper doorstep pounded on the panels, demanding entrance. One by one the motor cars, from shabby jitney taxis to luxurious limousines, drew up beside the curb and discharged their passengers, grave Jewish fathers with long, solemn-looking coats and short black beards; dapper Jewish youths with heavy ulsters, and derby hats cocked nonchalantly over one ear; Jewish women, some in humble, unfashionable apparel and others elegantly attired in satins and laces and furs, but all alike brilliant with cosmetics and with jewels, whether real or imitation; dear old Jewish grandmothers, their gay shawls wrapped tightly about their heads and shoulders; and lovely, dark-eyed Jewish children.

At length a handsome motor car bedecked with white satin ribbons appeared in view amid a clanging of bells and a shrieking of auto horns. An eager shout went up from the crowd.

"The bride! The bride! It's Rachel! It's Rachel!"

But a quick murmur of disappointment followed. It was not the bride. It was, however, her bridesmaids; and as they emerged from the car another shout went up to greet them:

"Look! Look! It's Rachel's bridesmaids!"

"There's Rose and Goldie!"

"And Becky and Yetta and Sarah!"

"Hello there, Miriam! Where's Rachel?"

"O my, but don't they look grand!"

The six young Jewesses did indeed present a striking picture as they stood there upon the snowy sidewalk with the feathery flakes falling thickly all about them. Rich-skinned and dark-eyed, their natural loveliness was enhanced by their bright, vari-colored chiffon frocks which fluttered gaily in the wind, as the girls, with much merriment, tried ineffectually to wrap their evening coats about them. The snowflakes clustered rapidly on their dark hair, covered only with lacy scarves. Their voices rang through the frosty twilight in silvery laughter.

When the arrival of the bridesmaids was shouted through the keyhole, the doors of the synagogue swung open suddenly and the crowd, bridesmaids and all, poured in. The six girls were extricated with difficulty and led into an anteroom, while the guests rushed excitedly down the aisles of the auditorium to find the choicest seats. In an incredibly short time the synagogue was filled to capacity. Late comers, invited and uninvited, crowded into the gallery or stood around the walls.

For the next three-quarters of an hour the guests relieved their impatience by exchanges of friendly greeting, by an appraising scrutiny of "who were who" and by a minute inspection of the simple but charming floral decorations. A restless motion and a ceaseless low hum of voices buzzed through the synagogue, accentuated from time to time by audible exclamations:

"Come back here, Rosie, you'll lose your seat!"

"Sit down in front there!"

"No, it's taken! I'm saving this place for my uncle!"

"Haven't they come yet? Where's Rachel?"

The wedding was scheduled for half-past five. At last, a few moments before seven o'clock the organist, who had been softly improvising on the keys, burst suddenly into the Lohengrin. A murmur of tensest excitement seethed through the auditorium.

"She's here! She's here! Rachel's here. They're coming! Look! They're coming!"

The large double doors at the rear of the synagogue opened wide, and the beautiful wedding procession started. Slowly down the long aisle it came to the high dais—over which was spread the red-velvet canopy embossed with the Jewish *Mogen Dovid*—which was raised directly in front of the altar.

At the head of the procession walked, with distinguished mien, the foremost *Rav* of the New York Ghetto—Rabbi Mordecai Moses—impressive in his long black silken robes, his flowing gray beard and earlocks, and his high silk hat. Behind him, also in the long rabbinical garments and the high silk hats, followed the assisting rabbi and the cantor. Gravely they mounted the carpeted steps and took their places upon the dais facing the assembled guests.

All eyes were eagerly strained as, following the three rabbis, and walking between his mother on the right hand and—his father being dead—his eldest brother on the left, came next in turn the bridegroom—Max Kalinsky.

Very pale he looked beneath his high silk hat, with the expansive white silk shirt-front, and the large white rosebud in his buttonhole. He looked, too, so slight and boyish—frail almost when one contrasted him with his brother Jacob's florid robustness, or with his mother's purple-velveted rotundity and self-possession. Deborah Kalinsky was nothing if not self-possessed. She rose above every occasion always; and to-night, at the marriage of the youngest of her live sons, she towered. The bridegroom himself was entirely eclipsed.

Next in the procession came six tiny flower-girls attired in fluffy yellow frocks. Like dainty butterflies they looked as they bobbed cunningly up and down, strewing roses in the pathway from graceful baskets hanging on their chubby arms.

And then, as the cantor, in his rich tenor voice, sang gloriously the Jewish marriage song, the six charming bridesmaids, each one escorted by a groomsman, followed in their rainbow-tinted gowns amid a wealth of flowers. Each bridesmaid carried in her right hand a lighted candle. As they came to appointed places in the aisle they stood at even intervals from one another and, upon a given signal, they suddenly raised their bouquets aloft in their left hands. The groomsmen standing opposite them seized the vari-colored satin streamers; and thus was formed a candle-lighted, rose-strewn, floral archway through which the bride would pass to meet her husband.

A moment of breathless suspense and then—a swelling

murmur of delight as she at last appeared in view within the doorway.

"Rachel! Rachel!" In suppressed excitement a hundred voices passed her name along. Every eye was turned upon the archway in admiring wonder as the lovely little Jewish bride passed slowly through it to the altar.

Rachel Mendelssohn was always beautiful. Among all the Jewish girls with whom she had grown from childhood not one was as beautiful as she. With her delicate features, the rich coloring of her creamy skin, and with her lustrous eyes and hair of deepest black, she was indeed fair to look upon. But never had she looked as lovely as she did to-night. In her simple white wedding dress, with the filmy veil drawn softly over her face, she seemed as exquisite as the lilies that she carried. In the wonderful dark eyes that shone through the lace there was a depth, an earnestness, but seldom seen in a girl of Rachel's tender years.

Except for her maid-of-honor by her side, Rachel walked alone. Alone! For she had neither father nor mother, brother nor sister nor grandparents to lead her to the marriage altar. Only a few miles away from the synagogue, in the Jewish cemetery at Cypress Hills, her father and her mother both lay sleeping in their humble graves. Her only brother Ivan, twenty-one years old, lay beside them. Three days before, according to orthodox Jewish custom, Rachel had visited their graves and summoned their spirits to be present at her wedding. Of her living relatives—uncles, aunts and cousins—all were in far-away Roumania, where Rachel had been born. She was entering a new family to-night, but of her own kinsfolk—her own near and dear ones—not one was with her to pray God's blessing on her marriage. In the vast city of New York, in the strange new world of America, Rachel Mendelssohn was all alone.

A hush of eager expectancy surged like a wave over the whole synagogue as the bride, with eyes straight forward and with queenly grace, slowly mounted the dais steps and took her place beside her bridegroom beneath the Jewish marriage canopy. The bridesmaids followed and formed a circle with their lighted candles around the youthful couple.

Within the circle, directly opposite the bride and groom, stood the three silk-hatted rabbis facing them. To the left of the rabbis stood the bridegroom's brother Jacob; and on their right, magnificent in her purple velvet and pearls, rose–was it ominously?—his mother, Mrs. Deborah Kalinsky. The maid-of-honor was just a step behind the bride upon her right. The six groomsmen and the six little flower-girls stood upon the front corners of the dais just outside the lighted circle.

The impressive Jewish marriage ceremony began. There was a brief moment's pause; and then out of deepest silence the rich, wonderful voice of the cantor rose upon the strains of the *Kaddish,* the Jewish prayer for the dead. In wailing minor he intoned the mournful chant to the memory of the departed relatives of the bride and bridegroom, thrilling every listener to highest intensity of feeling. Among the emotional Jewish audience many handkerchiefs became visible, and a sound as of low sobbing swept through the synagogue. Throughout the entire lengthy dirge, Rachel stood erect, as motionless as marble. Through the filmy veil there was apparent not so much as the quiver of an eyelash. Max, on the other hand, trembled violently while shining teardrops coursed their way rapidly down his white, twitching face.

The prayer for the dead sung, the ceremony proper proceeded the maid-of-honor, stepping close to the bride, very deftly drew her veil in thick folds across her eyes. Thus blindfolded she was led by Rabbi Moses three times in a circle around the bridegroom. Then followed a lengthy ritual composed of the reading of Scripture from the parchment scroll and the recital of many prayers. All was performed by the Rav in Hebrew. Finally, in conclusion the veil was drawn back from the bride's face.

Without any formality of benediction or other mode of dismissal the ceremony terminated abruptly. The guests knew that Max Kalinsky and Rachel Mendelssohn were man and wife.

From every seat in the synagogue there was an instant rush of friends to surround the bride and bridegroom. For the next ten minutes there followed a deafening chorus of congratulations.

With greatest difficulty Max and Rachel were rescued from the excitement. It was Mrs. Deborah Kalinsky herself, with her instinctive generalship, who finally cleared a pathway and marshalled them to the waiting limousine into which she and her son Jacob and the three rabbis also entered. She slammed the door vigorously and the car whisked up the avenue followed by a procession of other cars of every kind and sort. Up Clinton Street and Avenue B they went—the wedding party and the guests—through the now heavily falling snow, across Eighth Street to Second Avenue, up Second Avenue to Eleventh Street, and thence a few doors westward to the four-story basement red-brick home of the mother of the bridegroom, where the marriage supper was awaiting them.

Within half an hour the two hundred guests who were fortunate enough to have received invitations to the supper had all arrived and the house was full to overflowing. There were no tiresome reception formalities to mar the real festivity of the occasion. As the guests entered the house, just as soon as they had removed their wraps on the second floor, they proceeded with all possible rapidity down the back stairway to the main floor, and took their places immediately, as many of them as could be accommodated, at the festal board. The rest of the guests patiently awaited their turn visiting in the hallways or in little groups in the rooms on the two top floors.

The sumptuous wedding feast was spread upon connecting tables extending through the center and down the entire length of the two long, narrow parlors. They were profusely decorated with flowers and candles and with elaborately frosted Jewish layer-cakes and bowls of assorted fruit. At each cover there was a huge Jewish bread roll and a bottle of orange crush or ginger ale.

Across the head of the long table a transverse table was spread, at which were seated the bride and bridegroom, his mother and eldest brother, the maid-of-honor and the three rabbis. Just opposite them, at the upper end of the long table were the bridesmaids and the six little flower-girls. In front of the bride was a mountainous wedding cake; and in front of Rabbi Mordecai Moses there was an enormous loaf of Jewish bread and an equally enormous carving knife with which he cut it into small pieces. These were passed down the tables from hand to hand, every guest taking a piece to eat.

Amid much merriment and laughter the marriage supper

proceeded. It was served by Mrs. Kalinsky's three other sons—Joseph and Otto and Ben—and their wives, and by others of her near relatives. Of the gentlemen who served, some wore coats and some did not. All wore their high silk or derby hats.

The courses of delicious home-cooked Jewish food followed one another in rapid succession—fruit salad, noodle soup, Jewish *gefuellte Fisch*, delectable fried chicken with full accompaniment of vegetables and potato, another salad of green onions; and then for dessert, Jewish cakes with fruits and ices, all followed by strong black Jewish tea. As one guest finished he would promptly give his place to another who was waiting. Three relays of tables were served before the marriage supper was finally concluded just shortly after half-past ten o'clock.

During the supper, many telegrams poured in which were read by Jacob Kalinsky, as master of ceremonies. Many gifts came in as well, which were opened and displayed right at the bridal table.

Finally, the *Rav* himself rose with elaborate gravity and addressed his parting message to the bride and groom. His words were all in Hebrew, but to those who understood, the tenor of his counsel was very plain. Max and Rachel were to live together in mutual fidelity and love; they were to adhere strictly to all the tenets and observances of orthodox Judaism; they were to worship always and only the one true God. And, above everything, they were to be vigilant against all Christians—especially against those pernicious Christian missionaries who would seek to lead them astray into paths of idolatry and blasphemy—enjoining upon them the worship of three gods instead of one. The God of Abraham, Isaac, and Jacob must be their Light and Guide. He would bless and guard their earthly dwelling. He would lead them safely through this life below. He would bring them at the end to their eternal Home in Heaven.

Throughout the lengthy repast the entire wedding party remained at the table. Max and Rachel rose frequently in their places to greet the many friends who came to speak to them.

Rachel was very lovely. Her veil was now thrown back from her face, revealing the exquisite features softly flushed to deep wild rose. Her wonderful eyes sparkled with vivacity and happiness. In her every movement there was a graciousness and

13

charm, and ease of manner that bespoke innate refinement.

Max, seated joyfully beside her, was at his best. He was no longer pale or nervous as he had been during the marriage ceremony. His color was natural and his bearing composed. With his dark eyes, and fine teeth flashing white each time he smiled, he looked almost handsome. Adorned with his high silk hat and the new dignity of matrimony, he seemed invested with unwonted manliness and strength. During the entire supper his attentions to his bride were very gracious, very tender. Each seemed, in a way truly beautiful, to illume, to complete the other. They were indeed a winsome couple.

It was not the bride and groom, however, but the mother—

Mrs. Deborah Kalinsky—who was the focus of attention. Conspicuously and deliberately she made herself the center of magnetic attraction on this grand occasion of the marriage of her youngest son. The son himself and his beautiful bride were mere adjuncts to her glory. Above the purple velvet her swarthy, heavy-featured face beamed with complete self-satisfaction. The contrast between her stolid pridefulness and the gentle grace and sweetness of her new daughter-in-law was striking in the extreme.

Mrs. Kalinsky's all-penetrating black eyes swept over the scene before her. Not a detail escaped their eagle scrutiny. Every part of the supper arrangements—the seating of the guests, the serving of the food, the performance of the program—was deftly directed by her mere uplifted finger. Every bit of audible conversation that reached her eager ears, especially that of the bride and bridegroom, was carefully noted and stored for future reference. Nothing—absolutely nothing—escaped her.

And she it was who, when the last guest had finally been served and the marriage supper was ended, skillfully maneuvered the clearing of the room. With amazing swiftness everything was removed from the tables, the boards and horses forming them were dexterously stacked against the walls, brooms and dustpans were brought in and the floor swept. This provided ample room for all the guests to mingle with the new couple. Rachel's lovely face began to show traces of deep weariness, but she smiled and chatted gaily on.

It was twelve o'clock when Mrs. Kalinsky, her generalship

14

still unabated, finally drew Max and Rachel aside and bade them hasten their preparations for departure. So skillfully did she supervise every detail of them herself that within half an hour more the youthful bride and bridegroom—amid a storm of boisterous farewell—were off for their three days' honeymoon. The rabbis and the older guests soon followed, but the young ones remained.

But all good times must have an end, even a Jewish wedding. As the clock struck two, one by one the couples reluctantly left. Slowly they mounted the stairways, front or rear alike, procured their wraps and descended again to the lower hallway. A few moments more of merry leave-taking and then gradually, in couples or in groups of four or five, the guests all laughing gaily, emerged through the front doorway, down the high steps, and into the snowy street below. By two-thirty nearly every one at last had gone. Only the family and a few of the closest friends remained.

Chapter II.

A Mother in Israel

"Be not wise in your own conceits."
—*Romans 12:16.*

The big house in East Eleventh Street was strangely still. After the high-tide of life and merriment of the wedding feast, the emptiness and hush of the long, high-ceilinged rooms seemed almost weird.

In the front parlor Joseph and Otto and Ben Kalinsky with their wives, Rose and Goldie and Esther, all having just taken leave of their mother downstairs, were standing in a little circle for the last good-nights among themselves. Their children, long since grown weary of waiting for them, had curled themselves up in the rose plush Chesterfield and wing-chairs, and four out of the seven were fast asleep. Jacob and Sarah and their three children, Izzy and Becky and Solly, who lived in the big house with Mrs. Kalinsky, had retired to their rooms upstairs.

In the basement kitchen old Grandmother Kalinsky, who also lived in the same house with her widowed daughter-in-law, was dozing in her old-fashioned rocker by the stove, unnoticed and undisturbed by any one. Rachel it was who had always taken her tenderly to bed each night, but Rachel was gone now and there was no one else to care. Her gray woolen shawl was wrapped about her head and shoulders. Over her cheap black dress she wore a wide green gingham apron. Her spectacles had dropped low over her nose as she had nodded off to sleep.

At the other side of the kitchen, piled high with hundreds of unwashed dishes and the remains of the wedding feast, Mrs. Kalinsky sat down at the end of the table with her two dearest friends, Mrs. Sophy Yasnik and Mrs. Yetta Cash, to talk it all over. Following behind Sophy came a Mrs. Kalish, a cousin visiting her from Chicago, whom Mrs. Kalinsky had urged Sophy to bring with her to the wedding. Mrs. Kalish had not yet been presented to her hostess nor to Mrs. Cash. Mrs. Yasnik graciously performed the ceremony of introduction:

"Ladies, meet my cousin, Mrs. Kalish, from Chicago. Mrs.

In the kitchen old Grandmother Kallinsky dozed in her rocker.

Kalish, meet my friend, Mrs. Kalinsky. Mrs. Kalinsky, Mrs. Kalish."

"Glad to meet you, Mrs. Kalish."

"Same here."

"And Mrs. Cash, meet Mrs. Kalish. Mrs. Kalish, Mrs. Cash."

"Happy to know you, Mrs. Cash."

"Likewise."

Mrs. Kalinsky, with her never-failing Jewish hospitality, insisted upon tea. Her three guests demurred in chorus.

"Not any for me, thanks, Mrs. Kalinsky," said Mrs. Kalish politely.

"Not for me neither," added Sophy Yasnik.

"No thanks, Debby, I couldn't have nothing," vehemently protested Yetta Cash.

"Vot! No more teal Vot iss the matter mit all of yous? Sure you vill haf tea. Vy not?" Mrs. Kalinsky lifted the tea-pot from the stove, filled four glasses and set them down upon the table with decision. "Pass the lemon und sugar, Sophy. Yetta, hand that plate of biscuits. Und see, here it iss a leetle vedding cake yet. Eat it!"

Meekly the guests obeyed their insistent hostess and began to eat and drink. A sudden inspiration seized Mrs. Kalinsky. She got up quickly from the table and went over to the stove again.

"Vot you think? Here it iss a lot more shicken yet. You all vill haf it—joost a leetle shicken!"

"Shicken! Vill you make me die yet?" Mrs. Yasnik's tone was reproachful.

"No, no, Debby, I couldn't!" expostulated Mrs. Cash.

"Not any for me, please, Mrs. Kalinsky! I am telling you, I couldn't possibly eat nothing!" echoed Mrs. Kalish.

Their protests were ignored. The plates were filled with chicken and gravy and potato and quietly placed before them. "Come," commanded Mrs. Kalinsky, "you must eat it some shicken—it vill strength you!" A bowl of fruit was also set upon the table, and without further objection the Jewish women proceeded with their after-feast. They ate for a few moments in silence; then gradually their tongues loosened and the confidences flowed.

"Oi, oi, but it vus a grand vedding, I am telling you!" Mrs.

Cash began. "Rachel she look just *bu-tee-ful.* Like a angel she look!"

"Und the bridesmaids, Mrs. Kalinsky," Mrs. Kalish added, "the bridesmaids und the maid-of-honor they vus vunderful!"

"Und the fettle flowver girls they vus so sweet—und the music und the vedding march—oi, oi!" Mrs. Yasnik's powers of description failed her.

"Und the supper, Mrs. Kalinsky!" exclaimed Mrs. Kalish with happy reflection upon the delectable viands—past and present— of which she had eaten and was eating no small portion, "such a supper I haf nefer tasted—nefer. This shicken it iss vunderful!"

Mrs. Kalinsky beamed with inward satisfaction. She gloried in the praises of her cooking. "You like it? I cook it efery bit meinself," she added proudly.

"Yourself?" the three women exclaimed in amazed chorus.

"All by meinself alone, I am telling you," replied Mrs. Kalinsky. "All last night I stay up till five o'clock this morning yet cooking the shicken und the feesch; und all day long today eferythings else I cook. Sarah she help me und Goldie she help me und Esther und Rosie und mein sohns they all help me. Ve do ourselfs eferythings. But the shicken und the feesch I do all by meinself alone. I don't trust nobody!"

"It all vus grand, Mrs. Kalinsky—the shicken, the salat, the cakes—joost grand!" Mrs. Kalish's praise was fulsome.

"Oi, it must haf kostet you a lot of money, Debby!" The tone of Sophy Yasnik's exclamation was interrogatory. Mrs. Kalinsky needed no urging to satisfy her curiosity.

"Oi, oi, vot all that whole vedding kostet me!" She extended her small, plump hands, palms upward, in a gesture of despair. "You couldn't nefer guess vot it all kostet me—supper for two hoondred peoples—shicken und fruits, und the ices und eferythings—und then all the flowvers—und the vedding dresses und the wail—oi, oi!" She lowered her voice to a confidential whisper, "I vouldn't tell nobody—but mein dearest freunds, beliefe me I am telling you, that vedding to-night it kostet me—vot you think? It kostet me four hoondredund-tventy-vun dollars und tventy-seven cents!"

"Oi, oi, oi!" The other Jewish women rocked themselves back

19

and forth and gesticulated violently in expression of their mingled admiration, sympathy, and horror.

Mrs. Kalish's strong natural curiosity was aroused. "You pay for it yourself, Mrs. Kalinsky? You make yourself the vedding? Vy the bride not make her own vedding? Is she not rich?"

"Rich!" retorted Mrs. Kalinsky scornfully, "Rakkel? rich? Vy, mein dearest Mrs. Kalish, Rakkel Mendelssohn she ain't got nothings! I meinself haf gif her eferythings vot she efer haf... Vot? Vy I make so fine a vedding? I vill tell you vy. Ven Rakkel marry mein sohn Max I say I make for her meinself a vedding vhich it iss so fine it couldn't nefer be no finer possible... Vy I do it? Listen, I am telling you! All mein other sohns they marry rich girls und they haf grand vedding. Ven mein Maxie get married I say he must haf a grand vun also. That iss vy I make it all so fine a vedding. It iss for mein sohn Maxie that I make it!"

Mrs. Kalish's insatiable curiosity persisted. "But Rachel's parents, vy they not make the vedding?"

"Her parents!" answered Mrs. Kalinsky with crescendo inflection, "Rakkel, she ain't got no parents. Both her parents they iss dead yet, God bless them!"

"Oi, oi," murmured Mrs. Kalish pityingly, "und ven did her parents die, Mrs. Kalinsky?"

"They die ven Rakkel vus only of age von elefen years; und efer since I haf done for her meinself eferythings. I gif her home, I buy for her her clothes, her food, her medizines ven she iss seeck—eferythings! . . . Vy I do it, Mrs. Kalish? Belief me I am telling you."

Mrs. Kalinsky filled the glasses with hot tea and passed the fruit and cake. The three other Jewish women leaned forward closely on their elbows and all listened eagerly as she proceeded. Rachel's sad little story was perfectly familiar to Mrs. Yasnik and to Mrs. Cash. A hundred times they had heard it from their worthy friend; but they nodded their sympathetic approval of a fresh recital. Mrs. Kalinsky was excited.

"You vant to know vy I so good to Rakkel? I vill tell you. It vus because her mother, Olga Mendelssohn, vus mein dearest freund ven ve vus girls together in Roumania. Mein hoosband und Olga's hoosband they vus cousins. Mein hoosband und me

20

ve come to America—to Noy York. Olga und her hoosband they stay in Bucharest; but joost the year before the vor Mr. Mendelssohn he come to Noy York too. He here for five years yet. He make fine business—lots of money. He too old to be sent back to Roumania to the vor. Then ven the vor iss ofer, he send for his vife und two children, vhich it iss Rakkel who iss elefen yet und his boy Ivan of age von twenty-vun years. He get all ready for them a nice leetle flat in the Bronx—all fine new furniture—so nice. I help him pick it out meinself. Eferythings iss all ready for his family to come und he so happy. Oi, oi!"

Mrs. Kalinsky paused to pour herself a cup of tea. Mrs. Kalish was listening with eager sympathy. The keen edge of the sympathy of Mrs. Cash and Mrs. Yasnik had been dulled a bit by multiplied repetitions of the tale.

"Und then," Mrs. Kalinsky continued, "und then vot you think? You couldn't nefer guess! It vus so dreadful!—It vus the vinter of the flu—that awful vinter, ven hoondreds und hoondreds of people vus dying yet. Und ladies, vould you beliefe me I am telling you! Mr. Mendelssohn he vus tooken sudden mit the flu himself, und the very day vhich his vife's und children's boat should come through Sandy Hook, he die!"

"Oi, oi, oi!" the emotional Jewish women all exclaimed loudly in tragic chorus. "Oi, oi, that vus awful!"

"Beliefe me I am telling you it vas awful!" continued Mrs. Kalinsky. "I go meinself to meet the steamer at the dock in Hoboken, und I haf meinself to tell mein dearest freund her hoosband he iss dead yet. Oi, oi, oi!" Mrs. Kalinsky rocked herself violently back and forth at the terrible recollection.

Mrs. Kalish listened breathlessly. Mrs. Kalinsky composed herself and went on.

"I bring Mrs. Mendelssohn and Ivan und Rakkel right to mein house und here we haf the funeral. Und then I say to Olga they all must stay by me. Vy not? They haf no place to go, I am telling you! Mein freund Olga her hoosband he is dead yet! She haf no money! She haf no home! The rent vus not paid for the flat before Mr. Mendelssohn he die, und so the landlord he tooken it avay. Und they haf to sell the furniture to pay the funeral."

"Und then, you vouldn't nefer beliefe it vot vus happen! Ladies, I am telling you. In vun veek after his father's funeral,

Ivan he iss tooken seeck mit the flu also, und the very next day Ivan he die too."

"Oi, oi, oi!"

Mrs. Kalinsky disregarded the anguished exclamations of her friends and continued her story rapidly.

"Und then, listen I am telling you! Mein freund Olga Mendelssohn, vhich she iss now a widow und her only sohn iss dead, she joost do nothings but cry und cry und cry. She sit on the floor in a corner und say *Kaddish* all day long und then she cry all night. She try to get vork but she don't know no English und she is too veak yet. She vork vun day und then she haf to stay in bed for three. Then she get up und try to vork again und she seeck a veek. Und all the time she cry und cry und cry. At last, in the Spring it iss, she go to bed und nefer again she get up. I bring to her the Doctor und he shake his head und say it iss the qvick cum-sumption, und before the Summer iss gone yet mein freund Olga she die also! I bury her beside her hoosband und her sohn. I pay meinself the funeral!"

"Oi, oi, oi!" How dreadful, Mrs. Kalinsky! Und poor leetle Rachel! Vot iss she done?" Good Mrs. Kalish's sympathy was very genuine.

"Rakkel? I am telling you before. Efer since her mother die, I haf keep Rakkel here by me . . . . Vy I do it? Listen, I am telling you! Before her mother die she cry so hard vot vould became of Rakkel? She vould be a orphant all alone yet. Und so I promise her, because she iss mein dearest freund, I promise her I vill take keer of Rakkel. I vill gif to her good home until she iss grow up und then—vot else you think I promise her?" Mrs. Kalinsky's voice became very confidential, very impressive. "Ladies, beliefe me I am telling you! I promise Olga vhich she vus mein dearest freund ven ve vus girls in Roumania, I promise her ven Rakkel iss grow up, I vill marry her mit vun of mein own sohns!—Und then Olga she die happy."

"Und I haf keep mein promise. I gif Rakkel fine home. I buy for her eferythings. I make for her many good freunds. I haf been to her meinself a mother. I keep her in school till she iss fourteen yet und then I get for her fine job by a millinery. She been there efer since until last week."

"Und to-night, I keep the rest of mein promise vhich it iss I

22

make to mein dear Olga. To-night I marry Rakkel to mein sohn, mein Maxie. Rakkel she haf now a vunderful hoosband. Mein Maxie iss so good a boy vhich it couldn't possibly be better. Beliefe me I am telling you, Rakkel Mendelssohn—vhich it iss now Rakkel Kalinsky—she iss a fortunate girl!"

Mrs. Kalinsky's dramatic recital was finished. The four women sat for a few moments in silence pensively sipping their third glass of tea.

Finally Mrs. Kalish spoke. "Vell, Mrs. Kalinsky, you haf been a grand good vomans und I hope you vill be vell paid back. I hope Rachel vill make for your sohn a fine vife!"

Mrs. Kalinsky glanced up shrewdly. "Vot? A fine vife? Vy not?" she asked sharply. "Vy not she make for mein sohn a fine vife? Certainly it iss she vill! I meinself vill take keer of that, beliefe me I am telling you!—Of course," she continued reflectively, "Rakkel she haf got much to learn yet. She so busy mit her job by millinery—many nights she haf to vork till nine o'clock— she haf no time to do much housevork only Sundays. Und she iss very young yet—only sefenteen—mein Max he twenty-two. But Rakkel she iss clefer. She vill learn qvick—cooking, vashing, sveeping, scrubbing—all vhich it iss very necessary a good Jewvish vife must know. You need not to vorry, ladies, that Rakkel Mendelssohn not make a good vife for mein sohn. Certainly she haf got much vot she must learn yet. But I mein- self will learn her eferythings!"

The clock struck three. Mrs. Kalinsky's guests rose hastily. "Three o'clock!" they exclaimed in astonished chorus. Their hospitable hostess remonstrated gently, "Vot, you are not going? Vy you must go so soon yet?"

"It iss three o'clock, Mrs. Kalinsky," said Mrs. Kalish apolo- getically.

"Three o'clock!" echoed Mrs. Cash and Mrs. Yasnik.

"Oi, oi! Vot should you care?" urged the indomitable Mrs. Kalinsky. "Three o'clock iss only three o'clock!"

"But you must get some sleep, Debby," urged Yetta, "look at all you vill haf to do tomorrow!"

"Ach, tomorrow! Vy should I vorry about tomorrow? It iss only today yet!"

The good-nights were lovingly and lingeringly exchanged at

last, and by three-fifteen the guests had finally departed. In the meantime the Kalinsky boys with their wives and children had also gone. Poor old Grandmother Kalinsky, too, had shuffled off quite unobserved to climb the four flights of stairs to her little room at the rear of the top floor, where she got herself to bed as best she could, unaided for almost the first time in years by her loving little Rachel.

Mrs. Kalinsky was at last alone. She poured herself another glass of tea. She sat down—weary to exhaustion, but well content. She had done a good day's work. The wedding had been an unqualified success. She smiled with deep inward pride and satisfaction. Her whole life had been a success. Since her husband's death ten years ago she had carried on his wholesale clothing business by herself, and had built it up to a position of prosperity far beyond any ever attained by him. She had bought this fine house on East Eleventh Street. She had bought three cars. She had had a trip to Europe. She had established all of her five sons, Jacob and Joseph with herself, and each one of the others in a business of his own. And finally, by clever, unsuspected manoeuvring, she had successfully married her sons to wives of her own choosing.

And Max, her fifth and last son—and her idol—was married to-night. And his wife—Rachel Mendelssohn—Mrs. Kalinsky well knew was the finest of all the Kalinsky wives. Of every one of the five Jewish girls whom she had appraisingly determined upon for her boys, Rachel was by all odds the most desirable. She was the handsomest. She was the cleverest. She had the most attractive disposition. She was young. She was eager. She was strong. Yes, Mrs. Kalinsky reflected, in every way she would make a splendid wife for her Max.

Of course, she did not know much yet—but that would be all right. Mrs. Kalinsky was quite untroubled on that score. She reassured herself of the purpose she had announced to her friends over their tea glasses. She smiled knowingly. A look of calculating shrewdness came into her dark eyes. Aloud she uttered her determination—her fixed, unalterable purpose—"Yes, Rakkel haf got very much vot she must learn yet before she iss a good enough vife for mein dear Maxie—but I meinself vill learn her—eferythings!"

Chapter III.

Eden Amid the Ghetto

*"He leadeth me beside the still waters. . . my cup
runneth over."—Psalm 23:2, 5.*

In the tiny three-room flat on East Second Street, just west of Avenue B, the days that followed for Rachel were as days of heaven upon the earth. Each new day seemed happier than the last, Rachel had never dreamed it was possible for any girl to be so happy.

Max was so good to her. Every morning before he left home for his little newspaper shop on Second Avenue, he helped Rachel all he possibly could as she began her household duties. Their flat was on the top floor in one of the shabby, unmodernized tenement blocks with which the lower East Side abounds, whose only heat is such as is furnished by the tenants themselves. Accordingly therefore, the first thing each morning Max carried the wood and coal up the five flights of stairs from their bin in the basement, and lighted the fire for the day in the kitchen range. Then while Rachel was preparing breakfast, Max insisted always upon sweeping and dusting the entire flat. After breakfast he would help with the dishes, and perhaps run on an errand or two for Rachel before he started off for his long day's work.

And every night, promptly at half-past six, he would close up the shop and hurry home to his little bride. He could have made much more money had he kept open evenings, but—"what do I care about money?" he would ask Rachel. "I would rather be home with you, Raychen," he would murmur "than have all the money in New York!"

And always when he came home he brought her a treat for supper from one of the little Kosher shops on the Avenue. Sometimes it was a bit of *gefuellte Fisch*, sometimes fresh onions or celery or lettuce, or again it might be a Jewish coffee roll, or possibly a nice raw herring.

Then while Max was changing for supper, as Rachel always

gently insisted he must do, she would prepare the delicacy for the table, arranging it artistically in a dainty bowl if it were fruit or salad, or cooking it in the long-handled frying-pan if it chanced that evening to be fish or meat.

Very charming indeed the little Jewish housewife looked as she stood over the stove in her dainty blue dress and crisp yellow apron. The heat of the stove flushed her cheeks to richest pink while the light from the glowing coals was reflected in her sparkling black eyes.

The pretty kitchen was worthy of its fair little mistress. Her own artistic skill and dauntless energy had made it inviting indeed. The stove formed the center of the decorative motif. Polished and shining and glowing as Rachel always kept it, it was yet more luminous with the array of gleaming cooking utensils on top of it or hanging on the wall above it. The large tea-kettle, the stewing-pot, the soup-basin, the ladle, the curious old frying-pan with its enormous handle, several smaller saucepans and kettles, and finally the handsome samovar—all were reminiscent of Rachel's childhood in Roumania. They were of genuine Russian brass and very valuable—family heirlooms taken by Rachel's grandmother when she had gone as a bride from Russia to Roumania. Since Rachel's mother's death—she had brought them with her to America—they had been Rachel's most treasured possessions.

Opposite the stove was the white sink, with its polished faucets; and just beyond the sink, in the corner, a sort of ingle-nook had been improvised with two-high-backed old fashioned settles, painted a deep cream—two shades deeper than the cream-tinted walls—with a stencil design in burnt-orange and rich blue. Within this nook stood the little table attractively spread for supper with a snowy linen cloth and the daintiest of dishes—wedding gifts, most of them, from Rachel's many friends.

On the wall above the table was an open cupboard—also done in cream and orange and blue—filled with old blue china, likewise reminiscent of Roumania. Two slender Windsor chairs, a Windsor arm-chair with a bright blue cushion, and a pretty tea-wagon—all painted alike to match the settles and the table—filled the remaining spaces. Edging the cupboard and gracefully draping the two windows were glazed chintz curtains, figured-orange frilled with blue. A bright hooked rug above a neat blue and cream checked linoleum, a red geranium in each window, and a comfortable cat, curled sleepily before the fire, completed the delightful ensemble.

And it had all been so inexpensive, too. Rachel had been so skillful. "You are wonderful, Raychen!" Max had said to her with tenderness when—just a trifle apprehensively—she had presented the total reckoning to him, "yes, you are just wonderful, to make it all so fine for such a little bit of money. What a clever little wife I have!"

Max's praise was very sweet to her after all her hard work. For she had worked hard and faithfully indeed. She had spent many long hours browsing through second-hand furniture shops on Delancey Street, where whenever she had found a piece of furniture whose lines appealed to her, even though it might be sadly battered, she would order it sent home; and with untiring energy—Max helping her evenings—she would scrub and scrape it, and then with her skillful paint brush and her stencils she would transform it. The hooked rug and the curtains she had also made herself from materials she had bought at a bargain sale at Gimbel's. The linoleum had been a wedding gift from Jacob and Sarah.

But above and beyond all the material furnishings and adornments of the pretty kitchen and the other pretty rooms, there was that pervading them which money could never buy. There was the atmosphere of love—the atmosphere of home. Seated opposite each other in the little ingle-nook for their attractive evening meal, talking happily together of the day's activities— with the shades closely drawn, the brass tea-kettle singing over the glowing fire, and the cat purring contentedly at their feet, it all seemed to Max and Rachel a bit of Paradise. Right there in the heart of the sordid Ghetto of New York it did seem as if that little Jewish home were indeed an Eden, dropped down to earth from the heavenly gardens above.

Rachel and Max always lingered over their supper long after their appetites were satisfied, so dearly did they love their "cozy hour," as they called it. But finally they would rise reluctantly and clear the table, putting away the food and covering the

Max and Rachel always lingered over their supper.

dishes neatly in the sink. Rachel would wash them in the morning. Max would offer to help her with them after supper, but her evenings with him were too precious to waste one moment of them washing dishes.

Usually by half-past eight they would go out. They would stroll awhile on the Avenue.

Very occasionally Max would ask, "Where would you like to go, Rachyen?"

"Anywhere, Maxie," she would answer, smiling up at him lovingly.

"But where would you like to go?"

And then she would ask him timidly—eagerly, "Oh, Maxie, couldn't we go to-night to the Metropolitan Art Museum?" So Max would take her.

Her few evenings there she treasured fondly, for art was a deep passion within her. She had inherited a gift for art—from her mother.

Still another delight to Rachel was the wonderful Public Library at Forty-second Street. Just to saunter through the marble-arched colonnades with Max beside her, gave her a peculiar thrill of exultation; and to browse leisurely among the carefully selected pile of books the attendant brought to the reading table upon her written order—while Max, looking a bit bored, skimmed the newspaper he had carried in his pocket— furnished a rich feast to her eager mind, ever hungering for knowledge.

One evening a week—usually it was Thursday—Max and Rachel would always spend with Ben and Esther. Ben was Max's next older brother and his closest chum, and Esther, his wife of a year, was Rachel's dearest girl friend. Ever since Rachel had first come to New York as a child of eleven, she and Esther Ginsburg had been inseparable in their devotion.

The girls would decide over the telephone beforehand in which of their two homes they would have supper—Ben and Esther lived in the Bronx—and then usually by three o'clock they would meet and go to market for their traditional Thursday evening chicken. They would always buy a live one—haggling over the bargain as all good Jewish housewives do, while the long-bearded Kosher vendor weighed the bird and excitedly demonstrated its excellent culinary qualities. Then, the deal concluded to the satisfaction of all concerned except the chicken, that noble animal was carried along the street—now by Esther and now by Rachel—head downward, and flapping and squawking violently—to the rabbi, who killed it while the little housewives waited.

Then they would come home—usually to Rachel's—and pluck and dress the chicken and prepare it for frying. There would then be a couple of hours of happy visiting together—helping with each other's household sewing perhaps—until their husbands joined them after seven. The two boys would at once array themselves in big aprons, and caps made of paper bags, and armed with a formidable array of forks and spoons, would fry the chicken in the queer long-handled brass pan, while the girls completed the other preparation for their supper.

And then, everything ready at last after the merriest excitement and confusion, the four good friends would sit down together in the little ingle-nook for their happy—and boisterous—weekly feast.

On the Thursdays when they met at Ben and Esther's, they would gather around the piano and Rachel would play while all the rest would sing. Sometimes they would make Rachel sing alone, it was such a delight to hear her sweet, rich contralto as she sang the songs of old Roumania. At eleven o'clock they would have another little supper—fruit and honey cakes and cheese and nuts and tea—and then at twelve the friends would exchange merry and loving good-nights, and the happy little party would adjourn until another Thursday.

Other friends there were as well with whom Max and Rachel visited back and forth on occasional evenings. Both of them were popular with the younger Jewish set in the Avenue B neighborhood, and their little flat on East Second Street was a favorite rendezvous. With true Jewish hospitality Max and Rachel always kept open door and a welcome place at their table for whoever cared to come and at whatever hour. Not infrequently there were no fewer than a dozen friends visiting them at once. When the table—drawn out beyond the ingle-nook to fullest length—became crowded to capacity, the tea wagon was added to it, and if that were not sufficient, it could always be supplemented with the ironing board, extended from the edge of the wagon to the cool end of the stove. If there were still an overflow of boys and girls, they could camp in the little parlor beyond. Much to their disappointment however, for the kitchen was the center of attraction. Rachel was in the kitchen. Rachel it was, whether in her own little home or in the home of any of her friends, who always was the leader in the merriment. Hers was ever the gayest laugh, hers the blithest, gladdest song.

On Sunday afternoons Max and Rachel went to the big Kalinsky house on East Eleventh Street for the weekly family gathering. From the time that Mrs. Deborah Kalinsky's first son had married, it had been the established order that all the Kalinsky sons and the Kalinsky wives and the Kalinsky grandchildren should congregate on Sundays beneath the maternal roof. Even when Mrs. Kalinsky was away they congregated just the same, by force of habit.

She was away now—in California. She had a sister in Los Angeles who long had urged Deborah to visit her; but that excellent mother had never felt she could leave her family to go so far away. Finally, however, when the last one of her five sons was married and established, she felt free to go. Accordingly, therefore, she had left for the West only two days after Max and Rachel's wedding, before they had returned from their honeymoon or she had seen them in their little flat. She would be away six months.

Meantime, in her absence, the atmosphere of the big house was, to Rachel at least, noticeably different. Just what constituted the difference, Rachel could not exactly define. Sarah, as housekeeper, was a worthy successor to her mother-in-law. She was indeed, in many respects, a close counterpart to that good lady. The boys and their wives came in and out with the same informal irregularity; the children were just as noisy and saucy as ever; poor old Grandmother Kalinsky was just as pitiful and inconspicuous in her rocker by the kitchen stove; and the eating was as interminable as it always had been. Yes, everything was just the same exactly—and yet how vastly different! In Mrs. Deborah Kalinsky's absence the magnetic pole of influence was gone—that peculiar binding quality, that cohesive, compelling force which held the twenty-one Kalinskys all together as one organic whole.

Each Friday evening—the beginning of the Jewish Sabbath—Max and Rachel usually spent quietly at home alone. And of all the happy times of the entire week, this to Rachel was the very happiest of all. The evenings she went out with Max, the visits with Ben and Esther, or with other friends, the jolly little "togetherings"—not one was half so sweet to her as these quiet Sabbath evenings alone with her husband in their own dear home.

After supper, which on Fridays was particularly attractive, while they still lingered at the table in the ingle-nook, Max—as head, now, of a Jewish home—would open the Jewish Prayer-Book and together they would read aloud the Sabbath Scriptures and a Psalm of praise. Then they would recite in unison the great commandment of Jehovah to His Chosen People: Hear, O Israel: THE LORD our God is one LORD: And thou shalt love the LORD thy God with all thine heart, and with all thy soul, and with all thy might.

And then they would go into the cozy little parlor and Max would rest upon the couch while Rachel would sit close beside him in her big chintz arm-chair. The cat, peacefully purring, lay curled up on Max's shoulder. After a while Rachel would extinguish the electric lights, and the only light in the room would then be that of the Sabbath candles burning on the table, and the ruddy glow from the kitchen stove reflected in the polished surface of the beautiful Russian brasses.

In this soft light, the happy little Jewish couple would exchange sweet confidences. So much there was to tell each other—so many things to talk about! There were plans for the new piano they hoped to be able to purchase by next Fall; plans for the time when they should become very rich and would then travel back to see Rachel's relations in Roumania; plans for Max soon to begin his studies, for Rachel wanted him some day to be a scholar like her father. And still other plans there were they talked of in the slowly fading light—tender, wonderful plans of joys the future years would bring to their home and to their hearts.

On Saturday mornings they always went together to the synagogue. This was quite the accustomed and accepted habit, for

Max and Rachel had both been brought up in strictest orthodoxy. Max's attendance upon the service, however, was formal
and perfunctory. Rachel, on the other hand, esteemed the hour
of worship more than her necessary food. Hers was a deeply
soulful nature. Even as a little child when her father in their
home in Roumania had read to her each night out of the big
Hebrew *Taanach*, she had had an instinct for the things of God.
But her thoughts of Him were tinged with deepest awe and not
a little fear. As she grew older she experienced a conscious longing that she might know Him better. Like Job of old her heart
cried out: "Oh, that I knew where I might find Him!" But also,
even as Job, she knew not of the Daysman betwixt them
through Whom alone she might have boldness and access unto
God as Father.

During the hours through each day when Max was away at
work, Rachel was invariably busy. Just the housework alone
engaged much of her time, for the stove and the windows and
the brasses must always be kept bright and shining; the table
linen must be fresh and snowy; and Max's socks must all be
nicely darned and his buttons sewed securely on. He was such
a boy for losing buttons! Then, too, there were the trips to
market every morning—and the washing and the ironing. And
then, of course, there was the cooking. The cooking was the
hardest thing of all. Rachel's mother and grandmother in
Roumania had taught her something of it; but during the years
in Mrs. Kalinsky's house she had seldom cooked, and much that
she had known was quite forgotten. But Max was so sweet and
patient with her; and gradually, as she persisted, things came
back and she began to grow quite skillful.

Of course she made funny mistakes sometimes. More than
once she had forgotten to put the baking-powder in her cake;
but Max had loyally insisted that it didn't matter at all—it was
delicious, anyway, since she had made it. Another time she
forgot to move the soup kettle to the back of the stove when she
went out for the afternoon, with the sad result that Max had no
soup for supper. Instead, when he came home, only a black,
empty kettle awaited him and heavy fumes as of burning onions
filled the entire flat. And once there was a dreadful mistake.
Rachel had come in late from market one day, and, in her nerv-

ousness and haste, in some way or other—she couldn't explain to Maxie quite how it did happen—she got her two packages of meat mixed—the kidneys for Max's kidney pie, and the bits of liver for the cat. Accordingly therefore, Max's pie, when it was served at supper, was made of liver, while Miss Pussy regaled herself delicately upon the delectable kidneys.

After the household duties for the morning were finished, and Rachel had had her lunch alone—Max did not have time to leave his shop at noon—she filled many delightful hours with shopping excursions, or in visiting with her girl friends. Many hours, too, there were that were happily whiled away in sight-seeing, either by herself alone or in company with others. During the seven years that Rachel had been in New York, that great metropolis had never lost its fascination for her. It was a constantly unfolding wonder. Hardly a day passed that she did not discover something new and thrilling in it.

She loved especially to browse leisurely through the streets of the vast Jewish Ghetto. Division Street, Grand Street, Orchard Street—all held for her the keenest interest. Rivington Street especially possessed a subtle charm for her. It was always so exciting. Scores of women were hanging out of the upper windows of the tenements. Scores more thronged the side-walks—old Jewish women, from every country on the globe, with gaily colored shawls about their heads; long-bearded, patri-archal-looking Jewish grandfathers; and swarms of Jewish and foreign children playing in the middle of the street, entirely unmindful of danger until they were scattered like leaves before an autumn wind by the furious honking of an auto horn or the clanging gong of a fire truck as it bore down upon them. Often there were hurdy-gurdys or Italian organ-grinders. And, some-times-oh, how Rachel loved it!—there would be a little red-capped, red-coated monkey holding in his shrivelled, quiv-ering fingers a battered tin cup into which Rachel would delight-edly ring a few pennies, receiving in return the unctuous smiling and scraping of the Italian and the snarling show of the monkey's teeth.

But best of all on Rivington Street were the Jewish pushcarts. Rachel loved pushcarts. The people who attended them were fascinating to her. Usually the vendor was some elderly, greasy-coated Hebrew with long-flowing beard; sometimes it was a buxom Jewish mother. Once in a while a beautiful young Jewish girl would be in charge. It made no difference who it was, Rachel loved them all. They were her sisters and her brothers—her own dear Jewish people. She often stopped to chat with them in Yiddish. With her winsomeness and charm, she made friends easily; and as she came again and again, they began to look for her visits, and always greeted her eagerly with warm smiles and friendly words.

She frequently made little purchases. The wares were spread out upon the long line of carts in tempting and astonishing array—laces, shawls, shoe-strings, furs, rugs, buttons, pencils, shell combs, suspenders, children's dresses, and shoes, picture frames and mirrors; then fish, bologna, lettuce, cabbages, bananas, onions, apples, celery, cheese, and huge loaves of Jewish bread—all displayed in indiscriminate and democratic heaps.

Rachel frequently did her marketing in Rivington Street. One could get such excellent bargains at the pushcarts. Rachel gloried in bargains. They meant to her not only that Max would call her his clever little housewife, but also that more money would be saved each week from their household budget. Every Sabbath eve, whatever was left above the week's expenses was gravely put into a little padlocked savings-bank, which was kept carefully hidden in the dresser drawer. When this little bank became full, Max would take it to the large Jewish savings institution on East Broadway, where it would be unlocked by the teller, who alone possessed the key, and the heaps of dimes and nickels and quarters would be deposited to Max's account, to draw interest at four per cent. Eagerly Max and Rachel watched the balance in the little pass-book grow. In three or four years more, perhaps, they would have five-hundred dollars, which they would invest in dunams of land in Palestine. For Max and Rachel both were ardent Zionists. Every one of the Kalinskys was, in fact. All the boys were members of the local B'nai B'rith, where Otto held office as Vice-President. Mrs. Deborah Kalinsky was treasurer of her local branch of Hadassah, the women's Zionist organization.

Thus passed that happy first winter of their married life—all too rapidly for Max and Rachel. As the warm Spring and Summer days drew on, there were many added pleasures—picnic suppers in the parks, excursion trips on Saturday afternoons to the Palisades or Coney Island, or rides in the warm Summer evenings on the motor buses. Frequently after supper they would take the Fifth Avenue bus up Riverside Drive to Grant's Tomb. They would go to Washington Arch and board it there at the terminus so that Rachel would be sure of getting her favorite seat—the front one on the upper deck. Settled happily at that vantage point, high above the pavement and with unobstructed view, she felt, while they bowled up beautiful Fifth Avenue and Riverside, as if the very world were at her feet.

Often they would take a trip of a Summer evening on one of the many ferry-boats that throng the New York harbor. One evening in mid-June they took the boat to Staten Island. As they approached the Battery on the return trip, they stood on the upper front deck eagerly drinking in the wonderful scene before them. It was full moonlight, and the harbor was a shimmering flood of silver dotted all over with the sparkling lights of many boats. Great ocean liners, brilliantly illuminated, lay at anchor in the Hudson River or were moored alongside their berths. To the south of Manhattan the Statue of Liberty raised aloft her shining torch of welcome to America; to the east the lights of Brooklyn Bridge spanned the East River as with a jewelled girdle. As they drew near the dock the imposing skyline of lower Manhattan became clearly visible. The vast towering buildings loomed in massive splendor before them. There still were lights in many of the office windows, twinkling like a myriad of fire-flies.

Rachel's artistic soul thrilled to the wondrous beauty and to the stupendous magnificence of it all. The grandeur of America's metropolis—its colossal material achievements; its gigantic commercial enterprise; the marvel of its myriad peoples representing every land on earth; the vastness of its wealth, its influence, its power; the richness of its beauties, both natural and man-created; the never-ceasing wonder of its throbbing, thrilling life—all held for Rachel a tremendous fascination. As she stood there on the deck of the ferry-boat gazing upon it, as it seemed to rise up out of the water into the moonlight like a mirage of mist and pearl—she experienced a glow of happiness such as she had never felt conscious of before. It was her own beloved city—her adopted new-world home—her wonderful New York!

It was yet early—early, at least, for a Summer evening in town—so Max and Rachel, both feeling full of joyous vigor, walked up Broadway the entire distance from the Battery to the City Hall. They went through the "canyon" between the massive downtown skyscrapers, past Wall Street with beautiful Trinity Church at its head, and on still further until they came to Old St. Paul's. Above it towered the Postal Telegraph offices and the gigantic Woolworth Building. The full moon, in a sea of billowy, tinted clouds, poured its light impartially down upon the three imposing structures—the vast commercial piles, the epitome of twentieth-century financial achievement; and lying low by comparison beneath them, the exquisitely-modeled brown-stone church of long by-gone days, with its graceful spire pointing heavenward, as if it still would make its spiritual appeal amid all the din and God-forgetfulness of modern life. The moonlight flooded, too, the ancient burying ground surrounding the church, enclosed within the iron coping—shining down upon the graves where lay many of New York's distinguished dead—reposing in their last peaceful sleep in the very heart of the restless, rushing life of Broadway.

The still energetic young couple continued walking to the Post Office and the City Hall, and thence across City Hall Park to Brooklyn Bridge, where they took the "L" for home.

As the train sped through the congested lower East Side, Rachel, looking eagerly through the car windows, noted the pulsating life below. It was now nearly twelve, but still there were hundreds of children playing in the streets, and throngs of men and women on the sidewalks, or leaning from the windows of their tenements to catch whatever breath of air they could on that hot night in New York City.

The teeming population of New York! And one person out of every four a Hebrew! In the whole vast city of over seven millions, one-and-three-quarters-million souls were Jews—Jews in every walk and circumstance of life—Jews from every nation under heaven! Rachel thrilled profoundly at the thought.

For she was one of them! She with them was a descendant of Abraham, Isaac, and Jacob. They were her own people—her Hebrew kinsmen—her fellow-Israelites. And Israel was God's Chosen Nation—His peculiar treasure—the very apple of His eye! Rachel exulted with patriotic pride. Her race-consciousness was strong. Someone—a Gentile—had asked her one day, "Do you call yourself a Roumanian or an American?" And she had boastfully replied, "I am a Hebrew!"

The clock in the Metropolitan tower was musically chiming midnight as Max and Rachel reached their little flat. From their kitchen window they could see the great tower light, over fifty stories high. As they entered their door the moonlight flooded the kitchen and gleamed upon the brasses. . .the cat arched her back and rubbed against them purringly in welcome.

Then Max lighted the candles in the high brass candlesticks, while Rachel lighted the samovar to make their tea. The glow from both mingled with the silvery moonlight and illumined the room with a rich mellow softness, bringing out in beautiful relief the graceful furniture, the warm tones of the curtains, the blue heirloom dishes, and the bowl of flowers on the table. Rachel gazed fondly upon each familiar, well-loved treasure ... she slipped into her place in the ingle-nook behind the samovar and tea-glasses...Max took his seat opposite her...they waited for the water in the samovar to boil...Rachel hummed softly a love song of old Roumania.

Neither one spoke. The joy in both their hearts lay deeper than in words. It seemed to Rachel as if a very river of peace were flooding her soul to-night, even as the moonlight was flooding the beautiful kitchen. Her eyes were misty with happiness. It was all hers, this cozy little home—hers and Max's! And it was theirs forever. Nothing could ever rob them of it. Rachel's heart seemed almost bursting with a sudden thrill as of fierce, exulting joy. No! Nothing could ever rob them of their home, because nothing could ever rob them of their love.

The samovar was bubbling over . . . Rachel made the tea . . . they drank it silently . . .again Rachel hummed the love song of Roumania . . .again her eyes wandered lingeringly among her treasures—the Windsor chairs—the little tea-wagon—the dainty curtains—the cat—the brasses . . .

38

Ah, gentle little Rachel, gaze lovingly and yearningly upon them all—upon each prized possession—upon every object that you hold so dear! Impress its image indelibly upon your mind and heart—against that day, so swiftly drawing on, when all the wealth your dear home holds for you tonight will be yours only in precious, precious memory! For the storm is coming!

You are happy tonight, little Rachel—your heart is overflowing with youth and joyousness and love. But sorrow, dear, has claimed you for her own, and is bearing swiftly down upon you. The storm is coming, Rachel—the storm is coming!

Yes, the storm was coming. Though Rachel dreamed it not, it was coming—coming fast. Already signs of it—all unconsciously to Rachel—were appearing upon the horizon. Only a tiny cloud at first, no bigger than a man's hand. But other clouds were following in quick succession. Black, angry clouds were gathering—gathering. And soon they would break in pitiless fury upon that happy little Jewish home and upon Rachel's defenseless head.

Chapter IV.

Eden Invaded

"Abide now at home; why shouldest thou meddle...?"
–2 Chronicles 25:19.

M rs. Deborah Kalinsky came home from California in July. Her arrival, early one Sunday morning, was sudden and unannounced. The first Rachel knew of it was when Sarah called her on the telephone shortly before noon:

"Rachel, is that you at last! I called you up at nine o'clock and again at ten o'clock. Where were you?"

"I was at the shop with Max. He had to go up early to see about some papers. Why? What is it?"

"You could never guess, possibly—what has happened!"

"What? Tell me!"

"Mamma!"

"W-what?" asked Rachel lamely. Her knees suddenly went weak.

"Mamma!—Mamma Kalinsky! I am telling you. She has come home!"

"Oh, really, Sarah! When?" Rachel controlled her voice perfectly.

"At seven o'clock this morning. She is now eating some more breakfast. She wants I should call you and tell you and Max to hurry up and come and see her. She is very excited till you get here. So you hurry quick. Goldie and Esther and Rosie and the boys and the children are all come already and dinner is at one o'clock. So you and Maxie hurry up!"

"All right, Sarah! Thank you so much for telling us. We'll come right away. Max will be so glad to see his mother." Rachel's voice was held in hand well. Sarah could not detect in the faintest degree her true inward reaction to the news of her mother-in-law's arrival. She hung up the receiver with a peculiar sense of depression—the same feeling exactly that a child experiences when holidays are over and school begins once more. She glanced sorrowfully at the dainty luncheon-basket,

40

standing all ready packed upon the table. She and Max had planned such a wonderful time. They were going to spend the day at the Palisades. She resented this sudden, altogether unexpected blockade to their delightful Sunday outing. Somehow she had a vague fear that their plans for future Sundays—and other days as well—would be subject to amendment by Mrs. Kalinsky.

Max entered the kitchen. She greeted him—unflinching—with her usual bright smile.

"Oh, Max! Such a surprise I have for you! You will be so glad!"

"A surprise? What is it, Rachel?"

"Three guesses!" She forced the buoyant, playful tone.

"Is it a cake for our picnic?" asked Max hopefully.

"Wrong!"

"Is it—is it," Max reflected slowly, "is it something for supper after we get home?"

"No—wrong again! It's nothing to eat. It's a surprise—a wonderful surprise! Something that has happened."

"Happened? "—Max's brain registered slowly—" What has happened, Raychen?"

Rachel did not wait for the third guess. She would not prolong his suspense nor her own.

"It's your mother, Max! Your mother is home! Sarah just phoned."

"Mamma!" exclaimed Max with unfeigned joy. "Mamma home?—from California? When did she get here, Rachel?"

"At seven o'clock this morning. Sarah rang up twice while we were out. And she says your mother wants us to hurry and come up."

"Yes, let's get right off! Leave everything—the breakfast dishes, the sweeping, everything. Come, hurry up—don't touch a thing. Mamma will be so impatient till we get there." He glanced at the luncheon-basket a shade regretfully. "Our picnic! Will it keep until tomorrow night, Rachel?"

"Couldn't we still go today, Max?" asked Rachel hopefully. "Couldn't we see your mother now and then go late this afternoon?"

"No, Raychen, sure not!" Max's tone was reproving. "We will have to spend the whole day with Mamma, of course—her first

41

Sunday back. Why, she wouldn't think of letting us leave early."

With Max continuing to urge haste, Rachel left everything as it was in the disordered flat. She changed her picnic attire for a dainty street frock, and they started off shortly after twelve o'clock—Rachel's heart feeling far from light. Max hailed a taxi. Never before had they taken a taxi from Second to East Eleventh Street. Always they had gone on the street car or they had walked. Rachel protested mildly against the extravagance, but Max justified it promptly, "It's late, Rachel, and Mamma hates that anyone should keep her waiting. You know Mamma!"

As they drew up before the maternal abode, sounds of noisy mirth emerged through the open doorway. Max and Rachel were the last arrivals. The children greeted them excitedly, scream-ing their names upstairs, just as Mrs. Deborah Kalinsky, resplen-dent for the festive occasion in bright orange satin, was beginning proudly to come down. Her majestic approach was suggestive of a flood which sweeps everything before it. On her swarthy face was a broad, expansive smile of perfect satisfac-tion. Her arms were extended wide in effusive welcome.

"Mein Maxie, mein Maxie! Mein dear sohn! Mamma she iss came home to you at last—she iss came home to her own precious boy!"

She next turned upon Rachel and swallowed her up with a similar greeting—as quite befitted her newest daughter-in-law.

"Und mein leetle Rakkel! Mein beautiful leetle Rakkel— mein Maxie's bride—vhich it iss now mein own vunderful daugh-ter!"

By this time the entire family was surrounding the newly returned traveller. She flew from one to another of them, embracing them rapturously with excessive utterances of devo-tion.

"Meiri darling Jacob—mein Joseph—mein Otto—mein Goldie—mein Esther—mein leetle grandchilderns! It iss now here mein whole familee—mein five sohns—mein five dear daughters—mein ten darling grandchilderns! You are all came home to see Mamma yet! Come, ve vill go downstairs und make it the dinner ready. You all must be so very hungry." She led the way toward the rear stairway, deliriously excited almost to the verge of hysteria.

42

The Kalinskys, twenty-one strong, flocked into the large kitchen. Grandmother Kalinsky in her rocker made twenty-two. Sarah had suggested that the dinner be served in the state dining-room upstairs, in honor of the great occasion, but Mrs. Kalinsky insisted upon the kitchen. There every one felt more at home. And the kitchen was doubly attractive now—for the children certainly—by reason of the array of half-unpacked trunks and valises from which all sorts of mysterious packages were bulging. Every child and grandchild had a gift from California—candied fruits and nuts, big oranges and grape-fruit, and curios made from abilone shells. Poor little Grandmother Kalinsky was quite forgotten in the distribution, but Rachel quickly filled her lap with her own sack of oranges, and the dear old soul was overjoyed.

A gradual thinning-out process began, fortunately for Sarah, Rose, and Goldie, who were detailed to the cooking of the dinner. The children, one by one, went out to play in the street or in the back yard; the older boys went off for their Sunday papers. Rachel and Esther, chatting happily together, helped their older sisters-in-law in various ways with the dinner preparations. Mrs. Kalinsky had firmly annexed Max for the day, and she was now, in her orange satin, buried in the depths of the rose plush Chesterfield in the front parlor in confidential and earnest conversation with him. She was perfectly happy. Her twenty children and grandchildren had all gathered to do her honor; and her Max—her precious youngest son—her heart's idol—was beside her.

At length, soon after two o'clock, dinner was served, and the entire Kalinsky family sat down before the long, festive board. Mrs. Kalinsky, with Max next to her, graced the head of the table. Rachel sat at the foot, between Grandmother Kalinsky on the one side, and Little Moischa, Joseph and Rose's boy, on the other. For two full hours the viands and the festivity passed back and forth. While they were still eating, neighbors began dropping in—Yetta Cash and Sophy Yasnik, and another and yet another friend, who seated themselves around the room, until Mrs. Deborah, highly exulting in the welcome thus accorded her, was holding court as proudest queen.

Finally by four o'clock, dinner was really finished and then

Mrs. Kalinsky, together with her sons and her neighbors, ascended to the upstairs parlors; while the daughters-in-law were left below to wash the dishes. The older children were instructed to remain and help them, but their tenure of office was of short duration. So, too, was that of their mothers. The heavy end of the task fell eventually upon Esther and Rachel. The dishes seemed interminable. Although in loyalty to Max, Rachel had given no outward sign of displeasure, nevertheless she still felt an inward rankling over the disappointed Sunday plans, and a conscious regret in Mrs. Kalinsky's home-coming. Rachel's was a nature that was easily pleased, and as quickly grieved. Unhappily the grieving when it did occur, took the form of brooding and depression of spirit. She was brooding now as she stood over the dish pan. And for the best of reasons. Not one word had she had with Max alone all afternoon, so exclusively had his mother exercised her proprietorship over him. She was too proud to own her unhappiness even to Esther.

After the kitchen had finally been restored to order, the girls joined the others upstairs, and soon Rachel was asked to sing. She did so obediently, but there was no buoyancy in her tone, no accustomed cheer. Nor was her inward mood by any means improved when Max called attention to that fact. But still she gave no outward sign. She sang another song at Max's request—this time with forced gaiety and brilliancy, but with a secretly heavy heart. Then the children trooped in and wanted "Auntie Ray" to tell them a story. This she did rather more happily, for she loved the children. Then Mrs. Kalinsky drew her court into a close circle around her and for a couple of hours regaled them with the wonders of "Californien" and her rich relations there. And then that hospitable lady suggested it was time to eat again, and Rachel with the other young wives was sweetly asked if she would "please be so kind to make ready for us a leetle supper."

At eight o'clock the large Kalinsky family gathered once more around the table, their ranks this time being augmented by Yetta Cash and Sophy Yasnik and half a dozen other guests. The meal, as usual, was a lengthy one, and then once more for Rachel, the colossal stack of dishes. By eleven o'clock, when they were at last finished, her head was aching and her heart was heavy and sore. It was still nearly another hour before Max was finally released from the maternal wings, and they were free to go home.

They did not take a taxi back—not even the street car. Max was in the mood to walk the twelve blocks down to Avenue B and Second Street. Rachel's mood was not consulted. She was too proud and too hurt to urge it. Max talked volubly. One thought alone absorbed him—his mother's return from California and the wonderful plans she had formulated there and had today unfolded to him, whereby within a year he would own the finest paper shop on Second Avenue. He was too elated himself to note Rachel's unresponsiveness. He continued talking—eagerly, excitedly. Rachel was silent—silent and heartsick.

It was after twelve o'clock when they reached home. The picnic basket stood on the table just as they left it in the morning. The still unwashed breakfast dishes confronted them—the unswept, untidy flat. The cat miaowed hungrily. Rachel—for the first time since Pussy had come to live with her—had forgotten, before her hurried departure in the morning, to fill her saucer with cream. For the first time, too, she now failed to light the samovar and make Max's tea. Max looked at her puzzled and disappointed. But she didn't care, she told him—she couldn't help it—her head ached—no, she wasn't going to make any tea to-night. Her tone was petulant, her beautiful face sullen. There was a sudden sharp word of reproach from Max, a sudden unwonted burst of tears from Rachel. The first tiny rift had pierced their tuneful lute.

The next morning while they were at breakfast, Mrs. Kalinsky called up Max on the telephone. Her visit with him was so extended that his coffee grew quite cold. Rachel continued eating alone her fish and toast and celery, with mounting displeasure as, inescapably, she heard Max's cross-section of the conversation.

"It is so fine, Mamma, to have you home again. . . . Yes, w e had a wonderful day with you yesterday—we both enjoyed it a lot—and all the plans you told me for the business, how we can make money quick, they are all just great. You bet I'll do it, Mamma, exactly like you say! . . . What? When are we coming up again? Whenever you say, Mamma! . . . Next Sunday? Sure, every Sunday. . . When? Before Sunday? When do you want us?

45

What? Thursday night? Oh—Thursday—wait a minute, I'll ask Rachel."

Max shot a questioning glance toward the table. Rachel's eyes met his appealingly. "O Max, not Thursday, dear—we're to go up to Ben and Esther's Thursday." Max continued into the transmitter, "Mamma, Rachel says we've got another date then . . . Where to?—Why, we're going up to Ben and Esther's place for supper . . . What? Go there on Wednesday instead? . . . All right, I'll try to fix it with them. We'll see you then on Thursday . . . What's that? When will you come down to our house? Just as soon as you possibly can, Mamma! We're both anxious you should see our little flat. When will you come? . . . What? To-night? . . . Good! Sure it will be all right! We have supper about seven . . . What? . . . You'll come down early to help Rachel get the supper ready? That's awfully good of you. She'll be so glad, I know she will . . . All right, at three o'clock then! I'll tell Rachel . . . Good-bye, Mamma! We'll see you later!"

Max turned to Rachel eagerly. "Mamma is coming, Raychen, to have supper with us tonight—to see us in our flat. Won't that be great, dear? You'll buy something nice at the market won't you, and cook it just the finest you know how? Mamma says she'll come at three o'clock to help you—why, what is it, Rachel? What's the matter?"

Rachel tried bravely to conceal the inward tumult. "Nothing, dear," she answered, trying to smile her usual radiant smile. "It will be so nice to have your mother here. It is so good of her to come so soon." But Max's quick ear detected a strained note in her voice, and he knew that all was not quite well.

"Rachel, what is it?" he repeated his question anxiously, "what is the matter? You didn't mind my changing our night with Ben and Esther from Thursday to Wednesday, did you? I thought it wouldn't make any difference; and Mamma was so anxious to have us come to her house Thursday. You didn't care, did you, Rachel?"

"No—oh, no—it was all right. Max," she answered lamely. "I just—don't feel quite well today. I have such a headache . . . "

Max was all tenderness at once. "I'm so sorry!" he murmured, putting his arm around her. "You must go out for a little walk this morning, then have a nap after lunch before Mamma comes."

But Rachel knew there was neither walk nor nap for her that day. It was now nine o'clock, and she knew it would take her every moment until three to make fitting preparation for the great event—the first reception of her mother-in-law in her own home. She had no doubt that every smallest detail of the entire establishment would be subjected to minute and critical inspection. So the moment Max was gone she set to work. First there were the dishes—all of yesterday's still remaining over. She had been too tired to touch them last night. Then there was the sweeping and the dusting. For the first time since their marriage Max had failed to do it for her. Then everything, she reflected nervously, must be polished beyond all possibility of reproach. And then the supper must be planned and ordered over the telephone and cooked. O dear, O dear, why was Mrs. Kalinsky coming tonight? And why on earth did she say she would come at three o'clock? And why, oh why, couldn't she have stayed in California?

Everything went badly all day. The headache grew worse. Rachel broke one of her grandmother's teacups. She upset a bottle of frying oil over the stove and spattered all the brasses. She burnt her fingers opening the oven door. And worse, she burnt the cake. However, by dint of sheer grit and dogged perseverance, at three o'clock the little flat was shining, the fish loaf was all ready for the oven, the vegetables and the salad were prepared, and the cake, successfully grated off with respect to its burnt section, was frosted artistically. Max would bring some flowers home with him. Rachel herself was tastefully dressed in a becoming old-rose frock which especially pleased Max. Everything was in readiness for the distinguished guest of honor—just as perfect as the "clever little housewife" could make it. And yet Rachel felt uncomfortably apprehensive. Well she might!

Mrs. Kalinsky arrived at half-past four. Her greeting of Rachel was greasily effusive. Rachel bore it bravely. "Mein darling daughter! Mamma she is came to see you in your beautiful flat. Oi, oi, how fine it all iss— how vunderful!" She threw up her arms and clapped her hands over her head in ecstatic gesture. "Oi, but it iss all so grand! You haf made it sveet! Come, you

47

must show it to Mamma eferythings! Mein Maxie's home—mein own darling Maxie! He haf now a fine leetle flat vhich it iss all his own. Und he haf now too a beautiful leetle vife— vhich it iss mein own darling daughter Rakkel!"

Mrs. Kalinsky removed her hat and coat and combed her hair, and then proceeded upon her tour of inspection of every remotest corner of the flat, accompanying it with voluble comment. On this, her first visit, her appraisal of the material equipment was altogether favorable. Rachel's domestic activities, however, did not so easily pass muster. Within fifteen minutes of her entrance into the bride's little home, Mrs. Kalinsky started to make good her promise declared on the night of the wedding to Sophy Yasnik and Yetta Cash and Mrs. Kalish, that she would "learn Rakkel eferythings."

Her instruction began with noodle soup. After the minute examination of the flat had been completed to her satisfaction, Mrs. Kalinsky sat down in the kitchen and watched Rachel as she drew out her bake board and proceeded to cut into artistic shapes the little mounds of dough she had so carefully kneaded in the morning.

"Vot you making, Rakkel?" interrogated Mrs. Kalinsky sharply.

"I'm making noodles for the chicken soup," Rachel replied sweetly.

"Vot? Noo-dles? Them things ain't noo-dles! Vy you cut it all so qveer? Come, I vill learn you right." She seized the knife and the dough from Rachel's hands and began chopping vigorously. "See, Rakkel," she said, shaving the ball into the thinnest possible shreds, "you must cut noo-dles alvays so."

Rachel's spirit of independence flamed. "But," she protested, "I always cut them up in fancy shapes for Max. He likes them best that way."

Her appeal to Max's preference was not the most tactful reply. Rather, it was exceedingly unhappy.

"Vot," Mrs. Kalinsky exclaimed shrilly—her tone not quite pleasant—"vot? You think you know it better than his mother how mein Maxie like his noo-dles? For twenty-two years I haf meinself made noo-dles for mein sohn. I guess, mein dear Rakkel, you cannot tell me how mein Maxie vant his noo-dles."

Latent maternal jealousy was aroused. The cutting of the dough proceeded forthwith according to Mrs. Kalinsky's pattern.

Rachel's method of baking the fish loaf was next called into question. Likewise her choice of saucepans for the cooking of the vegetables—while her artistic arrangement of the salad upon the dainty individual glass plates was sniffed at as "foolishness." Every detail, in fact, of the preparation of the little bride's first dinner for her mother-in-law was subject to the displeasure of that estimable lady. By the time Max arrived and dinner was served, Rachel's nervousness and resentment had reached a high pitch. Her feelings were not soothed at all by Mrs. Kalinsky's observations to her son after they had started eating.

"It iss such a nice leetle supper. I meinself certainly haf show Rakkel how she must cook it. She iss going to be a very clefer housevife, Maxie, after Mamma vill learn her yet."

Max came manfully to his bride's defense. "Rachel is a wonderful little housewife already! You should see, Mamma, all the fine things she cooks for me."

But Mrs. Kalinsky shook her head stubbornly. "Rakkel, maybe she vill be a fine cook some day—but she haf very, very much vot she must learn yet. But nefer mind"—this to Rachel— "you must be very patient und I vill show you. I haf promise I meinself vill learn you eferythings."

Rachel's anger was dangerously near the surface by this time. But her loyalty to Max, combined with her innate pride, enabled her to conceal it from their guest.

The meal proceeded apace, Rachel outwardly very charming and gracious as hostess, while all the time she was inwardly raging. But the shoals and quicksands of the evening were safely passed at last, and by half-past ten Max escorted his mother home. He invited Rachel to go with them but she declined. His mother would want to have a little visit with him alone. In her heart she longed to get alone by herself—as quickly as possible.

And for good reason! She knew she was at the snapping point. The instant the door closed upon Mrs. Kalinsky and Max she gave way. All the pent-up anger and resentment and nerve strain of the past two days was released in a flood of violent weeping. Free at last, Rachel buried her head in her arms and sobbed hysterically. The poor child was thoroughly unnerved.

49

Her keen instinct and quick perception appraised the situation exactly. She saw before her a weary path. Her peaceful little home had been invaded, and Rachel knew that future invasions were as certain as that night follows day. Nor could she see any possible escape—none certainly while Max was so completely dominated by his mother. She looked ahead with dread. She knew the beautiful sweet road had met a turning. The pathway now would be beset with thorns. Nor were her fears in the least degree mistaken.

From that day forward, Mrs. Kalinsky's smouldering jealousy mounted apace. Her determination "to learn Rakkel eferythings" took definite action. Rachel's freedom was completely gone. No longer was she mistress in her own home. Her every movement was scrutinized, criticized, reproved.

Hardly a day passed that Mrs. Kalinsky did not either demand that Max and Rachel come to Eleventh Street, or that she did not go down to their flat. Sundays they must always spend with her at the big house, she insisted upon it. Their visit lasted usually from noon till nearly midnight, with all which that implied—hours of drudgery for Rachel over the big stove or the dishpan, and yet more distasteful hours of visiting in the family group in the ugly parlors, listening endlessly to Mrs. Kalinsky's smug self-praise. The worst thing of all about those "detestable Kalinsky Sundays" as Rachel resentfully called them—to herself, never to Max—was that she had no opportunity whatever to talk with him alone. All day long, from the moment they entered the house until they left it, Max was his mother's undisputed, proprietary possession.

Besides Sunday, there was one evening a week at least when they must go to Eleventh Street for dinner; and never less than two evenings that Mrs. Kalinsky visited them, which was worse. After the first gushing effusiveness toward "mein darling new daughter" wore off, Mrs. Kalinsky's natural colors came more to the fore. Never a visit was there that Rachel after it did not feel strained and almost ill. In her truly noble effort to conceal from Max her burning inward resentment, the nervous tension was constant and extreme. The pretty flat which upon Mrs. Kalinsky's first visit and a few succeeding ones met with favor, became gradually the object of her gruelling criticism. Nothing in it pleased her. The jealous cross-examination of its little mistress was detailed and insistent.

"Vy you keep your brass things on the stove? You should keep them alvays in the cupboard, Rakkel". . . "Vy you haf a rug on top of your linoleum? You don't need no rug mit linoleum; you should not haf vot iss not necessary." . . . "Vy you keep it alvays flowvers on your table? Flowvers they iss too expensive." . . . "Vy you cook your supper in the mornings? You should not make it your supper ready till you haf had your lunch yet.". . . "Vy you put it in your cake so much good oil? It iss not necessary that you use so much. Vun spoonful certainly iss all you vant." . . . "Vy you vear in the mornings, Rakkel, such fancy dresses in the house? You should vear always in the house dark dresses to save vashing!" And so on—endlessly. Nothing—absolutely nothing escaped her eye. And nothing suited.

Her pet aversion was the cat. She detested cats. Whenever she came she insisted that Rachel put hers down in the basement. One day she noticed Rachel pouring a jug of cream into the cat's saucer. This was more than she could stand. "Rakkel Kalinsky!" she demanded, "vot vus you gifing to that cat? . . . Krim! You gif to a cat krim! To a cat! Und I can't afford to buy krim for meinself. Nefer let me see you doing such a things again! Alvays you must feed cats only mit skim-milk."

Next to the cat, Mrs. Kalinsky's chief displeasure was the ingle-nook. Each time she tried to squeeze her portly bulk into it, behind the table, her ire was roused. More than once she had angrily jerked the table out of the nook into the center of the floor and placed the Windsor chairs around it before she would sit down.

And still another source of irritation were the glazed chintz curtains. "Such foolishness," was her comment upon these. "Vy you haf in your kitchen curtains which it iss so silly? These ain't no kind of curtains for a kitchen. They iss for a parlor. Vot they kostet you?" she suddenly demanded.

Rachel met the issue squarely, "Seven dollars!"

Mrs. Kalinsky's wrath exploded. "Vot! Sef-en dol-lars! Rakkel Mendelssohn Kalinsky! You pay sefen dollars for curtains for a kitchen!" Her voice rose to a shrill crescendo.

"You dare to told me you spend it sefen dollars of mein poor sohn's money vhich he haf to vork so hard for, to buy curtains for a kitchen! Oi, oi, you vill make him to be ruined yet—mein poor dear boy, mein Maxie!"

Mrs. Kalinsky seemed possessed with the very spirit of contradiction. Usually Rachel could throw off the weight of her visits as soon as she had gone. Her cutting thrusts had fortunately no lasting effect upon her young daughter-in-law. Once the door was closed upon her, Rachel would feel a keen elation in the thought that now, for a little while at least, she could again be mistress in her own home. But one act of Mrs. Kalinsky's there was—her master-stroke of domination—of such cruel consequence that it was impossible for Rachel to throw off the depression it created. It left in its train an abiding and an irreparable sorrow.

The occasion was Mrs. Kalinsky's second visit in the little flat. On her first visit with Max and Rachel the evening had passed without mishap. But the second time she dined with them she had said suddenly, just as they were finishing dessert, "Vot time do you go back to the shop, Max?"

"Go back—to the shop!" Max repeatedly blankly.

"Yes, after supper. Vot time do you go back to vork?"

"I—I don't work evenings, Mamma," faltered Max. "I always close the shop at half-past six." Instantly the red lights blazed. Mrs. Kalinsky turned upon him in shocked displeasure.

"Vot?" she demanded violently. "You don't vork efenings? Vot you mean by such a things, mein sohn? How you expect you vill get rich qvick like vot ve plan, ven you close your shop up efenings? Tonight it iss Friday, so you need not go to-night und you can vait also Saturday und Sunday. But Monday you vill start. You must get a boy to mind the shop till you get back from supper, und then you vill vork efery night till ten o'clock und Saturdays elefen!"

Thus the maternal mandate went forth. And there was no appeal. Forthwith, on the following Monday evening the little shop on Second Avenue remained open for business until ten-and on every evening thereafter. In consequence Rachel at home was lonely and sad.

She seldom went out now after supper. She would not go to the homes of their married friends without Max; and gradually these friends no longer came, with the old happy informality and frequency, to their house. Even Ben and Esther, after two or three very unsatisfactory suppers when Max had to rush off and leave them, finally found difficulty in getting down to Second Street; while Rachel of course could not go alone away up the Bronx to their home. She and Esther still enjoyed many happy visits together over their tea in the afternoon; but the jolly little suppers with the boys gradually diminished. Mrs. Kalinsky kept urging Rachel to stay at the big house every evening until Max called for her, but this she always avoided doing whenever it was diplomatically possible. She chose the lesser evil of staying home alone.

She whiled away the long hours reading or sewing or busying herself with various household tasks. She would play with the cat. She would try to sing. She would make a special treat for Max. At ten o'clock she would start the water boiling in the samovar. Sometimes it was eleven before Max reached the flat— so often it was that his mother wanted to talk over the day's business with him after the shop was closed at ten, and he would have to go away up to Eleventh Street before coming home. More than once it was nearly twelve o'clock before Rachel, tense and unstrung, at last would hear his steps upon the stairs. But whatever time it was, she invariably met him with a smile. He never suspected her displeasure. But though she succeeded so unselfishly and admirably in concealing from her husband her unhappiness, Rachel could not conceal it from herself. She was thoroughly unhappy and she knew it.

Chapter V.

Eden Disquieted

"For the word of God is quick and powerful, and
sharper than any two-edged sword, piercing
even to . . . dividing asunder." —Hebrews 4:12.

In her strange new loneliness Rachel's heart turned instinctively towards two of her dearest friends—an elderly Russian Jewish couple whose humble dwelling was in a basement tenement in Rivington Street. All who live in Rivington Street are not of Rivington Street. Full many a noble son and daughter of Abraham, many a true prince or princess of Israel is hidden, by force of cruel circumstance, in some drear and dismal corner of the Ghetto.

Such was the case with Mr. and Mrs. Saramoff. Like many another elderly man and wife, they had come to America to spend their sunset years with a dear son who had preceded them to the New World and its opportunity and had prospered. For two years they had been cherished tenderly and their every need had been abundantly supplied. Then suddenly—with terrific shock to the poor old father and mother—both the son and his wife were taken from them by accidental drowning, leaving but a slender fund of savings, and the care of their only child—a little girl three years old and crippled. The savings dwindled, and Mr. and Mrs. Saramoff thus were forced at seventy years of age, to fight life's battle alone in a strange new land. The result, after seven cruel years, was—in self-respecting preference to charity—a pushcart as their sole means of livelihood and as their sole abode, the wretched tenement in the basement rear on Rivington Street.

But miserable as it was, it yet bore evidence that gentlefolk were dwelling there. The pitiful furnishings could not conceal their true nobility and character. And Rachel loved to visit them. Just to be with them was a benediction.

She had first met the Saramoff's as she had made purchases at their pushcart. At the outset there were exchanges of friendly words between them, then gradually a warmth of sympathy, as Rachel instinctively was attracted to them and they to her. It was not long before she was invited into their poor little home, where she was cheered by many a chat with Mrs. Saramoff and refreshed by her fragrant Russian tea. As Rachel sipped it happily, Little Jessie, the crippled grandchild, would always lean her tiny crutch in the corner and curl up close beside her.

One evening late in October, when Max was at the shop, and Rachel at home was feeling particularly lonely, a great longing to see the Saramoff's came over her. Something in their presence there was—she could not define just what—that was peculiarly soothing to her. She knew that Max did not approve of her going out alone at night, but the mood was strong upon her and she went.

As she entered the basement kitchen in response to Mrs. Saramoff's cheery "come in" she perceived that another guest was present—a young woman of exceptional attractiveness—a Gentile—in her early thirties probably. Her face had a peculiar charm and winsomeness and her bearing clearly bespoke distinction. She and Mr. and Mrs. Saramoff and Little Jessie were all seated around the table. In front of them lay open books, the pages illumined by the light of two tall candles.

As Rachel advanced toward the table, Little Jessie screaming in delighted welcome, slid from her chair and hobbled to Rachel on her one small crutch. She flung her free arm around Rachel's neck joyfully while Rachel enfolded her in a fond embrace. Mr. and Mrs. Saramoff both rose also, and their genuinely cordial reception went straight to Rachel's heart. Already she felt warmed and cheered and strengthened.

Mrs. Saramoff then presented Rachel to their guest, "Miss Hamilton, this is my dear little friend, Mrs. Rachel Kalinsky, I was telling you of. And Mrs. Kalinsky, Miss Violet Hamilton is one of my very dear Gentile friends. I want you two girls to know and to love each other."

The attraction between them—the older Gentile girl and the younger Jewish one—was mutually instinctive and instantaneous. Violet Hamilton's warm, sympathetic handclasp, her radiant smile, her winsome personality captivated Rachel at once. She felt a glowing warmth—a sense of restfulness and peace. She was glad that she had come.

And then instantly, Rachel suffered a dreadful shock—a sudden, terrible revulsion of feeling. She was stunned, bewildered, grieved. For her eyes, always keen for the printed page, had glanced down at the book lying open on the table before her. To her horror she had noted what it was—the New Testament. She was struck dumb. She could not believe it possible. What was that Book doing here in the Saramoff home?—a New Testament on a Jewish table! She looked first at Mr. Saramoff and then at his gentle wife. In her eyes were mingled questioning, amazement, and reproach. Both of her friends met her gaze squarely, unflinchingly. Violet Hamilton, skilled missionary to the Jews that she was, was quick to discern the dramatic tenseness of the situation. She relieved it with charming tact. Offering her chair to Rachel, with her engaging smile she handed her the Testament. "Mrs. Kalinsky," she said, in the rich, sweet voice that had won its way to many a Jewish heart, "would you not like to join us in our reading? We were just enjoying together such a wonderful story about a Jewish young man and his two sisters in the little town of Bethany."

Rachel was overwhelmed with confusion. She could not show discourtesy to a kind young woman nor to her host and hostess in their home. But on the other hand her rigid orthodox Jewish convictions had been rudely assailed. She faltered lamely, "But Miss Hamilton, that is the New Testament, is it not?—the Christian Bible? I am a Jewess!" Again she looked questioningly, reproachfully at the Saramoffs. They remained silent while Miss Hamilton, with that rare intuitive sympathy which had made her missionary efforts so successful, handled the difficult problem. She smiled radiantly in response.

"A Jewess!" she exclaimed. "Oh, how wonderful, Mrs. Kalinsky, it must be to be a Jewess! A daughter of Abraham! One of God's own Chosen People—a jewel for His diadem! Dear Mrs. Kalinsky, if you only knew how I envy you that honor!"

Rachel gasped in amazement. Never before in her life had she heard a Gentile say such a thing as that. She had always believed firmly that the Gentile attitude toward the Jew was one of condescension if not of actual aversion. Miss Hamilton was quick to press her advantage. Her lovely brown eyes smiled into Rachel's bewildered black ones.

"Since you are a Jewess then, Mrs. Kalinsky," she urged, "the New Testament is the very Book that you would most appreciate."

"Why?" interposed Rachel in frank astonishment.

"Because," Miss Hamilton continued, "this is the Book that tells the story of the most wonderful Jew that ever lived."

"You mean—Jesus?" There was a shade of scorn in Rachel's tone.

"Yes! The Lord Christ Jesus! This Book tells us of Him." Violet Hamilton's eyes glowed with lovely light. She hurried on eagerly, "Do you know Him at all, Mrs. Kalinsky? Have you ever read of His wonderful, wonderful life?—of His compassion and tenderness towards all who suffered and were sad?—of His marvellous miracles?—His matchless teaching?—His lofty ideals and example?—and then of His cruel death upon the cross, and of His glorious, triumphant Resurrection? Dear Mrs. Kalinsky, do you know of these?" Her eyes—her voice—her charm held Rachel fascinated.

Quickly, before Rachel had time to interpose a word, Miss Hamilton opened the New Testament to the eleventh of John— while her heart swelled with intense and tender longing for this Jewish girl. "Here, for instance," she said smilingly, "is one story about the Lord Jesus that is marvellous. "Won't you just listen while I read it?" Again Violet Hamilton's winsome manner was consciously directed towards effective service for her Master.

Rachel was entirely disarmed. No further resistance was possible. She sat down at the table with her fellow Hebrews, the New Testament open in her hands, while the Christian missionary to the Jews unfolded to her for the first time in her life the treasures of God's Word concerning His Son from Heaven, as declared in New Testament writ. Little Jessie cuddled close beside her. The light of the two tall candles fell alike upon Rachel's beautiful face and upon the New Testament open in her hands.

With gradually unfolding wonderment Rachel listened to the story of Jesus' raising of Lazarus from the dead. Vividly, with dramatic power, Miss Hamilton portrayed the stirring scene— the grid-stricken sisters—the emotional Jewish throng beside

57

the grave—the compassion of the Friend—His quiet assumption of control—His appeal and thanksgiving to the Father—His voice of authority, "Lazarus come forth!"—the restoration of the dead to life!

As Miss Hamilton finished the reading and the exposition of the chapter, all sat for a few moments in pensive, reverent silence. Rachel was the first to break it. "Oh, Miss Hamilton—how marvellous a story! Jesus was—yes, He surely was, a wonderful, wonderful man!" She was profoundly moved. To the three who were watching her closely, that was clearly evident. Miss Hamilton seized the opportunity with challenge. "A man! Did you say a man? Oh, Mrs. Kalinsky, can you not see, on the evidence of that miracle alone—that He is infinitely more than man? What man could raise the dead to life? No, dear Mrs. Kalinsky, Jesus Christ is God—the Son from Heaven—the true Messiah!"

Rachel was completely silenced. Again she looked at Mr. and Mrs. Saramoff. And again they met her gaze unflinchingly. With her sweet, gentle smile the elderly woman nodded her head in affirmation. "Yes, dear, Jesus is the Son of God."

"And our Messiah!" joyfully added Mr. Saramoff—"the Messiah of our people Israel!"

Rachel attempted weakly one last defensive. "But you are Hebrews!" she exclaimed. "He is the Messiah of the Christians!"

"He is the Messiah of us all—of all who will accept Him," Mrs. Saramoff replied. "And we," she confessed gently with a radiant smile, "are Christians—Hebrew-Christians! Yes, dear," as Rachel stared at her in blank amazement, "for many years we both have been—believers!"

"And we believe, Mrs. Kalinsky," added Mr. Saramoff firmly, with the dignity of the true Christian gentleman he was, despite the tenement, despite the pushcart, "we believe on the evidence presented in this Book."

"Yes," affirmed Miss Hamilton, " 'these are written, that ye might believe that Jesus is the Christ, the Son of God; and that believing ye might have life through His name.' Dear Mrs. Kalinsky, will you not take this little Book, and search for yourself these things and prove that they are true?"

Half-eagerly, half-fearfully Rachel thanked her and accepted the proffered New Testament, carefully concealing it in an inner pocket of her hand-bag. As she did so she glanced at her wrist-watch. She gave a startled exclamation. "Oh, I did not know it was so late! I am sorry. I must hurry." Instantly her thoughts were frenzied. Whatever would Max say! It was the first time all evening that she had thought of Max.

She took her departure hurriedly. Little Jessie clung to her and begged her not to go. Mr. and Mrs. Saramoff both eagerly invited her to come back. Violet Hamilton, strongly moved by Rachel's appealing earnestness, voiced her longing that they soon might meet again. As the door closed behind Rachel, though she knew it not, many and ardent were the prayers that followed her.

As she sped homeward her emotions were in strange tumult. Uppermost was the sense of fear—fear of the streets so late at night and the greater fear of what Max would say should he have reached home before her. He would be very angry, she was sure of that. Then there was utter bewilderment of thought concerning those things which she had heard tonight. There had been tremendous impact of new and strange ideas against ancient orthodox tradition, accepted always previously without question. Had Rachel but realized it, it was the impact between light and darkness—the darkness of Judaism and the Light of Life.

Then too, there was much confusion in her sense of values. This mysterious Book—this New Testament—which all good Jews should hate—she had found, as Miss Hamilton had read and explained it to her, absolutely fascinating and enthralling. And this Jesus—Whose very Name was anathema on Jewish lips—confessed as Messiah by that beautiful Miss Hamilton, and even by her own dear Jewish friends, the Saramoffs. Yes, and even Little Jessie had said she loved Him! And Rachel herself was bound to confess, from the story of Him she had listened to tonight, her own tremendous admiration. If the record they had read of Him were true, if His raising of the dead to life could be authenticated, then the evidence of His Messiahship was indisputable. And yet, and yet—He was the hated Jesus, and she, Rachel Mendelssohn Kalinsky, was a Jewess—of the sect of strictest orthodoxy. As she sped on faster and faster, her mind, her heart, was in a whirl.

Fortunately she reached home before Max. Her relief was great. Now she would not have to tell him. It was the first time since their marriage that she had ever concealed anything from her young husband. There had been entire openness and candor between them on every subject, always. But this was different! Intuitively Rachel felt that this would raise a barrier. Anyway, she argued with her conscience, this was no concern of Max's. This was a matter of her own inmost soul—a question between herself and God alone. When she got it all worked out to her own satisfaction then she would tell Max. But not yet—not yet!

And work it out she must. She had to get it all thought through. If the New Testament were, as Miss Hamilton had claimed, equally with the Old Testament—the *Taanach*—the Word of God; and if by any possibility Jesus were indeed the true Messiah, then Rachel must find it out. She could not rest content until she knew the truth.

She would read the New Testament for herself. And she would go again to the Saramoffs. Mrs. Saramoff had so cordially invited her and had told her that Miss Hamilton was with them every Thursday night. Thursday!—the hardest of all the lonely evenings now, without the old happy parties with Ben and Esther. Yes, she must go down again some Thursday and read and study more with that wonderful Miss Hamilton. She had recalled how, at her wedding supper the *Rav* had warned her and Max against the Christian missionaries. But she did not care. Hers was a fearless mind, an independent spirit. Even Rabbi Mordecai Moses could not dictate to her conscience. She was determined that she would investigate this entire subject for herself.

And so as the Indian Summer wore away and the Fall was drawing on toward Winter, Rachel spent more and more time in the study of God's Word. Max was invariably away from her now—never an evening that he was home before eleven at the earliest. Rachel's spirit grew dull. The old happy vivacity was gone, the sparkle, the brilliancy, the continuously overbubbling joy that had welled up from her happy heart. Mrs. Kalinsky was constantly at the flat—to the gradual exclusion of Rachel's girl friends, who could not stand her—and her jarring presence cast a positive pall over the little home. Rachel became nervous and irritable and even quarrelsome with Max. When he came home at night he was always tired and jaded, and if he talked at all it was of the one subject that now was uppermost—his business and making big money fast. In the morning he slept late and therefore had no time to help Rachel as he used to do. Often she had even to carry the coal herself up the five steep flights. And through the day there was no longer the eager looking forward to Max's homecoming for their old-time happy evenings together. So, little by little, the former joyous camaraderie between them ceased.

And thus very naturally it came about that her one solace amid the loneliness was the little Testament. Every morning after Max had gone, and before there was any danger of Mrs. Kalinsky coming, and after she had locked the door carefully against any other possible intruders, she drew the New Testament forth from its place of concealment—the soft inner lining of her coat—the only place she could think of that would be safe from Mrs. Kalinsky's all-invading eye; and hour after hour she would study it with deepening absorption, comparing the New Testament Scriptures and the Old with gradual growing and irresistible conviction.

And then on occasional Thursday evenings when the coast seemed clear, she would run down to Rivington Street for an hour—she never risked longer—with the Saramoffs and her now very dear Miss Hamilton. Gradually she became bolder and went more and more frequently, but she always kept her visits there carefully concealed from her husband and her mother-in-law.

At length she summoned up sufficient courage to invite Miss Hamilton to call upon her in her flat. Mrs. Kalinsky was out of town for a few days. Esther and the other sisters-in-law never came unless they phoned her previously. Max never got home before six at the very earliest. Yes, she felt it would be quite safe. Miss Hamilton accepted the invitation joyfully. For months she had been praying for this very opportunity. She wanted Rachel to herself alone, away even from the Saramoffs.

And so it happened that the following Monday afternoon—the day before Christmas it was—found the two friends chatting together over their tea-glasses in the ingle-nook in Rachel's pretty kitchen. It was a happy occasion to Rachel to be thus entertaining Miss Hamilton in her own little home. And if it was happy for Rachel it was ten-fold happier for Violet Hamilton. To her it was precious beyond words. It was a God-given opportunity. It was answered prayer. Her heart swelled in praise and thanksgiving to Him. As she studied the sweet, eager face before her, she pleaded in a very agony of earnestness that wisdom from on high might be given her to speak aright—that her lips might be kept in safeguard—that no word might escape them which was not divinely led. She wanted to be only a humble mouthpiece—a willing, yielded instrument for the Holy Spirit's operation. But the work—however it might please Him to direct it—must be altogether His.

They had their tea together with sweetly deepening intimacy. Rachel was so happy in this dear new friend. And Violet Hamilton, looking upon Rachel Kalinsky, loved her. With unutterable longing she prayed that she might be used of God to win her for the King.

Tea finished, Rachel brought her Testament, still safely concealed in the lining of her coat, and Miss Hamilton opened her Bible. As she offered aloud a brief prayer to God for the Spirit's illumination of the Word, Rachel bent her head in reverent silence. Then together the two girls—the Jewess and the Gentile—studied from the Epistle to the Romans. Aloud and in unison they read the wonderful third chapter—"What advantage then hath the Jew? or what profit is there of circumcision?" So deeply absorbed did they become that they did not hear the door open and a firm step enter the room. The kitchen stove had become overheated and, off guard for a brief moment, Rachel had opened the outer door the merest crack for ventilation.

They had come to the twenty-fourth verse and were just reading it aloud together—"Being justified freely by his grace through the redemption that is in Christ Jesus . . ." when suddenly, feeling a presence near her, Rachel looked up from her New Testament. Her blood froze in horror. For standing close beside the table, towering above her in a fearful rage, stood her mother-in-law, Mrs. Deborah Kalinsky. She had come home the night before quite unexpectedly.

Before Rachel could rise or even speak, the vials of wrath and withering scorn were poured upon her head in rushing torrent.

"Rakkel Mendelssohn Kalinsky! How did you dare to? —Vot iss it you vus doing?—You cannot fool me nothings. I know it vot it iss—that Book vhich you vus reading yet. It iss a Noy Testament! Beliefe me I am telling you, I know it a Noy Testament ven I see vun! Vot for you dare to haf it in mein sohn's house?—a book vhich it vus a Christian's book—a Je-sus book? Und you a Jewvish vife! You vill answer me-vot you dare to mean by all such things?" In a fury she seized the Testament from Rachel's hands and flung it into the stove. Then she turned in violent rage upon Miss Hamilton.

"Und who vus you?" she demanded. "Vot vus you doing here by mein dear daughter-in-law, vhich she iss the vife of mein own sohn—learning her Noy Testament? Vot you trying to do mit her—to change her from Jewvish into English?—You need not to tell me! Beliefe me, I know you vot you vus—ein mees-ion-aire!—ein vicked mees-ion-aire!—I am telling you, you shall nefer learn mein dear daughter about Je-sus. You go avay!—you leave mein sohn's house qvick."

Miss Hamilton having meanwhile risen from the table tried in vain to impede the flood of angry words. As easily could she have stayed Niagara. Each attempt only added fresh fuel to the flame. The monologue continued. With volcanic fury the scorching, withering words burst forth in shrill crescendo.

"A Noy Testament—a Noy Testament! Vot for you bring a Noy Testament into a Jewvish house? Don't you know ve Jews nefer touch mit our leetle fingers such a book? It iss poison! Vot you mean coming here to mein dear daughter ven her hoosband he iss avay yet? Vy don't you stay home by your own house? You should ought to be ashamed of yourself making such a fool of yourself! How much you get paid for turning Jews to English? Vy don't you work at something real yet? Can't you get no decent job? I vill get for you a job. I vill get for you a job where you belong—in jail yet. In jail you vill not be telling Jewvesses they must beliefe in Je-sus!"

Once again Miss Hamilton attempted to speak. Mrs. Kalinsky cut her off furiously. "Vot! Vot you say? Je-sus! Je-sus He is the

Mescheach? How dare you go for to talk such vickedness? Je-sus He iss not Mescheach! Mescheach He iss not came yet . . . Vot! Vot you say?" she fairly screamed her scorn, "Jesus, He iss the Sohn of God? Vy you talk it such foolishness? Haf God got a sohn? How could God haf a sohn . . . Beliefe me, I am telling you, you are talking vicked, vicked foolishness! . . . Vot! How dare you say such a things? Je-sus He iss Himself God! . . .Vot! God iss Father, Sohn und Holy Speerit? Three Gods iss vun God? Iss three vun und vun iss three? Beliefe me I am telling you, you iss foolish.

With scarcely a pause for breath between, the torrent of furious words continued to belch forth: "Christians! Christians! I know all vhich I vants to know about Christians! It iss Christians vot gets poor little Jewvish childrens mit candy und ice-krim und then locks them up in cellars und burns Jesus crosses on them. Und it iss Christians vot kills all the Jews they can. You say the Jews killed Jesus. Vell, please, vill you let me ask you vun qvestion—how many Jews iss it vot the Christians kill? Beliefe me I am telling you, I lif in Russien und mein own brother und six cousins they vus killed in the pogroms by Christians. Don't you go for to try und tell me nothings about Christians!"

Rachel, chagrined beyond expression, had attempted here and there to interrupt her mother-in-law, but she was brushed back like a fly. Miss Hamilton flashed her many glances of loving sympathy and understanding, but Rachel's humiliation was complete. She tried to compose herself, to get a grip upon the situation, but she was conscious of miserable eclipse and defeat. At last, Mrs. Kalinsky, her breath almost spent and her flow of words exhausted, suddenly seized Miss Hamilton by the arms and savagely shoved her towards the doorway. "You get oudt of here," she screamed, "und don't you nefer dare to show your face in here again! Learning mein daughter about Noy Testament und Je-sus! Shame on yourself! You get oudt from here qvick!"

And then Rachel gathered strength and did assert herself. Her pride was stung to its very depths. She realized that here was a crisis. Either she was mistress of her home or she was not. With dignity, controlling her anger by a supreme effort of will, she placed her arm detainingly around Miss Hamilton and stood between her and her irate mother-in-law. Her voice was low and cool—but firm.

"Mrs. Kalinsky," she said quietly—she never would call her mother-in-law "Mother"—which fact gave added grievance—

"Mrs. Kalinsky, Miss Hamilton is my dear friend, and I say she shall not go. She is always welcome in my home."

This was a new torch to Mrs. Kalinsky's rage. "Vot!" she snorted in scorn, "your home! Your home iss it, I should like it to know? It iss mein sohn's home—mein Maxie's!"

"Yes," replied Rachel with dignity, "and I am your son's wife, and his home is my home, too."

"Your home, iss it?" Mrs. Kalinsky reiterated maliciously, "if you vant to know it, ladies, whose home it iss, I am telling you. It iss mein home! Und vy? Because I pay for it meinself the rent! Eighteen-dollars-und-fifty-cents efery month I pay. Und alvays two-dollars-und-sefenty-five-cents the very lowest for electrish! So that iss whose home it iss, I vill haf you both to know yet."

Miss Hamilton, having donned her hat and coat was tactfully withdrawing, signalling understanding glances to Rachel— when just at that instant the door was flung open and in walked Max! Never before had he arrived at five o'clock. But this day of all days he elected to come home at that hour.

Quickly he perceived the storm signals. He looked first at his mother's angry, flaming face and then at his wife. And then he looked squarely and questioningly at the young woman who was a stranger to him. He was not kept waiting long for the desired explanation. Upon sight of him, Mrs. Kalinsky's vials of fury burst forth afresh. Before the storm gathered full momentum, however, Miss Hamilton quickly and quietly left, as that seemed to her experienced judgment the wisest thing to do. As she went out the door she pressed Rachel's hand in a warm, loving, understanding clasp. She longed to take her in her arms—to kiss her—but she dared not. It would only make further trouble for the poor little Jewish wife. She did not even speak. All she could do was to commit Rachel Kalinsky to the Heavenly Father's care. This she did, day after day, fervently, pleadingly, longingly—claiming her by faith for Christ.

Miss Hamilton gone, Mrs. Kalinsky rehearsed the indignity in

Max's astounded, grief-stricken ears. Rachel! His wife! Visited by a Christian missionary! Reading the New Testament! And talking aloud of Jesus! How long had this fearful thing been going on? And he had never dreamed it! He looked at Rachel with sorrowful reproach in his dark eyes.

Rachel waited for his accusation and rebuke. She nerved herself as with bars of steel for what was coming. He spoke only nine words but they broke her heart. Looking full into her eyes he cried bitterly, "Rachel! And I thought that I could trust you!"

Bursting into a flood of violent weeping Rachel withdrew into the little inner parlor, closed the door behind her and flung herself face downward on the couch. There she gave way to passionate sobbing, her tense nerves snapped at last. As the storm gradually spent itself she listened to Max and Mrs. Kalinsky talking in the kitchen. The tones were excited but kept low that she might not hear the words. At length, however, there was a distinctly audible command from Mrs. Kalinsky, her voice purposely directed towards the door closed between them.

"Come, mein sohn—mein precious Maxie. You vill came home to Mamma's house. Mamma vill make you there a nice hot supper yet. Come, mein poor darling boy! You must came home mit Mamma!"

Rachel heard the door slam behind them. She gave way to another fit of weeping. At length, utterly prostrated, she stumbled her way into the kitchen and found herself some supper. Every mouthful choked her. With heavy feet and a heavier heart she washed her supper dishes and the tea dishes. At sight of the tea table as she and Miss Hamilton had left it, the tears started afresh. Mechanically she swept the floor. . . she fed the cat. . . she set the table for breakfast. . . she lit the samovar for Max's tea. . . and then because she had nothing else to do, she polished the already gleaming brasses.

Then she sat down idly and waited. Ten o'clock. . . eleven o'clock. . . midnight. . . still no Max. The fire went out. She was numb with cold and terror. Half-past twelve. . . a quarter to one. Again she lighted the samovar. . . At one o'clock he came. His face was terribly white and drawn. He looked down at her a full moment in mingled reproach and grief. Rachel waited tensely for the blow to fall.

Chapter VI.

Eden Desolated

*"If a house be divided against itself,
that house cannot stand." —Mark 3:25.*

Yes, the storm is coming, Rachel, it is coming fast! Bow your head beneath its fury as it bursts upon you, dear—bow your head and rend your heart—for already, little Rachel, the storm, the angry storm is on!

For full ten minutes Max spoke absolutely not one word. His silence was more terrible than speech. Rachel waited in tensest suspense. He sat down at the table in the ingle-nook, an object of abject despair. His shoulders were dejected and limp; his elbows rested on the table, with his chin buried in his cupped hands. His derby hat was shoved back from his forehead aslant over one ear. His face was ashen. The mouth was drawn. The feverish dark eyes stared straight ahead, seeing nothing. He saw nothing; he said nothing; he was numb.

Rachel could stand it no longer. She poured his glass of tea and placed it before him. "Maxie dearest," she pleaded sorrowfully, "your tea! Won't you drink it?"

Savagely he thrust it from him. Still he saw nothing, said nothing . . . Then slowly he drew the glass back to him and toyed with the teaspoon while Rachel, aghast, stood looking at him dumbly. Suddenly he raised the tea to his lips and choked it down at one rapid draught . . . And then he broke the dreadful silence.

He laughed! Bitterly, scornfully, reproachfully.

"Well," he exclaimed in a sardonic voice, as suddenly he stood up and confronted his trembling little wife, "we won't be having our tea many more times in this house, Rachel! We're moving out!"

Rachel did not grasp the import of the words. But Max's menacing attitude, and his tone so strange and dreadful, struck terror to her heart.

"Wh-what?" she faltered. "What do you mean, Max?. . .Oh, do not look at me like that! I cannot bear it. What is it, Max?

What do you mean?"

"That's what I mean," he retorted harshly, "exactly that! We're moving out. And it's all your fault," he added bitterly.

"Moving? Out?" Rachel echoed in a stunned, hollow voice, "moving out? From here, Max? Moving? Oh, Maxie, Maxie, why?"

"Why? Because you can't be trusted to be left alone, that's why!"

"Oh, Maxie, don't say that—don't, don't! Oh, listen to me, dearest, you do not understand!" Pleadingly she lifted up her face to his.

With an oath—the first he had ever addressed to his beautiful little Jewish bride in his life—he pushed her away. A torrent of angry words burst forth.

"A lot you ever cared for me, Rachel Mendelssohn! . . . Yes, I understand all right!. . . I thought I had married a true Jewish wife, and here all the time you have been mixing up with Christians, bringing missionaries right to my own table even, when you thought I was safely away and would never know it. Allowing them to read from that accursed New Testament and to talk to you about Jesus Christ. And you my wife! And this a Jewish home! Ha—a home!" Again he laughed the bitter, heart-broken laugh. "Well," he continued, "I hope you're satisfied now with what you've done. It's our home no longer. You have broken it up by all your deceitfulness. Broken it up, I say—you have— you!" He flung himself into the chair again and burying his head in his arms upon the table, he sobbed aloud.

Rachel stood transfixed with horror. Her senses reeled. But as always in a crisis, her strength of character held firm. By a supreme effort of will she commanded her stunned faculties to face the situation. Here was no time for weakness or hysterical display. Too much was at stake. Her home, her love, her very life—all within one instant tottered on the brink of ruin.

She waited for Max's storm to spend itself. Then quietly she crossed to where he was sitting. Consciously she breathed a fervent upward prayer to God for wisdom and for strength. She must be guarded. Of the cause of the catastrophe—her growing interest in the claims of Christ—she knew she dared not breathe one word. All that must come at some later opportunity—but

68

His very Name even she dare not mention now. Also she must guard carefully every word she uttered concerning Mrs. Kalinsky. Rachel perceived clearly that her influence it was which had precipitated the present crisis; but not one syllable of reproach must drop. She was Max's mother.

"Max, our home is not broken. See, it all is here. You are here. I am here. Our love is here. No one can ever break that, Max— our wonderful love. And no one in all the world can break our home."

"It is broken, I am telling you," Max retorted bitterly. "We are moving out."

Again Rachel held herself in strong control. "When, Max?" she asked him quietly. Her voice, perfectly cool, gave no suggestion of the fire raging within. Breathlessly she awaited her husband's answer. He gave it in a mournful tone.

"In eight days! Today is the twenty-fourth. Tomorrow is the Christians' Christmas, and then their holiday week. Before it is over we'll be gone. Our lease is up the thirty-first and then—we leave!"

Still that wonderful poise, that perfect outward calm which was Rachel's most distinguishing characteristic. She stood erect and motionless as marble. And just as cold. With her next question an icy clutch was at her throat. "Where are we going, Max, from here?"

Max's reply confirmed her most terrible fear. "Why, to Mamma's house, of course. Where else could we go but Mamma's?"

The poise gave way. The wonderful calm collapsed. A moan of anguish burst from Rachel's heart.

"Oh, why, Max, why? Why must we give up our own dear, precious home? Who said so?"

"Mamma said so!'

"But why?"

"I told you why—because she says you can't be trusted to be left alone!"

"She says so?"

"And I say so, too! You make me have to say so by what you've done. You know it is the truth."

Max's anger was quite spent now, but in its place there

remained what was yet more terrible to Rachel—broken confidence and grief. Valiantly she set herself to do battle against these, as once more, by heroic effort she controlled her inward fury. Burning anger and resentment, outraged self-respect and pride, bitter hatred toward her mother-in-law—all these were in raging tumult within Rachel's breast. But again she held herself strongly in hand.

"Maxie," she argued gently, "if I can prove to you and to your mother that I can be trusted, then may we not stay here in our own dear home? Won't you urge your mother, Max, to let us stay?"

A hopeless shrug of his shoulders was Max's only answer.

"Oh, but Maxie darling, try," pleaded Rachel, as she gazed beseechingly into his eyes. "You must try, to save our home—our beautiful, beautiful home. Oh, we can't give it up, Max, we can't, we can't!"

He looked into her face. The bitter mood was entirely past, but a settled sadness brooded over him.

"Do try, Max," persisted Rachel, "try to make your mother change her mind."

But he only shook his head sadly as they wept together. "It won't do a bit of good, Rachel, anything I say. I did try all evening—to persuade her that everything would come all right—that you really didn't know what you were doing—and that after this you would leave all those Christian ideas alone. But I couldn't get anywhere. Mamma's mind is made up. And you can never change it. You know Mamma! Once Mamma's mind is made up, then believe me, I am telling you, it is made up."

Yes, Mrs. Deborah Kalinsky's mind was quite made up. And no power under Heaven could avail to change it. All too cruelly was Rachel made to realize that fact when next she met her mother-in-law, which was early the following morning. Mrs. Kalinsky lost no time. Once her mind was "made up," action was always prompt and decisive. Rachel was not to be trusted. It was necessary therefore that Mrs. Kalinsky herself assume active generalship over the preparations for moving, which she did forthwith, the redoubtable Sarah standing with her as her efficient and sympathetic ally.

To Rachel the eight days were a never-to-be-forgotten nightmare. From her mother-in-law's determined verdict there was no appeal. For Deborah Kalinsky herself constituted the highest court. When Rachel realized the futility of opposition, hope became despair. The effect was physical prostration. For days she was too ill to stand upon her feet. Hour after hour she could only lie upon her bed watching dumbly and hopelessly through the open doorway the steady destruction of her paradise.

At stated intervals Mrs. Kalinsky or Sarah would bring her food, or minister to her needs in other respects when absolutely necessary. Beyond this, Rachel was as impersonal and as inconsequential to them as the boxes and the barrels they were roping.

Rachel could hear them discussing her between themselves in low, excited tones—as one who had touched the accursed things of Christ and had therefore put herself outside the Jewish family pale. To her direct they addressed scarcely a word. Max's attitude toward her when he was at home was strained in the extreme. Whenever his mother or Sarah was present—and it was seldom that either one or both of them were not—he dared not speak with her at any length; which fact made his truly genuine efforts at kindness, when he and Rachel were alone, clumsy and altogether fruitless.

Mrs. Kalinsky's method in the disposition of Rachel's possessions was ruthless. The first treasure she disposed of was the cat. She was not going to have "that beast" under her feet while she was packing. Accordingly therefore, at the outset of her operations the grocer's errand-boy was paid five cents to "take it off." Pussy had had no breakfast—Rachel had not dared to give her any—and her hungry, frightened meow mingled with Rachel's moan as the boy gleefully carried her away.

The decks thus cleared for action, Mrs. Kalinsky and Sarah proceeded happily forthwith upon their self-appointed task of wrecking Rachel's home. Between them they handled all of her affairs quite satisfactorily.

One by one, Rachel, utterly helpless and heartbroken, watched all her treasures disappear from view. Mrs. Kalinsky's appraisal of the household goods was shrewd and calculating, and her decision concerning them wise accordingly. Anything

71

that might he used to good advantage at the big house was carefully sorted out for consignment thither. Things that did not suit her critical fancy were sold to second-hand men who were ordered in. Three separate times Rachel had to undergo the anguish of listening silently to her mother-in-law as she haggled with a Jewish vendor over the price of some cherished object.

The glazed-chintz curtains were ripped down and sold for two dollars and a quarter. The beautiful blue flower bowl went for forty cents; a lovely luncheon cloth that Rachel had embroidered herself for ninety-five.

With bated breath Rachel awaited the disposition of her precious heirlooms—her grandmother's dishes and brasses. These she was resolved that she would fight for, however terrible a scene it might produce. But happily she was spared this indignity. Mrs. Kalinsky herself was too keenly appraising. Every second-hand man grasped at them avidly, but Mrs. Kalinsky appreciated something of their worth and refused all offers however tempting. She had no immediate use for the dishes and brasses in the big house, her kitchen being already overstocked, but she would store them safely in her attic against future occasion. She packed them therefore in a barrel. The samovar was wrapped carefully in cotton wool and packed by itself in a large wooden box.

It was all over soon. The last day came—cold and bleak and dread. A sleety rain was pouring down. The wind moaned dismally. The atmosphere within the flat was all one with out-of-doors. Inside as well as out it was cold and bleak and mournful. The last home-fire had burned itself out through the night, and Rachel's stove, always warm and glowing, now stood black and dead, shrouded over with a film of ashes. The cupboards and the walls and floor were stripped and grim. Nothing was left but the barrels and boxes stacked in the middle of the kitchen, and the last few pieces of furniture required till the end. The moving van called for these at noon. One by one, Rachel, stunned with grief, saw them lifted out . . . . The last piece was gone! Nothing remained of Max and Rachel's Eden— nothing except the two painted settles which had formed the beloved ingle-nook. An hour later, after tensest waiting on Rachel's part, a second-hand dealer called for these. Three other men came with him. Together they lifted the heavy pieces from their places. Rachel, all dressed and ready for her own departure, watched these last two treasures being carried through the door.

She followed them out into the hallway and gazed after them with passionate regret. In the dim light, as the two settles were borne down the long, steep stairs, one man at either end of each, to Rachel's sickened brain they looked like coffins. She stood at the top of the stairway straining her eyes after them while her fingers clutched her throat convulsively. Coffins! Yes, that was exactly what they were—coffins. And in the first lay Max, and in the second one—herself.

By two o'clock it was all over. The last meal had been eaten— a cold, stand-up lunch of rolls and herring and onions, brought from the Kosher shop in paper bags by Max. The last suit-case had been closed, the last light turned off, and Max and Rachel, escorted by Mrs. Kalinsky and Sarah, were "moving out." Mrs. Kalinsky herself turned the key in the lock as the door closed forever upon their paradise. The heartbroken little wife, through blinding tears, stumbled her way down stairs—out into the cold, desolate rain. It was the thirty-first of December—the last day of the year—and the first anniversary of Max and Rachel's wedding.

They took a taxi to the house on East Eleventh Street. As they drove in silence through the dismal downpour, Rachel recalled bitterly her last trip in a taxi to Mrs. Kalinsky's home. It was in July—on that dreadful Sunday when her mother-in-law had returned from California. Rachel groaned aloud as she remembered. Oh, but that she might have stayed there—always!

"Abandon hope all ye who enter here." Had these words been blazoned in letters of fire on the lintel of the house on East Eleventh Street, they could not have scorched Rachel's heart more than already it was scorched and torn by retrospection and anticipation, as she mounted the steep steps, passed dully through the doorway, and was engulfed within the home of Mrs. Deborah Kalinsky.

Mercifully, the first few hours were spent alone. Max after hastily depositing the suitcases inside the door, rushed off to his shop. Mrs. Kalinsky, stopping only long enough to give Rachel her first instructions, went off with Sarah in the same taxi which had brought them, to a meeting of Hadassah. Jacob was at work. The children were at the Hebrew school. Grandmother Kalinsky, as usual, was sleeping in her kitchen rocker. Rachel would not disturb her for the world! How good to be asleep! Would that she too might have that sweet oblivion!

As in an awful dream she mounted the long stairs-four flights—in obedience to Mrs. Kalinsky's directions. She and Max were to share the top floor with Grandmother Kalinsky and the rats in the attic. A green skylight in the roof poured a wierd light down upon the upper staircase as wearily Rachel climbed it. When at last she reached the top, exhausted, her way was almost blocked by her barrels and boxes which congested the hallway outside the attic door.

She entered her room, the front one . . . Her artistic soul writhed. In the dull light from the two northern windows facing the leaden sky, the outlines of the dark, old-fashioned furniture stood out hideously. Sickly green hangings clashed violently with the frayed blue rug. The heavy bed was covered with a canopy and spread of purple satin. Ugly china ornaments cluttered the marble-topped dresser and table. A stuffed red-velvet armchair, with the stuffing bursting copiously from the arms and seat, graced the center of the room. In one cornet a rickety washstand held a cracked pink basin and an orange water-jug. The handle of the jug was broken off. Cheap chromos, each one dangling by a rusty wire at its own peculiar angle, adorned the walls, from which the dull tan paper was peeling off in many spots. A brass piano lamp, with a frayed rose silk shade, completed the scheme of the harmonious interior decoration.

With a bitter moan, Rachel flung herself face downward on the bed to shut it all out. Oh, if only she could shut out all thinking too! She tried to sleep but her brain pounded too heavily— also her heart. She tossed feverishly for an hour. Then she dragged herself up slowly and turned on the lamp. It gave a trace of comfort. But only for a moment. Still her brain pounded. She must do something—anything. Any activity whatever was better than this thinking. She went into the hall and started tugging at the boxes. She got one half unpacked, placing the contents—her table-linens—in a dresser drawer.

Then she heard noisy voices below. The children were coming in from school. Would they come upstairs, she wondered? Did they know that she was here? . . . But suddenly the voices stopped. The children had run out. Everything was quiet again—everything except the steady downpour of the rain upon the skylight and the scuttling of the rats. Rachel hated rats. She went into her room again and closed the door to shut out all of the distressing noises. She could not touch the boxes further. Later perhaps, but not now. It was all too sickening.

Once more she flung herself upon the bed, and this time she fell asleep. But it was a sleep without repose. Every kind of horror scuttled through her brain, much worse than the scuttling of the rats. Then the sleep became heavy and she was oblivious to commotion going on downstairs. . . She woke to see Max bending over her. Clumsily he tried to be comforting.

"Did you have a good sleep, Rachel? Come, dear, supper's ready. Mamma sent me up to bring you down."

"O no, Max, no! I don't want any supper! And I can't come down! O Max, I can't, I can't!"

Max looked unhappy. "Do come, Rachel," he urged "Mamma said so. Now that we are here, it is best that we should always do as Mamma says. You know Mamma, Rachel."

Yes, Rachel knew Mamma well. But she was to know her better still.

She bathed her tear-stained face and re-arranged her hair, then stoically she followed Max downstairs. She steeled herself for what might be awaiting in the kitchen—it did not matter what. Nothing mattered now.

What did await her was the unexpected. Reproach, scorn, cruelty, avoidance—Rachel was prepared for any one or all of these. But the actual staging of the drama swept her off her feet.

As she entered the kitchen, perfectly poised to outward view, but tumultuous within, a startling sight met her bewildered gaze. The long table was spread in holiday array with the best china, and adorned with flowers and candles. Around it were seated the entire Kalinsky family, sons, wives and grandchildren. Mrs. Kalinsky's two dearest friends, Yetta Cash and Sophy Yasnik—the unfailing news-reporters—were there as well; and of course Grandmother Kalinsky also. Mrs. Deborah, in the seat of authority and honor at the head of the table, was attired in her festive orange satin.

Upon sight of Rachel, five or six of the children rose and ran forward screaming excitedly to greet her, "Auntie Ray, Auntie Ray!" Mrs. Kalinsky, beaming expansively, motioned Max and Rachel to the vacant chairs on either side of her. Then she presented them to the assembled company as the guests-of-honor of the evening.

"Mein dear childrens und mein leetle grandchildrens und mein two dear freunds, certainly it iss to-night ve all vus vunderfully happy. It iss to-night that mein darling sohn—mein Maxie—und mein darling leetle daughter Rakkel iss came home to lif mit uns."

"To live? For good?" Excited exclamations ran around the table.

Rachel was speechless. But speech from her or from anyone else was quite unnecessary. Mrs. Kalinsky ably filled the gap.

"Ja, for gut—for alvays. Mein darling leetle Rakkel she iss not so strong, und it iss too hard for her to keep house all alone yet. Also the stairs by her flat iss too steep for me to climb, und mein darling Rakkel vants that Mamma should be always mit her. Und so ve all haf make it up together that Maxie and Rakkel they shall both came here. It iss a beautiful surprise vhich I haf keep all veek for efery vun."

Thus was explanation given and thus was it accepted. Curious and excited cross-examination failed to shake it. The strange and sudden action was given further plausible defense, "Mein Max is going for to make his business bigger, und he can safe it so much money, gifing up his flat."

Rachel said nothing. There was nothing to be said—certainly at least not now. Even her present dumbness was kindly and reasonably explained by her solicitous mother-in-law.

"Mein dear little Rakkel—she has had all day such a dreadful headache—all the packing und the mofing it has been so very hard. Ve vill excuse you, darling, to go right after supper back to bed yet."

It was a merciful release. Through the ordeal of that first awful meal Rachel clutched eagerly at the hope of quick escape at its conclusion. Therefore when the last nut was cracked and the last glass of tea was sipped, she fled. She did not even wait to speak with Ben and Esther or to heed the children flocking around her. Max would explain when she was gone.

Back to the hideous room beside the attic with the rats she went; and there for a full week of feverish days and nights she stayed. Every one was very kind to her. Attractive trays were brought and every attention possible was shown by different members of the household. Mrs. Kalinsky was the kindest of them all. Her devotion was as untiring as it was unctuous. Rachel's keen intuition perceived her tactics well. By her flattery and indulgence she would cajole her daughter-in-law into meek submission; and she would allay from the other Kalinskys, all possible suspicion regarding the true state of affairs between them. Sarah alone, outside of Max, was in Mrs. Kalinsky's confidence. For reasons of her own she would never let anyone else know of the disgrace which had threatened their proud family honor. By disdainfully ignoring all reference to the painful subject of Rachel's recent treachery, its evil consequences could best be stayed, and Rachel brought back to paths of orthodoxy.

Rachel was grateful for this respite. She felt too ill, too utterly broken-hearted for open combat. But something warned her that the respite could not be enduring. Permanent peace between her and Mrs. Kalinsky was possible on only one condition: complete submergence of her personality in that of her dominating mother-in-law. Rachel's fearless, independent spirit never could submit to that, especially in the realm of faith. And the claims of Christ, as Violet Hamilton and the Saramoffs had presented them, had stirred her to the depths.

She was in no position yet to defend them. Not even could she define clearly to her own heart and mind her answer to them. Complete silence regarding the entire subject was the necessary present program. And yet—even in spite of all that her interest in the Christian faith had thus far cost her—it gripped her thought tremendously.

As she lay through the days of fever and prostration, with anguish of mind and heart, there seemed to persist an under-current of longing that Christ Himself might be made real. Somehow she seemed to feel that were He actual and present, were He indeed the true Messiah, He could help and comfort even now in this dark hour. . . Later, when she was stronger she would try to talk alone with Max. . . perhaps Max would understand her . . . and together they might find Him.

Through the weary weeks and months that followed, Rachel gradually accepted the inevitable new order of existence. She fitted dumbly into her place in Mrs. Deborah Kalinsky's home. And the place was that of household Cinderella. Mrs. Kalinsky herself and the capable Sarah were constantly off upon their various Zionist committees; and the task of cooking and dish-washing, cleaning and scrubbing, even of the family washing, fell frequently to Rachel's unhappy lot. But she accepted it, as she accepted all else now, with utter apathy and deadness. If she were tired, it did not matter. If her head ached, that didn't matter either. It always ached. If Mrs. Kalinsky was ingratiating, or if beneath her sinuous caresses Rachel was conscious often of the adder's fangs, it was all the same. Her heart was dead, and nothing else was either here or there.

Max she scarcely ever saw alone. Mrs. Kalinsky took good care of that. Rachel was not to be trusted, that fact she was never allowed to forget. Nor was Max allowed to either.

She seldom saw her friends now. A little one had come to bless Ben and Esther's home, and Esther was held in the sweet captivity of motherhood. In the painful new surroundings of the house in East Eleventh Street Rachel's other friends were ill at ease. And Rachel had no heart herself to visit.

One friend supremely she longed for—Violet Hamilton. And the Saramoffs as well. All trace of them she feared was lost, for Violet would never venture another visit after that last disastrous one. And Rachel could not go to Rivington Street, for two good reasons. First, she dared not go. And second, the distance was too great from East Eleventh Street for Rachel in her present weakened condition to walk. And carfare she had none. Max was making his "big money" now but not five cents even could Rachel call her own. With no household budget, Max was assured by his mother that Rachel had no need for money. Mrs. Kalinsky herself provided all her clothes and other personal requirements. And Rachel was too proud to ask anybody for a cent.

In her terrible loneliness, Rachel's one solace was poor old

Grandmother Kalinsky and her Hebrew Bible. Since her mother-in-law had burned Rachel's New Testament on that dreadful day of the discovery, Rachel had had an unquenchable longing for the Word of God. Especially did she yearn ardently that she might see the New Testament again—a vain longing in the home of Deborah Kalinsky—but in the Old there was at least the promise of the New; and together with the aged Jewish woman, through many hours Rachel searched its pages diligently.

Rachel and Grandmother Kalinsky were kindred spirits in their loneliness and—to her great joy Rachel discovered it—in their trust in God and in the Messianic hope. The aged mother-in-Israel, beneath her silent inconspicuousness was conspicuous before her God for her great piety and faith, as daily, in reverent and zealous prayer, she waited for the consolation of her people Israel. In deepest secrecy, but with trembling gladness, as alone together they frequently sat either in Rachel's room or hers upon the top floor of the big house, Rachel told her all that she knew herself of Christ as the Messiah; and the dear old Grandmother received the good tidings with great joy. These little secret hours were Rachel's greatest comfort.

And then suddenly even this comfort was taken from her. Grandmother Kalinsky died. It was Rachel herself who found the dear old soul asleep in her accustomed rocker, early one morning as she came down to make the breakfast. Grandmother Kalinsky had stolen down alone in the night for her warm place by the stove. There she had fallen asleep as usual—but this time it was that last sweet sleep, from which awakening she would behold her own Messiah face to face.

In the orthodox Jewish home there followed the traditional eight days of mourning. They were terrible days for Rachel. All the shades were closely drawn and the house was hushed and weird. No member of the family went out of doors. Friends and neighbors all came in to mourn with them, sitting around the dreary parlors on boxes, or on the floor as they wailingly intoned the *Kaddish*—the Jewish prayer for the dead—while the long wax candles burned heavily. Amid all the perfunctory and professional evidences of sorrow, one heart there was that grieved sincerely—Rachel's.

The days of mourning ended, Rachel slipped back into the usual round of heartless household tasks, with the ugly room upstairs her only oasis between them. This room was very dreadful to her now. Besides its hideousness and the noise of the scuttling rats, it now held an added horror. It was just across the hall from the recent abode of death. Rachel had no fear of death as such, but the room so lately connected with it conveyed to her—very lonely now without the dear little Grandmother near her—an uncanny and depressing atmosphere.

At last the long, sorrowful Winter drew to a close, and the return of the robins found Rachel just a bit more white, more thin, more sad than when she first had come to East Eleventh Street.

With the balmy days of Spring Rachel ventured on occasional short walks. Her favorite one was over to Fifth Avenue, and home again by way of Wanamaker's. The great store fascinated her—even though with her empty purse its appeal was hopeless.

One day her eye was suddenly caught by a striking window display of English Bibles. There were several stacks of them in the background, and in the center foreground were half-a-dozen rare editions. On either side were open Bibles—open at various places in both the Old Testament and the New. Eagerly Rachel read all the text—then read it yet again.

The effect upon her was a quickened longing to possess a Bible—Old and New Testament together—for herself. Fight it down as she might, the longing would not be denied. A Bible she had to have. But how attain the impossible?

For days and nights she pondered over the problem—making many secret trips to the Bible window in the meantime—and finally the solution flashed upon her. And before her resolve could falter she put it into execution.

Carefully watching her chance, she stole up to the attic one afternoon, when Mrs. Kalinsky and Sarah were out and the children were at school, and there selected from among her household goods, a large, square, wooden box. It was very clumsy and it was heavy, and it excited wonderment and curiosity as Rachel hugged it in her arms and carried it along the street.

Nevertheless ten long blocks she went with it—to a Russian place she knew in the lower Ghetto. There, exhausted and breathless, she deposited it upon the counter before the astonished gaze of the dealer in Russian brasses, who opened it at her command.

The dealer's eyes grew eager and Rachel's eyes grew misty, as he drew from its folds of cotton-wool and tissue paper—her precious samovar. A bargain was quickly struck, the dealer eagerly seized his new art treasure; Rachel seized the crumpled ten-dollar bill he gave her in exchange. The samovar was easily worth fifty. The dealer's eyes grew big with satisfaction. Rachel's dear eyes grew wet with grief as she went out.

Back over the ten long blocks she retraced her weary steps, then steadfastly onward still another four or five, until she came to Wanamaker's. The clerks in the bookstall watched in admiring wonder the beautiful young Jewess as she searched diligently among their handsome leather Bibles, reading hungrily in the meanwhile from page after page of the New Testament. At length she found the Bible that exactly suited. The price, too, was exactly right—ten dollars. The exchange was made, and Rachel carried home triumphantly her dearly-purchased treasure. Surreptitiously she made her entrance through the upper doorway, her package carefully concealed inside her coat. Happily the coast was still quite clear, as Rachel found for the forbidden Book a safe hiding place within the attic.

No longer were her hours lonely now. Eagerly she treasured every moment she could spend within her ugly room when, as frequently happened, she had the house to herself. She would wait till she was absolutely sure, then she would draw the cherished Bible from its niche of concealment, and carry it lovingly to her room. Then, carefully locking the door as a further precaution, she opened the sacred Volume and pored over its pages hungrily.

She set herself to diligent and systematic study. One goal was ahead of her. She was going to get this question settled definitely and conclusively once for all. Was Jesus Christ truly the Son of God and Israel's Messiah, or was He not? Were His claims authentic or were they blasphemous and false, as she had always been taught, and had believed until she met Violet

Hamilton? She could not rest satisfied in mind or heart until she knew.

Hers was a quick and steady brain; her perceptions were clear and rapid, and her deductions therefrom were logical and sound. It was not many days, therefore, before she had arrived at a definite intellectual conviction that the claims of Jesus Christ were true.

Her assurance brought entire peace of mind. The questionings, the doubts, the strange perplexity were all removed. Her intellectual assent to Christ's Messiahship was now unqualified and clear.

But this was not enough. Her mind was satisfied but there yet remained a deep heart-hunger, indefinable but real. She longed that she might know Him for herself—that she might experience Him as a living, vivid Person, even as Violet herself so wonderfully knew Him. The Christ of Bethlehem, of Galilee, of Bethany—she reverenced profoundly and accepted as the Son of God. But He lived long ago—and Him they crucified. It was a living, present Christ she longed for—One Who might draw near to her even now in this dark hour as Comforter and Friend. Oh, that she knew where she might find Him! Her heart cried out in ardent longing.

It was one evening early in April that this longing reached its climax. Rachel was in her room, exhausted after her hard day's work. Max and his mother had gone away. Max had gently urged Rachel to accompany them but she had been too tired. Jacob and Sarah were away. The children were asleep. Rachel was weary and heartsick. A peculiar sense of loneliness enfolded her. Oh, that she might find Him—the living Christ— even now as her Consoler. Fervently she lifted up a prayer: "O God, reveal Him to me! Reveal Thy Son from Heaven. I know He is Thy Son, and Israel's true Messiah. I know it, dear God, I know it. But I want Him for myself—my own Messiah—my Saviour and my King! O God, reveal Him to me even now!"

She was kneeling at her bed, her Bible lying open in front of her. The light from the rose-shaded lamp cast a warm glow over her upturned face. Her eyes were luminous and soulful.

In answer to her ardent petition, the Spirit Who guides into all truth opened her eyes to behold wondrous things out of God's law, and ordered her steps in the Word where she sought to find the living, present Christ. Verse after verse He tenderly revealed to her, His own voice whispering to her eager heart each promise and assurance.

"I am he that liveth, and was dead; and behold, I am alive for evermore. . . I am the resurrection, and the life, he that believeth in me, though he were dead, yet shall he live. . . Before Abraham was, I am. . . Jesus Christ the same yesterday, today, and for ever. . . Why seek ye the living among the dead? He is not here, for he is risen. . . In him we live, and move, and have our being. . . I will not leave you comfortless, I will come to you . . . Come unto me, all ye that labour and are heavy laden, and I will give you rest. . . And the Spirit and the bride say, Come. And let him that heareth say, Come. And let him that is athirst come. And whosoever will, let him take the water of life freely . . . Surely I come quickly. . . The grace of our Lord Jesus Christ be with you all. Amen."

Rachel felt a warm glow within her heart. . . there seemed to be a Presence drawing near. . . she waited breathlessly.

She turned off the lamp, that she might better see. She buried her head in her arms and closed her eyes, that she might shut out every thought save thought of Him. Again and yet again His voice rang clear in tones that thrilled.

"I am the resurrection, and the life. . . I am he that liveth, and was dead, and behold, I am alive for evermore. Come unto me, all ye that labour and are heavy laden, and I will give you rest."

The room was entirely dark, Rachel knew. The lamp was out and the shades were closely drawn that not a ray might penetrate.

Yet gradually her heart became suffused with light. Flickering and faint at first, then ever richer and warmer it glowed, until it burst into a heavenly radiance—a light even as the light of resurrection morning. It was the Resurrection Morning in Rachel's joyful heart! For in that moment, as she hearkened to the Spirit's voice declaring unto her the Word of God, and as she opened wide the door to Jesus Christ, receiving Him by faith as her Messiah—her Saviour and her Lord and King—in that moment the darkness of Judaism fled before the Dawn—the Light streamed in—and Rachel Kalinsky passed from death to Life.

Chapter VII.

Light Amid the Darkness

"I will not leave you comfortless: I will come to you."
—John 14:18.

Pesach—the Jewish Feast of the Passover—was late that year. Seder, its opening evening with the Passover Supper, fell on Saturday, the twentieth of April, the celebration continuing through the following seven days. For weeks in advance, however, preparations for *Pesach* were in full progress. All over the great city of New York, in every Hebrew dwelling, the housewives were vigorously busy. The annual rites of house-cleaning were on, and no interruption short of fire or death might halt them.

In Mrs. Kalinsky's commodious abode on East Eleventh Street the *Pesach* cleansing was conducted with that good lady's characteristic force and determination. Not an inch of the big house escaped her vigorous onslaught. The walls and ceilings must all be carefully brushed down, the woodwork scoured, the upholstery vacuumed, and everything in sight scrubbed and polished to the last degree.

The dishes and cooking utensils used ordinarily through the year were all put away, and the barrels of those sacred to Passover were brought down from the attic and unpacked, and their contents sterilized and placed upon the pantry shelves. Every bit of "leaven" was searched out; and on the day preceding *Pesach* the usual Jewish bread was replaced by *matzoth*, and loaf cakes were baked with special unleavened *Pesach* Hour. Four ounces of flour to thirteen eggs.

To Rachel, as usual, fell the heavy end of the domestic work. In the Passover preparations her task it was to wash every window in the big house, to wash and iron and rehang every one of the fifty-six long curtains, and to polish all the metal. To Rachel also was given the commission to "make *Kosher*" the big kitchen range. This process involved the boiling in soapsuds and soda of every removable portion of the stove, and the burning

84

Rachel was put to polishing floors.

out of the oven with pans of red-hot coals. Last and most difficult of all the tasks, Rachel was put to polishing the floors. Many
a weary hour she sat bending over them, aching in every nerve.

But she never complained now. No longer either did she give
way to those quick outflashings of her naturally hot temper in
which formerly she had indulged under stress of Mrs. Kalinsky's or of Sarah's inconsiderate cruelties. Both of them noted
with suspicion the new spirit she manifested toward them—the
docility, the gentleness, the sweetness. To them it was uncanny.
It betokened ill. Mischief was brewing somewhere. "I am telling
you, that girl's qveer. Ve must vatch her, Sarah!"

But the secret of it all lay hidden deep within Rachel's joyful
heart. She had found the Christ! And finding Him she had found
the inward peace. No longer did she feel that sense of utter loneliness. No longer did she feel baffled and beaten by the over-
whelming forces of her new environment. No longer did she
have to fight singlehanded against odds that were impossible. In
Him she was more than conqueror over every circumstance,
every conflict, every foe. She had found the living, present, all-
victorious Christ! She had found her Comforter—her strong
Defender—her Counsellor—her Friend.

Ever since that night in her room when He had revealed
Himself to her and when she had joyously received Him into
her heart as her own Messiah and her Lord, Rachel's life had
been transformed.

Outwardly everything was just the same; the monotonous
drudgery went on as usual; the fragile little body grew just as
tired; Mrs. Kalinsky's jealous taunts were as caustic and as cruel
as ever; Sarah's sharpness just as stinging; the children were as
untidy and as noisy as they always were; Jacob just as dictato-
rial and harsh; and Max—her own dear Max—her husband—as
completely dominated as ever by his doting mother, and in
consequence thereof, aloof and strained in his relations with his
wife.

But something new had entered into Rachel's being. With the
coming of the Christ there had come His all-sufficient grace. As
simply as she had accepted Him as her Saviour so simply did
she accept, with eager child-like faith, all the gifts He waited to
bestow. And among the gifts, none was more precious than His

gift of peace—the peace above all pain—the peace of God that passeth understanding.

For several days Rachel basked in the sunshine of it. She forgot that she was tired. She forgot that she was homesick and heartsick for her little flat, where she and Max had been, oh, so happy. She forgot how much she was suffering in the home of Deborah Kalinsky. One consciousness alone absorbed her, flooding her soul with heavenly radiance—the consciousness of the indwelling Christ.

Day by day He became more real, more precious to her. His presence was actual and vivid, His power gloriously felt. The study of the Bible became more and more enthralling. It held new meaning now. It was God's own Word direct to Rachel's heart, concerning His dear Son. Each page disclosed to her some new loveliness in Him. Each word revealed afresh His love for her. Even for her—Rachel Mendelssohn Kalinsky—whom He had redeemed from the awful darkness of Israel by His own precious blood.

Rachel's intense nature never did anything by halves. And the same thoroughness which characterized everything she undertook, was expressed now in her new life as a Christian. Her one absorbing passion was that she might please the Father—that she might do His holy will. Eagerly and joyously, therefore, she endured all things for His dear sake Who had given His all for her.

When the household tasks exhausted her frail strength she rested in His omnipotence. When the loneliness and longing became unendurable she endured as seeing Him who is invisible. When the stinging subtleties of her mother-in-law left her tender heart so sorely wounded, she found her healing in His smile. His "well done, my child" at the end of a long, weary day, was ample compensation for all the cruelty the day had held.

Her life of bondage under Deborah Kalinsky became invested with a strange new glory. In Christ, its dreadful experiences assumed new values. His strength made perfect in her weakness, Rachel realized the paradox of taking pleasure in infirmities, in reproaches, in necessities, in persecutions, in distresses. For His dear sake she now could suffer all things with an actual albeit wondering gladness, rejoicing in this, that she was counted worthy. Thus day by day she experienced His peace in ever-increasing measure.

But peace demands its price. The peace of God is abiding only as long as there is full obedience to the will of God, as He reveals it step by step. And Rachel's obedience was soon to meet its fiery test.

She had sincerely believed her will to be in entire conformity to His. With each new morning she had prayed with sweet submission: "Let Thy perfect will, O Christ my Saviour, be done in me this day. Have Thine own way, dear Lord, have Thine own way. Oh, make me one in whom Thou canst delight!" The harmony between will and will—the divine will and the human—had been unbroken; the union between the Father and His child complete and beautiful. All had been well—thus far. All had been perfect peace.

And then suddenly God revealed to Rachel Kalinsky His deeper purpose for her life. And just as suddenly she shrank back in startled fear. Peace became panic. The wonderful harmony was broken. Between Rachel Kalinsky and her new-found Lord and Saviour Jesus Christ there had risen— controversy.

It was just one week before *Pesach*—and a rainy Saturday morning. Mrs. Kalinsky and Max, and Jacob and Sarah, with the two older children, were at the synagogue. Little Solly was spending the day at Auntie Goldie's house. Rachel had been left at home to cook the dinner. The house was quiet. Likewise safe.

While the gefuellte Fisch was boiling, Rachel stole up for a precious fifteen minutes in her attic with the Book, as she always did steal up at every possible opportunity. She drew the Bible—her now most priceless treasure—from its hiding place beneath the eaves, and crouched with it near a low window behind a trunk. She no longer ventured carrying it to her room. The risk was too great. She had had a narrow escape one day when suddenly and unexpectedly she had encountered Sarah face to face in the hallway, as she was holding her Bible, uncon- cealed, under her arm. Happily Sarah had been deeply engrossed in other matters than Rachel's behaviour at that pres- ent moment, and had passed with unseeing eye. But Rachel had trembled with a chill of terror for an hour afterward. From that day on she did her reading always in the attic where the Book could be slid instantly into its hiding place at the sound of approaching footsteps.

On this Saturday morning she would be quite safe, she was sure, for an hour at least. The rain was pouring heavily. The light through the little attic window was gray and dim. Rachel strained her eyes over the blurring pages.

But suddenly two verses from Matthew seemed to flash as with fire, and leaped before Rachel's eyes with vivid distinctness. As quickly as she read them so quickly did they strike home to the heart of this new-born babe in Christ with stunning conviction.

"Whosoever therefore shall confess me before men, him will I confess also before my Father which is in heaven."

"But whosoever shall deny me before men, him will I also deny before my Father which is in heaven."

Confess! The word seared and scorched into Rachel's brain. Confess Christ? Here? In the home of Deborah Kalinsky? Confess Him before her? Before Max—her husband? Oh, no, it was impossible! Not that, dear Lord, oh, not that surely!

Rachel tried in the gray light to read some other meaning into the words, but again they flashed their command to her.

"Whosoever therefore shall confess me before men, him will I confess also before my Father which is in heaven."

"But whosoever shall deny me before men, him will I also deny before my Father which is in heaven."

Uncomfortably Rachel closed the Book and put it back into its pocket under the eaves. For the first time since she had owned it, she experienced a secret sense of relief as she closed the door upon it and almost ran downstairs to the comfortable kitchen stove.

But though the Bible was thus hidden from her view, those two verses from Matthew were burned indelibly upon her heart. Escape from them was impossible. Day and night they rang in her ears as with a voice of thunder.

"Whosoever therefore shall confess me before men, him will I confess also before my Father which is in heaven."

"But whosoever shall deny me before men, him will I also deny before my Father which is in heaven."

From that moment in the attic when first she had tried to run away from them, the words haunted her. In consequence, the perfect communion with her Lord was destroyed; the beautiful inward peace was gone. Life reassumed its former dreariness. The tasks reassumed their heaviness. The heart realized afresh its ache. Rachel Kalinsky was in controversy with her God.

Earnestly she strove to overcome it. It was so dreadful to her. Christ seemed suddenly so far away. She grieved for Him—for His return—for the old-time sweet communion. Oh, she could never bear this separation! She must find Him again—Him Who now was her Beloved!

Diligently upon her knees she sought to win Him back. She first tried argument. For hours she strove in prayer, rehearsing before Him the reasons why she could not possibly confess Him yet.

It was so much sweeter to keep their union secret. Her fellowship with Him, apart from anyone suspecting it, had been so infinitely precious. To confess Him now would end that joy.

Then too, she of course must shield his dear Name from those who would dishonor it. What? Subject Him to the scorn and ridicule of Deborah Kalinsky? Oh no, dear Lord, no, no! I love Thee far too much for that!"

And Max! She longed so deeply that he too might know the Christ. Max, too, must find their own Messiah, and together they would serve and honor Him. "Oh, but not yet, dear Lord, not yet! It will be so much better to wait until we get away from here—until he gets far off from the influence of his mother. Just as soon as I can have him to myself again, I will tell him everything. I will confess Thee, oh, so gladly, then!"

But Rachel's every argument and counter-argument was futile. To every one the dear Voice answered, as the dear Eyes gazed down in gentle, yearning sorrow.

"Whosoever therefore shall confess me before men, him will I confess also before my Father which is in heaven.

"But whosoever shall deny me before men, him will I also deny before my Father which is in heaven."

And then followed three dreadful days in the wilderness whither Rachel tried to flee from Him—away from those dear Eyes, away from that dear Voice. For three whole days she would not read her Bible, she would not pray. For three whole days and nights in consequence she could neither eat nor sleep. Everything became unutterably dreadful. In Rachel's heart, more dreary than all the former wastes, was the present fearful desolation. Rachel Kalinsky was in controversy with her God.

And then she came back. Back to Him Who was her soul's Beloved. With humility and contrition for her disobedience, she bowed in deepest penitence before her Lord. And the dear Eyes looked down upon her with forgiving love; and the dear Voice whispered words of tenderness and hope, and Rachel Kalinsky's heart was glad once more. The controversy between her and God was ended, and His peace — the peace that passeth understanding—now like a river was flooding her very soul.

With full obedience and in absolute surrender she yielded up her will to His. "Have Thine own way, Lord—at whatever cost"—this alone was now her prayer.

Nor was she ignorant of what that cost might be. Merely her interest in the Christian faith, her friendship with a Christian missionary and her investigation of the New Testament and the Messianic claims of Christ, these had already cost her dear. Her precious home, her liberty, her husband's confidence—all these and more had been included in that cost. What price then might she not have to pay for actual confession of the Lord Christ Jesus in that home of strictest and most bitter orthodoxy? She dared not think; she dared not weigh the consequences lest her resolution falter.

But Rachel's resolution would not falter, for Christ would hold her strong. She had definitely promised Him, in coming back, that she would follow now wherever He would lead—no matter what the cost. Therefore come what might, pay whatever price should be required of her, endure whatever loss for His dear sake she must, Rachel's face was set like a flint to go all the way, if need be, to her Jerusalem.

"Whosoever therefore shall confess me before men, him will I confess also before my Father which is in heaven."

"But whosoever shall deny me before men, him will I also deny before my Father which is in heaven."

No longer did the words hold terror now. No longer did Rachel seek to flee from their importunity. As she knelt in reverent awe before the open Book she registered definitely her consent to God's command.

"Yea, Lord, I will confess Thee before men. With all my heart I love Thee, and I will confess Thee as my own Messiah. Do Thou but make me strong and open up the way."

She smiled trustingly up into the Father's face; and the Father smiled down in tender favor and in love upon His child. Their communion, one with the other, was very close and infinitely sweet. The inward peace lay deep within Rachel's heart—the peace of God that passeth understanding. The way lay dark ahead—dark and mysterious and full of pain—of this fact the Spirit in her heart gave witness. But He would go before and He would follow after, all the days. The Light of Life would illumine all the bitter pathway as Rachel step by step would steadfastly go forward. Hand in hand with her Beloved she was unafraid.

It was on the Sabbath evening just before the beginning of *Pesach*. Tomorrow evening would be *Seder*. Could she, Rachel wondered, make confession of the Christ at this important Jewish season? Well, the Lord would guide. Her will was now wholly His and He would open up the opportunity in His own appointed time and way.

Saturday dawned bright and clear. Rachel awoke with a sense of impending crisis. *Pesach* was nearly here at last; at sunset it would begin. Might she not confess her Lord today before it started? But if she did, what then? What would her husband say? What would be the effect upon Mrs. Kalinsky and the others? What for Rachel herself would be the consequence? She did not at all know. But He knew, and He would hold her firm to her resolve. Her part now was but to hearken obediently to His voice giving command when she should speak. He would take care of all the rest.

All through the day the family were busy with the final *Pesach* preparations. The cleansing had been thoroughly completed. From attic to cellar the house was gleaming. But certain last things must yet be done. One last thorough search for any possible remaining leaven must yet be made; the *matzoth* and the *Pesach* cakes must be set forth; the *Seder* supper must be cooked and the *Seder* table spread. Then all the household must array themselves in holiday attire.

During the morning while Rachel and Mrs. Kalinsky and Sarah were busy in the kitchen with the cooking, a knock came at the door. Rachel opened it. An attractive-looking young man—a Gentile—stood outside. Graciously he extended to Rachel a folded letter inscribed across the top in large Hebrew characters with the text: "Hear, O Israel, The LORD our God is one LORD."

The visitor smiled engagingly. This was a Jewish home, was it not? And the Jewish Passover was just beginning if he understood correctly. Would the ladies not accept this Passover greeting from interested Christian friends?

Rachel thanked the young man courteously, accepted the letter from his hand and closed the door. She unfolded the sheet and noted the words printed in large type in English across the bottom of it: "Christ our Passover is sacrificed for us."

But before she could read more Mrs. Kalinsky had rudely seized the letter from her and torn it into shreds. She had heard the one word "Christian" and it was as a spark to dynamite.

"Vot for you take it such a things?" she exploded violently. "Don't you know that vot it iss? It iss a letter vhich iss wrote to Jewvish peoples from a missionary. That man he iss a missionary—a Christian. Und beliefe me I am telling you, I hate all Christians just like they vus poison. Don't you nefer dare, Rakkel, to open the door on vun again!"

Was this Rachel's opportunity? Should she now confess the Christ? She grew hot and cold at the thought. But yes, she would try. With her heart pounding violently she began to speak. She would pave the way for confession by defending this Christian young man. But Sarah joined her mother-in-law in loud outcry against him, and Rachel, perceiving that the time was clearly inopportune, held her peace.

In the afternoon Esther dropped in for a few moments on her way home from the synagogue to her own *Seder* feast. Here was Rachel's chance now, surely! Esther was her dearest friend, and she would be the easiest one to speak to of the Messiah. But at the first mention of the Name "Christ" Esther raised astonished eyebrows, and Rachel, conscious of a sudden distinct chill in the atmosphere, was again rebuffed.

Sunset came at last and with it the great Jewish Feast of the Passover began. At seven o'clock the immediate Kalinsky family—Mrs. Kalinsky, Jacob and Sarah and their children, and Max and Rachel—gathered in the long state dining-room upstairs for their *Seder* supper. The other Kalinskys ate theirs in their respective homes, every household apart.

With Jacob at the head, and Mrs. Kalinsky at the foot of the table, the family stood silently behind their chairs with their Hebrew prayer-books lying open before them. The men and boys all wore their hats. Jacob, as nominal head of the family—Mrs. Kalinsky the actual head resigning in his favor for such occasions as this only—read aloud the Passover ritual, his elder son, Izzy, asking the traditional question, ordained of God in Egypt and handed down through every succeeding generation of Israelites: "What mean ye by this service?" A long prayer followed, and a *Pesach* hymn.

The family then sat down before the festal board which was spread with the special Passover dishes and silver, and upon which gleamed the sacred seven-branches silver candle-stick. Upon the tables, together with the elaborate supper, were the traditional Passover requirements. There were the dishes of bitter herbs, speaking of the Egyptian bondage; the egg, symbolic of resurrection; the unleavened bread; the salt; the lentils, and at each place there was a goblet of wine, with the extra goblet for the prophet Elijah, for whose desired coming the door was left wide open. Everything was in gala array, and all the Kalinskys were in gala dress and mood.

All save Rachel. Upon her heart there rested a deep sadness. She was feeling a very genuine sorrow for the blindness of her family—and for her own dear Max—and sorrow as well for the unutterable darkness of her whole beloved Jewish race. The Passover was the memorial of Israel's redemption from the cruel bondage of the land of Egypt. And the symbol of redemption had been the blood upon the doorposts. But throughout all Israel tonight the celebration of the Passover was altogether bloodless. In place of the paschal lamb of that first Passover feast in Egypt, their remained in Jewish homes now but a meagre shank of mutton roasted in ashes. And the true Passover Lamb—the Lamb of God slain from the foundation of the world—of Whom

94

the paschal lamb had been but the type and promise—He was still despised and rejected by His Jewish brethren.

Even there in the Kalinsky home that night, the lavish celebration, for which there had been weeks of elaborate preparation, was but an empty, lifeless form—a hollow mockery. Not one of the entire family realized the true significance of the Passover observance. Not one save Rachel. For she alone knew Christ and His redemption. She alone had His blood sprinkled upon the doorposts of her heart.

Oh, could she not confess Him even here and now? Could she not just quietly affirm before her husband's family, "Christ our Passover is sacrificed for us"? Two or three times, as she lifted up her heart in prayer for courage, she did try earnestly to confess. But each time as she began to speak a dumb spirit seemed to seize her. A curious sense of depression stole over her. She was conscious of miserable failure. Her Lord was counting upon her to confess Him before men. She had promised Him she would. And yet here, where they were actually dishonoring Him in their bloodless Passover feast, she—a Christian—was keeping silence. And by that very act of silence, denial was implied.

As the meal proceeded her sense of failure and of wretchedness increased. Finally it nearly overmastered her. Every one else was gay and even boisterous. But Rachel sat inarticulate and thoroughly unhappy.

Before the lengthy repast had quite reached its conclusion, other members of the Kalinsky family dropped in, having finished their own *Seder* suppers earlier. First came Joseph, then Otto and Goldie and their children. And then the inevitable Sophy Yasnik and Yetta Cash arrived and, following them shortly afterward, came the most honored friend of the Kalinsky family—Rabbi Mordecai Moses. These all sat around the room while the family continued eating supper at the table.

At last the feast was finished—all except the tea. Their guests must join them for this, Mrs. Kalinsky hospitably insisted. No, it was no trouble whatever. Rachel could quickly boil another kettle of water. A happy thought struck Sarah.

"Mamma, the teapot is too small, why not use Rachel's samovar? We've never used it since it came here and it is so handsome. It's just what we should have for *Seder*."

Yes, surely! Why had they never thought of that before? "Go get it qvick, Rakkel," Mrs. Kalinsky commanded. "You know it vhere it iss—in the big sqvare box by the vestern corner in the attic!"

Rachel's senses reeled. She was struck dumb.

"Go Rakkel, vill you hurry up?" reiterated her mother-in-law sharply.

"I—I don't know where it is," Rachel faltered miserably. "Vot! You don't know it vhere it iss—your own grandmother's samofar vhich your mother brought it ofer from Roumanien! Listen, Rakkel, I am telling you! It iss in the box—the big vun—by the vestern corner—in the attic—near the vindow. You go for to hurry up und bring it down!"

Sarah saved the immediate situation. "Here, I'll go. I know exactly where it is. Put the kettle on, Rachel; the water will boil more quickly on the stove."

Rachel fled to the kitchen, her heart beating wildly. What would they say when Sarah returned without the samovar? What possible explanation could Rachel make? Had her moment come at last? Was this now her opportunity to make confession of the Christ?

Slowly she filled the tea kettle and placed it on the range. She remained as long as she dared, then reluctantly returned to the dining-room upstairs and slipped silently and tremblingly into her place.

A moment later Sarah returned from her fruitless search in the attic. The samovar was certainly not there. But she had brought down something else!

"Look!" she screamed excitedly. "Look here, will you, what I found up there—beneath the eaves. Just look!"

All eyes were turned toward her as she stood with melodramatic pose within the doorway, extending at arm's length with unfeigned disgust and anger—Rachel's Bible.

The sight of it had a paralyzing effect upon Rachel. It was so sudden, so absolutely unexpected. The reaction of the family and their guests—particularly of Mrs. Kalinsky and of Rabbi Mordecai Moses—was so terrific that Rachel was rendered utterly speechless.

"A Bible? With the New Testament in it? Here—in Deborah Kalinsky's home? And at *Pesach*? Where did it come from? Whose was it? Was there any name in it? Look!"

Yes, there was a name. Rabbi Moses read it out in awful tones, "Rachel Mendelssohn Kalinsky."

Every eye was fastened upon her in stern and terrible rebuke. Mrs. Kalinsky's eye portended swift and fearful retribution. Rachel quailed before it. Max turned upon her one long gaze of heartbroken reproach.

Mrs. Kalinsky snatched the sacred Book from Rabbi Moses' hands and flung it violently into the fire burning on the hearth. Rachel uttered a sharp, quick cry of grief and protest. Instantly a buzz of shrill, angry voices burst upon her as all the witnesses of the strange scene crowded menacingly around her chair. She grew dizzy before them. She tried to speak. She must confess her Lord. This was the time, yes, right now, she was sure. "O Christ, give strength, give strength," she breathed in fervent prayer. But the words of confession choked in her throat.

The buzz of voices grew more shrill, the angry outcry more insistent. Rachel became more and more dizzy. The room spun round and round. She was suddenly weak . . . she felt herself slipping. . . slipping. . . falling to the floor the faces became dim . . . the voices sounded far away then everything went black.

When Rachel came slowly back to consciousness some hours later, the process was a strangely bewildering one. She did not at all know what had happened. The voices still were far away, the faces indistinct. She was vaguely aware of a numbness both of mind and body.

Then gradually things and people began to assume reality. The voices became distinguishable—Mrs. Kalinsky's high-keyed and shrill, Rabbi Moses' deep and authoritative, Sarah's petulant.

Then Rachel began to remember. Yes—they were eating *Seder* supper. They had the goblets of wine. . . and the *matzoth*. . . and the seven-branched silver candlestick. . . why, where were they? They were no longer there! . . . And the table, too, was gone! . . . And then Rachel discovered she was no longer in the dining-room, but in her own ugly room upstairs, and in bed. And then she knew that she was sick, yes, very, very sick.

Gradually the faces became more distinct. They were no longer crowding angrily around her, but one by one they were emerging from different parts of the room. The first she recognized clearly was Max's. He was bending over her, ardently pressing her hands and sobbing brokenly.

"Rachel, forgive me, forgive me! Oh, don't die! I do love you so much! Oh, Rachel, come back, come back!"

Yes, that was what it was. She was very sick. And she was going to die. That was what all the people were talking about in excited little groups.

The other faces became quite distinct now—Mrs. Kalinsky's and Rabbi Moses' and Jacob's on the other side of the bed, and Goldie's and Sarah's at the foot. And Yetta Cash's and Sophy Yasnik's over by the window. Jacob was holding his back firmly against the door through which the children were trying excitedly to squeeze. Through the open transom above the door, Izzy and Becky were peering in curiously.

And then Rachel began to remember other things—the samovar—the Bible. Oh, her precious, precious Bible! And that dreadful Mrs. Kalinsky had burned it, just as she had burned her Testament!

And then at last Rachel remembered her Bible verses—those two verses from Matthew which for days before had scorched her very brain.

"Whosoever therefore shall confess me before men, him will I confess also before my Father which is in heaven."

"But whosoever shall deny me before men, him will I also deny before my Father which is in heaven."

A sudden stab of pain shot through her heart. She had denied Him before men! Yes, by her silence at the *Seder* supper she had denied her Lord. She had promised Him she would confess His Name—before the Kalinsky family—even there at the beginning of the *Pesach* feast. It would have been such a wonderful opportunity when Mrs. Kalinsky burned her Bible. But she had failed—she had failed her Lord—miserably, miserably failed!

Great teardrops coursed down her checks for sorrow. Max's mingled with them as again broken-heartedly he pleaded with her not to die.

Two more people entered the room and came quickly to the

bedside. Rachel recognized them at once—Dr. Levi Goldstein, the aged Jewish physician, the same one who had attended her mother on her death-bed, and with him a Jewish nurse. There was a rapid, skillful examination, and then a whispered consultation between them. Rachel caught the one word "Operate."

Others caught it too, and a buzz of hysterical voices followed. Mrs. Kalinsky, Sarah, Goldie, Yetta Cash and Sophy Yasnik—all were in seething excitement. The men as well were stirred. Rabbi Moses alone retained his poise and dignity. The children tried vociferously to push past Jacob and Otto, who still formed a strong bodyguard at the doorway. Above their voices the voice of Mrs. Kalinsky rose in shrill demand that they keep quiet in the sick room.

Yes, Rachel understood it now quite well. She was going to die. That was why Max was crying. That was why she could not speak. She was going to die. Soon she would be in the presence of the King. In His very presence! A wave of terror convulsed her. She was going to meet the Lord Christ Jesus face to face—with her faith in Him as her Messiah unconfessed!

A deep moan escaped her lips. Oh, could she not confess Him even yet? Even now it might not be too late. With fervent prayer she pleaded: "Dear Lord, give strength, give strength!"

The physician gave the nurse a signal. Quickly she drew from a case an anaesthetizing cone and passed it to him. Rachel, her mind now keen and alert, perceived exactly what his purpose was.

He uncorked a bottle. . . he began pouring the ether on the cone. . . one moment more. . . ten seconds only. . . and it would be—forever—too late!

In an agony Rachel poured out her heart in pleading petition, "O Christ, give strength, give strength! I will confess Thee before men, I will, I will! I love Thee, Lord, with all my heart. I will confess Thee as my Saviour and my King. Oh, I will, I will! Do Thou but give me strength, dear Christ, give strength!"

Gravely the kindly old physician approached toward Rachel and bent over her. Swiftly the nurse made deft adjustments. One instant more . . . and the anaesthetic was pressed to Rachel's face.

Suddenly with a strength not her own, but strengthened with

all might by His Spirit in the inner man, as He heard and answered her prayer, Rachel thrust the doctor and the nurse aside, drew herself to sitting posture and began to speak. Raising her hand aloft with commanding gesture she electrified every one of the Jewish witnesses within the room listening breathlessly to her words. With eyes luminous with inward spiritual light, in clear and ringing tones she cried aloud.

"Wait! Wait! Before I die I want to tell you all—Max, Mrs. Kalinsky, Rabbi Moses, everybody—I am a Christian! I believe in Jesus Christ! I confess Him now before you all as Israel's Messiah and my own Saviour. I love—and worship—Him—with all—my heart. I—am—going—to—Him—now—my Lord—my—K—ing ...."

The last words trailed into an almost inaudible whisper. The strength, supernaturally given, had accomplished its desired purpose and now was spent. Exhausted, Rachel fell back among the pillows as the faces about her all registered horror.

A heavenly smile illumined her lovely countenance. All was well at last. She had confessed Christ before men, and He would confess her now before His Father which is in Heaven.

The blackness gathered fast, but Rachel had no fear. Again she felt herself slipping. . . slipping. . . slipping. But she knew that underneath her were the everlasting arms. And in her heart was peace.

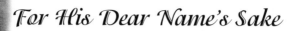

Chapter VIII.

For His Dear Name's Sake

"Let us go forth therefore unto him without the camp,
bearing his reproach."—Hebrews 13:13.

Underneath her were the everlasting arms. Rachel was blessedly conscious of them and rested content in their omnipotence and tenderness while, during many days, life and death waged over her grim battle. But at last life won. Life won because love won. Love, first and foremost always, for her Lord and Saviour Jesus Christ, Whose she now was, body and soul and spirit, and Whom she longed to serve with entire consecration of her life, would He but give it back. Love, next, for Max— her own dear, dear husband. So weak he was—ah, Rachel knew it!—so infirm of will, so vacillating, so altogether disappointing; and yet, despite it all, so infinitely precious to her. For his sake she must live. And the one supreme purpose in her living now, was that she might win Max, too, for Christ.

And finally, there was that wonderful Heaven—sent love newly dawning in Rachel's heart—the love of a mother for her first-born son. As she lay day after day weak and helpless, but quite happy now, he slept in his little crib beside her or curled within her arms. And his plaintive, feeble cry upon awakening was sweetest music to her ever-listening ear.

They named him Abraham Moses Max Kalinsky—Mrs. Kalinsky did the naming. It would be a long time, however, before the wee morsel of humanity could measure up to the dignity of such a lofty patronymic. And so for the present he was merely "Little Abie." And Little Abie soon had won all hearts.

And for Little Abie's sake his mother was held in favor by the entire Kalinsky household and by the large Kalinsky following. The most anxious solicitations were expressed for her recovery; the most tender care was lavished upon her.

Her strange confession of the hated Jesus Christ on the night they thought her dying—on *Seder* it was—was tacitly overlooked. It was of course but a wild raving of delirium. With returning of health there would be a full return to sanity.

Of the Bible hidden surreptitiously in the attic, and of Rachel's very evident guilt concerning it, it was as well that this, too, be ignored. The Bible was safely burned; and if Rachel herself dared ever again to make mention of it or of anything else connected even remotely with Christianity, all that could very easily be attended to later. But just at present for Little Abie's sake there must, of course, be no undue excitement. Mrs. Kalinsky and Rabbi Mordecai Moses, Jacob and Sarah, in secret conclave, all agreed to this. They agreed, too, that it wasn't necessary to say anything to Max. Max had worries and troubles enough already, poor darling boy—his business, Rachel's illness, the new responsibilities of fatherhood—without bothering him with this unhappy performance. There wasn't any occasion for alarm, Rabbi Moses assured them. Had Rachel been entertaining any secret leanings toward that blasphemous impostor, Jesus, the new cares and joys of motherhood would quite dispel them. Leave the whole sorry affair alone. Just watch her carefully, that was all. And so they said nothing.

Rachel, too, said nothing. But she thought much. She was not at all deceived by these new tactics of the family. Something was back of it, she knew. Between the extreme graciousness of every one—Mrs. Kalinsky's the most pronounced of all—on the one hand, and his or her most studied avoidance of the entire subject of Rachel's interest in the New Testament and in Christianity on the other hand, it was not difficult to perceive that storm areas were gathering. Storm signals were in the air. To Rachel's naturally sensitive intuition there now was added her rapidly deepening spiritual discernment. And she read the signs aright. She had made confession of the despised and hated Jesus Christ in Deborah Kalinsky's home. And she knew the die was cast.

But still her heart was kept in perfect peace. She had confessed her Lord before men. She was His forever. And He would guard His own. All unknown the future lay before her. But safe within His keeping she could face it without fear. Step by step He would lead her forward. However rough the path of His appointment for her life might be, His love and tenderness would be unfailing, His grace her all-sufficient portion to the end.

She would not run ahead of the Spirit's leading. Neither would she shrink and falter when the pillar of cloud and of fire might beckon her forward. The present pathway was made very plain. For Little Abie's sake, until he was well established and until her own health and vigor was restored, she must lie still and rest. Just that and nothing more. In quietness and confidence would be her strength.

And so the days—the weeks—of resting were very precious ones indeed. During the many long, quiet hours that she lay with her baby on her breast, she had sweet communion with her Lord. His power was present to heal; and body, mind and spirit gradually and graciously were restored by the great Physician's skill.

May passed, and June began with burning heat. For days and weeks the City lay within its deadly grip. Not in years had New York experienced such a sultry summer. There were many heavy storms. Thunder was constantly in the air, with depressing effect upon every one. By August Rachel's strength again began to languish. The baby, too, was often ailing.

The atmosphere within the Kalinsky home grew more and more oppressive. For thunder was there as well as in the clouds. Low and distant at first, its rumbling became day by day more ominous. Not yet had the storm clouds burst, but they were gathering in volume and in blackness. The storm was on its way—the most fearful storm of all.

Yes, dear Rachel, the storm is soon to reach its climax now. Already the thunder is rolling in, in deep reverberation. The lightning flashes angrily across your sky. Dear Child of God! Confessor of Jesus Christ His Son! All you have suffered thus far for your love and loyalty to Him is as nothing compared to the storm that yet must come. But it is all within God's plan, as you have yielded up your life to Him, and you may dare to face it undismayed. He will give you grace and strength in Christ to endure steadfast to the end—for His own dear Name's sake. In Him you will be more than conqueror.

Little Abie was his grandmother's chief joy. Even her precious Max held but second place now in her devotion. Proudly she exhibited her youngest grandson to every one who entered the house, holding him on her lap or generously passing him around for critical inspection.

"Did you efer see a baby vhich it vus so vunderful?" she exclaimed rapturously. "Oi, oi, he iss perfect. He iss so bu-tee-ful—so vise. He iss a true Kalinsky. See! He haf got the Kalinsky chin, the Kalinsky nose; his eyes they iss exactly like mine own. Und vould you joost look at the shape of his head yet! I am telling you that baby he haf got brains!"

"Come darling, come to your own Grandmamma! Mein precious Leetle Abie—vich it vus mein leetle grandsohn— mein Maxie's boy. Come to Grandmamma, darling, come!"

Mrs. Kalinsky took upon herself full responsibility for the care of the baby. All of his mother's ministrations to him were strictly under his grandmother's jealous jurisdiction.

"Vy you don't put more voolens on him, Rakkel?" she would ask querulously. . . "Vot, it iss too hot? Nonsense, I don't keer if it iss hot. Babies they must vear alvays heaps of voolens in August efen. . . Vy you not gif him oftener his food? I am telling you, you are starving that baby until death. . . Rakkel! Vy you let him cry like that? Vy you don't you pick him up und rock him?. . . Come, mein poor darling Baby, mein precious Leetle Abie, come to your own Grandmamma. Grandmamma she knows how leetle babies vants to be took keer of. There, there, mein own poor leetle lambie, there, there, there!"

Many a time Rachel had to endure the indignity of having her baby snatched from her arms by her disgruntled mother-in-law. Many a time, too, the sleeping infant was lifted from his crib and carried triumphantly downstairs solely that Mrs. Kalinsky might feed her greedy vanity on the fulsome praises of some neighbors who had just dropped in.

But the hours when Rachel did have her baby to herself were precious ones indeed. When Mrs. Kalinsky and Sarah were off upon their Hadassah affairs, and the children were at school and the house quiet, she would feel then that Little Abie was really her own, and she feasted her hungry heart upon him.

Yes, he was wise indeed! Mrs. Kalinsky was quite right upon that score. How very understanding and intelligent he did look as, curled in his mother's arms, he crowed up into her face with approving baby gurgles, agreeing perfectly with everything she said. To him alone Rachel confided her deepest secrets.

"Little Abie! Mother's own precious baby boy—mother's own dear little son! You are mine, Little Abie— mine and my darling Max's—our own beloved first-born child!

"And you are His, dear, you are Christ's. Do you know that, darling? Yes, Little Abie, you are Jesus Christ's. You belong to Him. Mother gave you all to Him even before she saw you, before she held you, darling, in her arms. Yes, Little Abie, you are going to be a Christian. Mother is a Christian—a Hebrew-Christian, dear—and some day Daddy is going to be a Christian too, And then, Little Son, we shall be, oh, so happy, all together. We won't have to stay here always, Baby, in this dreadful house. Some day very soon we are going to have our own dear home once more. And then we all shall live for Christ— Daddy and mother and our precious baby boy."

"And soon, Little Abie, you will be a big, big laddie and go to school and learn many wonderful things. And you will go then, too, to Church and Sunday School and learn the most wonderful things of all—all the lovely stories about the dear Lord Jesus. Once He was a little baby too, dear, just like you, and then a fine, strong boy just as you are going to be some day. And then, darling, when He grew up to be a man He died upon the cross for you and me and for our dear, dear Daddy. And that is why we must all love Him so—because He is our Saviour, our own Messiah and our King."

"Yes, Little Abie, the Lord Christ Jesus is the true Messiah of the Jews. Only the awful thing, Baby, is that so many of our dear, dear people do not believe in Him. It was the Jews, darling, who crucified Him. 'He came unto His own, and His own received Him not.' But some day, Little Abie, they will believe because you are going to tell them. Yes, dear, when you are old enough and when you are a big, strong man that is the wonderful work that you are going to do for God. You are going to tell our own dear Hebrew people about their true Messiah, the Lord Christ Jesus. Yes, my Son, you are going to be a Missionary—a Hebrew-Christian Missionary to the Hebrews."

But Mrs. Kalinsky had plans quite otherwise.

"Oi, oi, mine own Leetle Abie" she would say to him, you vus so clefer a baby vhich it couldn't be no cleferer baby possible. Und some day soon you vill be a big, big boy mit pockets yet, und then you vill go to Cheder und to Talmud Torah. You vill learn it there the Talmud und the Taanach. Und you vill learn to read und write in pure Hebraish. Und ven you iss thirteen you vill make it then *bar mitzveh*. You vill get to be of age yet and then you vill haf to became yourself responsible to keep the law vhich it iss your dear parents they now keeps for you.

"Und then later vhen you vill be sixteen already, you vill go to the College of the City of Noy York, vhere it iss so many Jewvish boys yet. Und vhen you make it finish, then your darling father he vill be by that time very rich. Und he vill send you for two more years yet to the great noy Hebraish University in Jerusalem. Und then vhen you came home a great, strong man already, ve vill get for you a fine big Synagogue like Temple Emanu-El by Central Park, und from all over the whole vorld peoples vill came to Noy York to hear it preach the vunderful noy Rabbi Abraham Moses Max Kalinsky!"

Rachel's plans were whispered secretly into Little Abie's ear alone. Mrs. Kalinsky's were broadcast freely and jubilantly to all her friends and neighbors. Frequently, also, with significant emphasis they were rehearsed to Max and Rachel. Though no open word of opposition was ever spoken between the mother-in-law and the daughter-in-law, each very keenly sensed the other's antagonism. Thus through that first sultry summer of Little Abie's life, there was strong atmospheric disturbance in the Kalinsky household. The electrical elements, positive and negative, were swiftly approaching collision, and heavy thunder soon began to roll.

The first real cloudburst came in mid-September. And between Rachel and her Max.

Since her convalescence in the early summer one thought had greatly troubled Rachel. She had made confession of her faith in Christ at *Pesach*, but not once since by word or act had she confirmed it. For the first few weeks when she lay so critically ill it was quite all right, her silence. For the baby's sake, until he, and she herself again would both be strong, she knew that God would have her do nothing more than rest and have quiet, sweet communion with Himself.

The vigor gradually returned, but Rachel argued with herself that on little Abie's account she must even yet avoid all possible excitement.

When, however, by midsummer she still had spoken not a word, her sensitive heart discerned a grieving of the Spirit. She was not standing true to her colors. Her banner, far from being gloriously unfurled was dangerously near trailing. Her very silence was giving occasion for triumph to the enemy. Rachel realized it suddenly with keenest penitence.

Firmly she resolved to make amends. She would honor her confession. She would make good her claim to faith in Christ. As she had named His Name before men, so now she must continue to proclaim it. But she found it far from easy.

It was vastly harder than her first confession. Then her illness had been a protection. They all had made allowance, "Rachel is in high fever; she is delirious; she is not responsible for what she says."

But there was no such wall of defense now. She was perfectly lucid; she was almost completely restored to health; she was fully accountable for all she said or did.

Before, too, she had confessed Christ in the face of what she had believed to be certain death; now she would have to confess Him with life before her.

Also, when she first had made confession, the baby had been her silent plea for mercy. For his sake they, of course, would never harm his mother. But now, however, the baby himself had become—next to Rachel's loyalty to Christ—the most insistent reason for her open allegiance to Israel's Messiah.

With growing alarm Rachel noted the frequent earnest conclaves between Mrs. Kalinsky and Rabbi Mordecai Moses concerning the immediate and future training of this promising Hebrew child. She resolved that the strong orthodox current must be deflected and a stream of Christian influence made to flow around her son.

And so, for Little Abie's sake, as well as for her loyalty to her Lord, Rachel steeled herself to speak. And therefore, not only because he was the child's father, but also because he was the one least inflammable in that orthodox Jewish household, Rachel resolved that she would speak to Max.

For several days she watched her opportunity. At last it came one Sabbath evening. Supper was just over. The candles burned upon the table. Jacob was reading the evening prayer when Rabbi Moses entered. Jacob turned the devotions over to him, and he made them an occasion for a lengthy discourse upon Hebrew parents' duties toward their firstborn son, Little Abie on his grandmother's lap furnishing the inspiration and the object lesson.

As the most rigid orthodoxy was insisted upon as the foundation stone in Hebrew child-training, Rachel burned with indignation. She held her peace before the Rabbi and the family, but as soon as she and Max and the baby were alone upstairs she expressed her unbridled resentment with vigor and directness.

"Max," she said decisively, "I do not like it."

"You don't like what, Rachel?" Max asked blankly.

"Their interference! I tell you I will not have it!"

"Whose interference—about what?"

"Rabbi Moses' and your mother's about our Little Abie. He is our child, Max, not theirs."

"Yes, of course. But Rachel, aren't the Rabbi and Mamma the best ones to say how we should bring him up?"

"No," replied Rachel hotly, "they are not!"

"Why not?" asked Max with mild astonishment.

"Because I tell you, we are Little Abie's parents. And they are planning an orthodox Hebrew training for him; and Max, I do not want it. I tell you, dear, I cannot, cannot have it!"

"What on earth are you talking about!" Max's astonishment was no longer mild. His dark eyes flashed with a warning glint of anger. "Tell me, Rachel, what do you mean?"

"O Max darling," pleaded Rachel, "you know exactly what I mean. You know, Max—by now you must know surely—that I am a Christian, and I want my child—our child—to have a Christian training—never, Max, a Jewish one."

Max's reaction was terrific.

"You are not a Christian. And my son shall never be a Christian—never on your life!"

He wheeled upon her sharply. "Are you crazy, Rachel? I thought that you were done with all the Christian stuff, You ought to be—all the havoc you have made with it. I tell you, girl, to forget it. Forget it!"

Quietly, with steeled composure, Rachel faced the storm. "No, Max," she said firmly, "I will never forget it. I am a Christian. I love the Lord Christ Jesus with all my heart, for I know, dear Max, that He is our true Messiah."

Max's reply took the very breath from Rachel's body.

"Well, suppose He is—what of it?"

"Max!"

"Oh, you needn't look at me like that. Of course He's the Messiah! I know it, Rachel, as well as you. No one can help knowing it if he reads the New Testament at all intelligently, as I have done, out of curiosity, a dozen times. Jews everywhere are reading it today. John's Gospel alone, clinches the question of His Messiahship absolutely. Certainly He is the Messiah. Without a doubt He is. Thousands of Jews believe it. Jewish rabbis believe it, lots of them. Why, I'd be willing to wager this very moment anything I've got that Rabbi Moses himself is a secret believer in Jesus Christ. But does he confess Him? It would mean his bread and butter. You can't hold down a job as Chief Rabbi of a synagogue and say that you believe in Jesus Christ!"

"O Max, Max!" Rachel looked at him with heartbroken reproach. But he ignored it and continued quite indifferently.

"Yes, He's the Messiah all right enough—but that is not the point. The point is, what has all that got to do with us? We are Jews. And no Jew can be an open follower of Jesus Christ. I tell you, Rachel, no Jew can be a Christian."

"Oh, but Maxie," exclaimed Rachel eagerly, "indeed he can be! In the Lord Christ Jesus there is neither Jew nor Gentile. The middle wall of partition is broken down. We are all one in Him."

But Max shook his head stubbornly. "I tell you no, Rachel. Now don't misunderstand me. I have no fault at all to find with Jesus Christ. In fact we Jews should all be proud of Him. He's the finest product of manhood that Israel has ever had. He's the flower of our Hebrew race. I grant all that. And what is more, as I've already intimated, I believe His claims were all authentic. I believe, without a doubt, He is the Son of God. But just the same—in spite of all of that—I tell you, Rachel, I can never be a Christian."

"Oh, but Max, Max," cried Rachel pleadingly, "why not, dear?

If you accept Him with your intellect, why will you not receive Him with your heart? Why will you not yield your soul—your life—to Him? Ah, Maxie darling, He longs so for your love, for your allegience to His Name. He is lonely, dear! He came unto His own and His own received Him not. We crucified Him, Max! And we today are crucifying Him afresh each time we close our heart against Him. Oh Max, He longs so to come in! He died for us, dear—for us; and oh, we must surely give our all to Him, Dear Max, He is standing even now outside the door of your heart, knocking, knocking patiently, for you to let Him in. Oh Maxie darling, won't you? Won't you give yourself to Him, your Lord and Saviour-your own Messiah—Jesus Christ?"

A wistful look came into Max's eyes. As Rachel pleaded with him it deepened and grew very tender. Almost it seemed that he would yield. But suddenly his eyes grew cold. His mouth hardened. His jaws and shoulders set. With finality of decision he shook his head.

"No, Rachel, no! I tell you I can never be a Christian. It would cost too much!"

"Suppose I did. Suppose together we both confessed our faith in Jesus Christ. All right, what then? You know what, well enough. We would be Meshumed to our Jewish people. We couldn't stay here in my mother's home another night. We would lose our business. We would lose our friends. We would lose our membership in the Hebrew synagogue. We would lose the respect of all the neighborhood. We would lose the prestige the Kalinsky family has always held. We would lose all the wonderful chances we have for our Little Abie's future. We would be cut off, I tell you—cut off and scorned by everybody— yes, and even cursed. I tell you, Rachel, we never can be Christians. It costs too much."

Rachel sat silent, stunned with chagrin and grief. But Max persisted in his argument.

"And then, Rachel, look at it from another angle. Suppose we were willing to pay the price. Suppose in spite of all its costs we still decided that we wanted to be Christians. All right, what then? What would we gain by it?"

"When our own Jewish people did cut us off and cast us out, what then? When we should go out of this house homeless and

110

friendless and accursed, would the Christians take us in? Would the Christians open up their homes to us and give us food and warmth and shelter? Would the Christians give us aid and comfort in our sorrow? No, they would not. Why not? Because we are Jews. Jews aren't welcome in the homes of Christians.

"Would the Christian business men give me a job? No. Why not? Because I am a Jew. Christian business organizations don't want Jews. Would the Christian women hold out a loving, helping hand to you? Would they receive you into their exclusive social circles? No, certainly they would not. Why not? You are a Jewess. Jewesses cannot mingle socially with Gentiles."

"Would the Christian schools extend a welcome to our Little Abie? No, they would not. Why not? Little Abie is a Jew. Christian mothers do not want their children to play with Jewish children."

"Just one thing more! Suppose, Rachel, we did confess our faith in Christ. Suppose we did come out openly as Christians. All right, what then? Would the Christian Church take us in? Would the Christian ministers who preach the Gospel of Jesus Christ, a Jew, show love to us who are His Jewish brethren? Would the Christian worshippers, bowing piously in prayer to Him, make welcome room for us within their pews? Would they? Tell me, would they? Sit down a bit and think it over. Go to a few Christian churches and find out. Find out for yourself how warm a welcome you would get from them. Find out how keen it is—the Church of Jesus Christ—to win the Jew."

"And Rachel, you and I are Jews. And Jews we'll stay. We'll stick to our own people. We'll stay where we have friends. Every one in this old world needs friends. And believe me, I know where to find them. Among the Jews. The Jews have love. The Christians talk a lot about love—about the love of Christ—but it takes the Jew to show it. You never yet saw a Jew refuse to give another Jew a helping hand when he was down. You never yet saw one Jew turn a hungry Jew away. You never saw a Jew that was sick or homeless or helpless very long. That's what I call love."

"And that's the kind of love I want. That's what I call the love of Christ. I tell you, Rachel, I have seen more of the true love of Jesus Christ in the heart of an orthodox Jew than I have in thou-

111

sands of Christians who claim to follow His example. Jesus Christ Himself is all right. I haven't one word to say against Him—not one single word. But believe me, those who call themselves by His Name are not like Him. There are very few Christians, Rachel, that I have any use for."

"So once for all I ask you, please, to stop all this talk about you and me becoming Christians. I tell you I will never be a Christian. And you won't be a Christian either. We're Jews! And Jews we stay."

The last words were punctuated with a sharp slamming of the door as Max went out.

Rachel sank upon her knees distressed and torn. Her heart and brain alike were in raging tumult because of Max's stand and because of her ardent yearning for Max's soul. But above the confusion one fact alone stood out in clear and bold relief. Though every man might be a liar, though every one who named His Name might yet prove false, Jesus Christ her Lord was true. And Him she was resolved that she would follow wheresoever He might lead. And to the very end. Him she would from this time forth faithfully confess at every opportunity, no matter what the cost. Steadfastly she set her face as a flint to go all the way forward with Him and for Him.

Another cloudburst came the following week. And this time the one who precipitated it was Jacob. Upon arising in the morning, Rachel had centered her devotions upon the first chapter of the Acts of the Apostles. She had been without a Bible since hers had been burned by Mrs. Kalinsky at *Seder*—for she had had no money for a new one. But the Word of God was stored richly in her heart. And through the wonderful eighth verse the Spirit spoke directly to her, "Ye shall receive power. . . ye shall be witnesses."

"Power." Dynamite, the word meant literally. "Ye shall receive dynamite!" the Master promised. With thrilling joy Rachel consciously realized herself to be a chosen channel for the mighty operation of the Holy Spirit.

"Ye shall be witnesses." She—Rachel Mendelssohn Kalinsky—a witness for her Lord Christ Jesus! Oh, the wondrous privilege, the honor of it!

"In Jerusalem." Right here among her own dear Jewish

people! Was that God's plan for her? As she communed with Him in prayer, the vision deepened in Rachel's awestruck soul of what He might do through her life, fully yielded up to Him, for Israel in New York City.

And to this heavenly vision she was not disobedient. That very afternoon Rachel Kalinsky began her missionary ministry as ambassador for Jesus Christ her King. And at once she was challenged by the Enemy. The immediate result of her witness was the cloudburst of Jacob's wrath.

It was pouring heavily outdoors and the children consequently had to play inside. They got tired. Wouldn't Auntie Ray please tell them some nice stories? Auntie Ray did—one story after another—nature stories and Bible stories from the Old Testament.

And then she ventured boldly. They had just had the story of the little Samuel. Would they not like to hear a wonderful story now about Another Little Boy?

Yes, they would. Eagerly they listened as still more eagerly Rachel, with a lovely light in her dark eyes and a glow in her heart, told them the story of the dear Lord Jesus when He was twelve years old. Her back was turned toward the doorway so that she did not see Jacob peering through it stealthily. The three children lined up before her on the chesterfield did see him and gave a guilty giggle. Then Rachel turned quickly—and faced the cloudburst.

Jacob was choking with rage. His ugly face was purple. The veins stood out upon his neck and forehead like whipcords. With a savage growl he suddenly rushed forward and struck the children brutally, ordering them off upstairs instantly. They fled from the room screaming. Then Jacob seized Rachel viciously by the shoulders and shook her until her teeth chattered.

"You Meshumed," he hissed. "You dare to! Don't you ever dare to talk to my children ever again about that blasphemous Jesus Christ."

He drew away and confronted her menacingly. "Look here, my girl," he snarled, "I am telling you just one thing. There ain't no room in this house for Jesus Christ. And there ain't no room for Christians. I ain't got nothing more to say at all—just only that—Jesus Christ and all his tribe gets out. Y'understand me, don't you? All right then, think it over!"

The children, of course, told their mother and Jacob told his mother; and from that hour thenceforth the thunderbolts crashed from every quarter. Cloudburst followed cloudburst. Through them all Rachel was sustained in wondrous peace. That the die was cast—that her hour was come—she knew beyond a doubt, but she was kept calm and unafraid. Steadfastly she stood true to her Lord—not aggressively or with any suggestion of defiance, but in her own quiet, forceful way speaking His Name with perfect naturalness at every possible opportunity. In consequence of which the storm increased in fury and momentum.

And at last the lightning struck.

It was on *Yom Kippur*—the great Day of Atonement—the day of humiliation and abasement. Throughout the Ghetto of New York, and throughout the world, Jews everywhere were gathered in their respective synagogues, from early morning until sunset, with weeping and fasting and penitential prayer—as they confessed their sins.

Yom Kippur fell this year on Sabbath—early in October. On Sabbath and *Yom Kippur* eve, before sundown, the Kalinsky's had partaken copiously of their elaborate supper as fortification against the long day of fasting on the morrow. At the table Mrs. Kalinsky outlined the *Yom Kippur* program. The men and children would go to the synagogue at seven and of course would stay all day. Yes, certainly they had to, she insisted, in response to the children's loud outcry of protest. It was the great *Yom Kippur*. Didn't they want to get forgiveness for their sins? She and Sarah would go in the morning, then one of them would come home at twelve o'clock to take care of the baby and let Rachel go from then till sundown, when *Yom Kippur* ended.

Rachel suddenly went cold! She knew—the hour was about to strike! A paralysis of nameless terror crept over her. Icy fingers seemed to grip her throat. She made no reply to Mrs. Kalinsky's plan. Escaping as quickly as possible to her room she flung herself upon her knees and pleaded with her Lord for strength.

Tenderly He drew near as He had done so many times before when the forces of darkness had almost overwhelmed. Over and over again He whispered to her heart, out of His own Word so richly hidden there, sweet promises of help and strength and peace:

"I will never leave thee nor forsake thee. . . When thou passest through the waters, I will be with thee; and through the rivers, they shall not overflow thee; when thou walkest through the fire, thou shalt not be burned; neither shall the flame kindle upon thee. . . Be strong and of a good courage; be not afraid, neither be thou dismayed; for the Lord thy God is with thee withersoever thou goest. . . He knoweth the way that I take. . . he performeth the thing that is appointed for me. . . The Lord is my shepherd; I shall not want. . . Thou wilt keep him in perfect peace, whose mind is stayed on thee; because he trusteth in thee. Trust ye in the Lord for ever: for in the Lord Jehovah is everlasting strength. . . For this God is our God for ever and ever; he will be our guide even unto death."

When Max, an hour later, entered the room, Rachel met him smiling. The victory was won. She was calm and strong.

Max looked glum. "Well," he said peevishly. "I suppose we've got to go through with it."

"Through with what, dear?"

"*Yom Kippur.* Having to stand up all day in a crowded, stuffy synagogue. It's too hot. Children crying all around you—everybody reading prayers and whimpering—nothing to eat all day long—it's rotten!"

"Max!"

"I can't help it. I hate it. It's a bore."

"Well, don't go then," answered Rachel quietly.

"What!" exclaimed Max, astounded, "Not go? To the synagogue? On the Day of Atonement? What are you talking about? Why, every Jew has got to go!"

"I am not going!" With perfect control Rachel spoke the fatal words. But Max did not grasp their import.

"Of course you're going, Rachel. Mamma said she would arrange things so you could. We've got to go, both of us, to make confession of our sins and get atonement for another year."

"Ah, dear Max," urged Rachel, "we have received full atonement forever through our Lord Christ Jesus. We need no yearly sacrifice. He offered up sacrifice for all when He offered up Himself. By one offering He hath perfected forever them that are sanctified. Our sins and iniquities He remembers no more forever against us. Now where remission of these is, there is no more offering for sin."

"Rachel!" exclaimed Max in consternation, "I tell you if you keep on with all this Christian business you will wreck our lives! Mamma, Jacob, and Sarah are already wild about it. Now do, dear, quit it! Believe what you like, but keep quiet in this house! And you must go, Rachel, to the synagogue tomorrow."

"I can't, dear."

"Why not?"

"You know why, Max. I am a Christian!"

"Well, what if you are? You can go to the synagogue on *Yom Kippur* just the same, can't you? You must go, Rachel, to keep peace."

"No, Max," answered Rachel with quiet firmness, "it would be compromise."

"Compromise!"

"Yes, compromise. I am a Christian. I am free from all the Jewish law: free from the ceremonial and the Talmud and the synagogue. If any man be in Christ, he is a new creature: old things are passed away; behold, all things are become new. Never again, Max, shall I be entangled in the yoke of Jewish bondage. I am free in the liberty wherewith Christ hath made me free."

Max groaned aloud. "But Rachel," he argued, "if you persist in being a Christian, at least you need not be a narrow one. I know Hebrew-Christians who keep up their Judaism just the same. Look at Otto Goldberg. He's been a Christian thirty years—but Otto will be at the synagogue all right tomorrow."

"Yes, I know he will. But I won't be. For all Otto claims to be a Christian—and I believe he is sincere—he is nevertheless entangled in the bondage of tradition. I have come farther out of Judaism in six months than he has in his entire thirty years."

"No, it's not that at all. Otto Goldberg has consideration for the feelings of his family. He knows the grief it would cause them if he were to separate himself from their orthodox observances. It is the offense of that, more than anything else, Rachel,

116

that breaks up Jewish families when a Jew becomes a Christian."

"Ah no, dear Max! That is not the offense. The offense is the Cross of Jesus Christ! And I have taken up that Cross. If in consequence I, too, must meet offense—amen, dear Lord, so be it!" Deeply moved she bowed her head in reverent prayer.

Wildly Max made one more attempt. "Rachel! Won't you stop it! Please! And if you don't go tomorrow it will mean—I warn you—just one thing. We can't stay one day longer in this house!"

"Oh, but Max," cried Rachel eagerly, "I do not want to stay. Oh, can't we leave, please? I have been so terribly unhappy here. Oh Maxie, can't we go and have our own dear little home once more? Just you and I and Little Abie? And can't we make it, Max, a Christian home? You do believe in Christ—you've said so. Oh Max, won't you take Him—just right now—as your own Messiah—your Saviour and your Lord and King! If only you would, He will make our life together in our own Christian home, more beautiful than we can dream of."

But Max promptly dashed cold water on Rachel's ardent hopes. "I've told you once for all, Rachel, I can never be a Christian. And you know why. I can't afford it. Religion is religion, but business is business. And with Little Abie coming on, we've got to get the business. And that's the reason, too, why we can't leave this house. We can't afford to. If we leave here because we're Christians, it means, of course, we leave the business too."

"Well, start a business of your own!"

"How can I when I haven't got the capital? Talk sense. You know that every cent I've got I get from Mamma. I tell you, Rachel, we don't dare to get in wrong with her. So we can't think of being Christians. She would never stand for it."

"Oh, Max, Max," pleaded Rachel, "be a man! Be independent! Are you never going to stand on your own feet? Are you never going to have an opinion of your own? Must you be anchored to your mother always? Oh Max, I want my home! I want my husband and my child! I want my home! And I want a Christian home!"

She looked at him imploringly, broken-heartedly. But Max had had enough. It was too hot tonight for quarreling. He picked up his hat and fanned himself with it vigorously. Then he opened the door with an air of finality and went downstairs.

The end came quickly. The next morning—the great Day of Atonement—Max and all the others had already gone to the synagogue before Rachel rose and dressed. After her devotions and her attending to the baby, she went downstairs and—while Jews world-wide were fasting in their synagogues—she got herself some breakfast. Purposely she left the dishes and the food on the kitchen table that the family, returning, might see and understand. Then she spent the morning alone with her God and with her child.

At noon Mrs. Kalinsky and Sarah both returned from the synagogue. Rachel could go now. They would both look after the baby. What! She wasn't going? Why not? And then they spied the dishes and the food and understood why not.

The lightning struck! With red-hot vitriolic fury it poured forth. Food on *Yom Kippur*! And breaking kosher too! Eating meat and milk together! And using the same knife to cut both meat and butter! Horrible! Horrible! And daring not to go to the synagogue! Refusing to confess her sins before her God! Well, He would surely damn her now! She was no longer a Kalinsky! Forever she would be Meshumed! Their wrath—Mrs. Kalinsky's and Sarah's—scorched, burned, and blazed. Just wait till Max came home! And Rabbi Moses! He would know of this fearful thing! He himself would attend to it! Just go back upstairs and wait! The waiting wouldn't be long—not with a Meshumed in the house!

Upstairs again forthwith Rachel went—and waited. And while she waited the conflagration spread. Back to the synagogue they flew—these two righteous mothers in Israel—they whose sins that day were all forgiven for a year. And there they wafted on the breeze the scandal: "Rachel Mendelssohn is Meshumed."

Meanwhile the gentle Rachel made her preparations. Her heart was torn, but underneath the pain was God's deep peace. Not one ray of light pierced the darkness of the future pathway. Everything beyond that day was absolutely black. But the Light Himself would be her Guide. Having Him she dared go forward undismayed.

Quietly she set everything in perfect order—her lavish

wardrobe, her trunks, her cherished books, her heirlooms, her wedding gifts and all her sweet, girlish treasures. She would leave them all. She would take nothing with her but the clothes that she and the baby wore. Nothing save such of the baby's little garments and her own articles as she could pack into a small hand-satchel. Into the top of it she slipped her father's, her mother's, and Max's pictures and her empty purse.

She bathed and dressed the baby carefully. His little white coat and bonnet were folded ready, with her own dark-blue hat and coat and the hand-satchel beside them.

Then for the remainder of the afternoon she gave herself to prayer. She must be fully fortified. She knelt beside Little Abie's crib. One last terrible fear convulsed her. Suppose—suppose! But she dared not think of such a thing as that. Her one ewe lamb! "O God of love, have mercy! O my Father, let this cup pass from me: nevertheless not as I will, but as Thou wilt." She rose from her knees comforted and strong. And then she waited.

She waited long. Once again she slipped downstairs and took some food. She must have it. She must have strength for the journey—whither? This time she cleared away the dishes and the food.

Still she waited. At last, after sunset, they came—all the family and many friends besides—and at their head walked Deborah Kalinsky and Rabbi Mordecai Moses. Rachel could hear them entering the house and going to the kitchen. And for full three hours she could hear their angry outcry. Wave after wave of roaring mounted upward, with one word always on their crest—"Meshumed."

And still she waited. . . But no one came. Ten o'clock. . . eleven o'clock. . . midnight. The crowd dispersed. . . The house became quiet. . . Still she was left alone. She lay down beside her little child, and soon her sleep was as peaceful and as sweet as his.

The morning broke with blistering heat. By nine o'clock Rachel herself was dressed—in purest white. The baby too was dressed and everything was ready. Still no one came. Through the window Rachel could see one after the other arriving—the entire Kalinsky family, Yetta Cash, Sophy Yasnik and other friends and neighbors, and finally Rabbi Mordecai Moses. And soon again she could hear the angry waves roaring.

They were waiting for her to come down!—the thought suddenly dawned upon her. All right, she would go down. Five minutes more in prayer for strength; then taking the baby on one arm and their coats on the other, with the satchel in her hand, she started. She paused in the doorway for a last farewell to the hideous room. Suddenly it became invested with strange glory. Here she had met her Lord; here she had confessed Him before men; here she had suffered for His dear sake; here her child had been born. She thanked the Father for it all—rejoicing that He had counted her worthy.

Then with firm tread, and with God's own peace garrisoning heart and mind, she went downstairs—toward the kitchen—and into the den of lions.

Yes, they were waiting for her, the whole fierce pack. As she entered the doorway they hissed and screamed with one accord, "Meshumed!"

They were all there—Jacob, Sarah, Goldie, Otto—all the rest. And they all looked at her with cold eyes. Even the children. And alas! with anguish of heart Rachel saw her—her precious Esther—her dearest girl friend. And Max! Her own beloved husband—the father of her child! He stood with his mother, a trifle apart from the others. He alone would not meet Rachel's eyes. With a skulking air, he hung his head. Swiftly the court was officially convened by Rabbi Moses. The lamb was thrown to the lions. A semi-circle was formed about her. Together with the Rabbi she stood within the center. Mercifully the agony was not prolonged. Swift and decisive was the judgment.

"Rachel Mendelssohn Kalinsky"—Rabbi Moses made indictment in a voice of thunder. "You have forsaken your God. You have gone over to the blasphemous apostates. You have confessed the name of Jesus Christ within this house. You have transgressed our most holy Law. You have broken fast on *Yom Kippur*. You have broken kosher. You have defied the worship and commandments of the synagogue. You have embraced an alien faith. You have proven traitor to all the holy traditions of your people. You have proven false to your husband, to his family, to your friends. You have renounced the one true God. In His Holy Name I pronounce you now Meshumed—accursed of God and man."

As a lamb before his shearers is dumb so the Messiah opened not His mouth. Like Him, His little lamb stood silent, without a quiver, through the terrible ordeal.

"Max Kalinsky, stand forth!" the Rabbi thundered his command; and Max, still avoiding Rachel's gaze, took his place beside her. His head was bowed with shame.

"What shall this righteous Israelite do with this apostate woman?" The Rabbi appealed the question to the court.

A chorus of frenzied cries responded instantly.

"Dee-worce her! Dee-worce her! She is Meshumed! Dee-worce her, Max, dee-worce her!"

Even the children screamed in shrill crescendo echo, "Dee-worce her, Uncle Max, dee-worce her!"

To Rachel's anguished heart the scene recalled another court—another angry crowd—another infuriated cry, "Crucify Him! Crucify Him! Crucify Him!"

"Dee-worce her! Dee-worce her! Dee-worce her!"

"Crucify Him! Crucify Him! Crucify Him!"

She experienced a thrill of holy joy above the anguish. She was being crucified with Him. She was one with Him in the mysterious fellowship of suffering.

And then came the most crucial moment of all. The baby was lifted from her arms and held aloft.

"What shall be done with this apostate's child?" the judge continued. Rachel's heart stopped beating while the lions sniffed for further blood.

A roar of divided opinion ensued. The baby was a true Kalinsky. He must be saved from such a mother. But no, he had drunk his mother's milk. He was Meshumed also. For a terrible instant Little Abie's fate swayed in the balance of a hair. And then the question was decided by himself. Mrs. Kalinsky took him from the Rabbi. Whereupon he screamed. Violently— angrily—convulsively. The once doting grandmother pushed him into Rachel's anguished arms with disgust.

"You take it avay qvick! Ve will not haf it here a baby vhich it iss such a brat! He iss Meshumed also!"

In a convulsion of joy and thankfulness, Rachel pressed her darling to her heart. Swiftly, sentence on them both was then pronounced.

"Rachel Mendelssohn, you are accursed! Your child is accursed! You are divorced forever from this family. You are cut off from Israel. You are cut off from God. Go—both of you—to your damnation!" Fiercely Rabbi Moses pointed to the open door.

Rachel drew herself up and held her baby close. Calmly she looked around at every face within the circle and as calmly said "Good-bye." She walked toward Max and stood before him. She compelled his gaze.

"Max," she pleaded softly, "will you not come with us too? Come, dear, come!"

The good angels and the evil angels fought desperately for Max Kalinsky's soul. For him it was an awful moment. On the one side were orthodox tradition, family ties, fear of consequences. On the other side his wife, his child, his Lord.

He looked at the sweet-faced girl he truly loved. He looked at his first-born son. He looked at the gentle Nazarene Who entreated him with pleading eyes. For an instant the good angels and the evil angels hovered over him with bated breath.

"Come, Max—my own dear husband—come! Come, Max, with your own Messiah, the dear Lord Jesus! Come, come! Come with your wife and with your child!"

Almost he yielded. And then he caught his mother's terrible eye. He quailed before it.

"You are not my wife! That is not my child! You are both Meshumed!"

It was the last cruel blow—the final bitter anguish. Rachel uttered a low, heart-broken moan. For an instant she reeled dizzily. She would have fallen, but swiftly and strongly she felt herself upborne by a mighty force. She realized that underneath her were the everlasting arms. Round about her, safely, holding, was the Saviour's love.

Tenderly He drew her to His breast. Strongly He held her, pressed close against His riven side. She was there—safe hidden in the cleft of the Rock. She was sounding now the depths of anguish—the depths of joy—in her fellowship with her Saviour's sufferings. She was crucified with Him. She looked up into His dear face. She heard His voice whispering comfort to her heart. Instantly she was made strong.

Once more her gaze swept over the circle of cold, angry eyes. Once more it fastened upon her husband who cringed before her, broken and sobbing, his face buried in his hands. Once more she said "Good-bye" to all.

Then she turned toward the doorway. Holding her baby and the coats within her arms and picking up her satchel, with a firm step and without a backward look—penniless, hungry, weak and friendless—victoriously she passed forever from Deborah Kalinsky's home.

Thus did the loving little Rachel, confessor of Jesus Christ, go forth unto Him without the camp, bearing His reproach.

Chapter IX.

False Shepherds of Israel

"Woe be to the shepherds of Israel that do feed themselves! should not the shepherds feed the flocks? . . . ye feed not the flock." —Ezekiel 34:2, 3.

It was high noon. The sun poured down upon the New York streets with burning heat. The temperature of the unprecedented Summer still continued unbroken into Indian Summer. It felt more like August than October. The glare from the high brick walls was dazzling. The pavements fairly smoked.

As Rachel and Little Abie passed through Mrs. Kalinsky's kitchen doorway the heat seemed to leap upon them like tongues of fire. But Rachel's head was cool. And her heart, though torn with anguish, was brave and strong.

With Little Abie heavy in her arms, she turned aimlessly eastward. Before she had gone a quarter of a block all the Kalinsky children were at her heels shrilly screaming "Meshumed." Other children joined in the excitement and took up the cry, and soon a lengthy, noisy procession was following her. Some of the boys were throwing sticks.

Where could she go? What could she do? The sense of exalted triumph with which she had forever left the Kalinsky family circle went down before a sudden wave of depression and terror. The vast city lay before her like a burning octopus. Traffic rushed and roared around her. She felt dizzy and confused and weak—a mere chip in a rushing, swirling Niagara.

Northward up Second Avenue she turned, her feet now heavier than lead. And heavier and heavier grew her heart as the awful pain kept stabbing—stabbing.

She tried to concentrate upon some plan, but her thinking became chaotic. Her throat was parched. It felt as if some one were choking her. She was faint, too, with hunger. She had eaten no food since three o'clock the day before. And the baby kept getting heavier. . . and the sun blazed fiercely. Here—she would just sit on this doorstep for a moment. She must rest. . . she would faint.

But still the children were at her heels and swarmed around her, still screaming "Meshumed" as she sat down. So she remained only a moment and then trudged on—past Twelfth Street and Thirteenth.

Oh, but she was so thirsty! And the baby—she must get water for him somewhere. This heat was awful for Little Abie. . . he would die!

Oh, how good! Here was Mrs. Einstein's house. She and Mrs. Einstein were old friends. Mrs. Einstein would gladly give her water for the baby. . . and perhaps she would ask them in and give them food. Rachel rang the bell hopefully.

But ill-report has wings. Already it had blazed its way up and down Second Avenue: "Rachel Kalinsky has turned Meshumed!" And not Mrs. Einstein's door alone, but several other Jewish doors as well were closed indignantly upon the renegade and her child, by women—Jewish women—Jewish mothers—whom she had counted friends.

Near the corner of Sixteenth Street stood Mrs. Kotzen's little kosher shop. The window was filled with delectable Jewish bread and herrings and cabbages. The sight of them made Rachel almost faint with longing. She must get food—she had to have it. She would buy something here on credit. Mrs. Kotzen would let her have it, she knew. Rachel had often bought on credit here for Mrs. Kalinsky. She would ask for just a little bread—she wouldn't need much—and a bottle of milk, and she would pay Mrs. Kotzen next week. She would be able to buy then surely—somehow.

Rachel went in. Half a dozen other Jewish customers stood waiting. Some of them Rachel knew, but they turned their backs upon her. Mrs. Kotzen stared at her across the counter.

"Vell?" she demanded with cold eyes.

Tremblingly Rachel made her request. Some bread, if she didn't mind—just the smallest loaf would do—and a pint of milk and she would pay for it next week. Would that be all right, please?

Mrs. Kotzen broke into a shrill outcry.

"Vot! Brodt? Mein brodt you vant? Vot for you think I should be selling it mein brodt to a Meshumed?"

"Meshumed!" shrieked the other women in chorus. "Iss she

Meshumed?" They hugged their head-shawls close in horror.

"Certainly it iss so that she iss Meshumed," Mrs. Silverman assured them. "Yesterday by the synagogue from *Yom Kippur* Yetta Cash she tellt me—und it iss so," she added triumphantly. "Rakkel Kalinsky she iss Meshumed!"

"Oi, oi, oi," screamed the women, "Meshumed! Meshumed! Meshumed!"

Mrs. Kotzen's husband opened the door wide and pushed Rachel outside. Solly Kotzen threw a rotten orange after her. The shrill cries of the women and a remnant of the children followed her up the street: "Meshumed! Meshumed! Meshumed!" A little dog snapped at her heels.

On she went—Seventeenth Street, Eighteenth, Nineteenth, Twentieth. Following Twentieth westward Rachel and her Little Abie reached at last the grateful, cooling shade of Gramercy Park. Just a few more exhausted steps and Rachel's hand was plunged eagerly into the sparkling fountain. She dripped the water from her fingers into the baby's parched mouth, and bathed his face, and then drank deeply herself.

Greatly refreshed, farther into the Park she went to a secluded place, and with a deep sigh of relief she sank exhausted upon a bench beneath a spreading shade tree. She ministered to her baby, then rocked him in her tired arms until he fell asleep. Then she spread her coat upon the grass and laid him on it, covering him carefully with his own coat. And then she lay beside him and almost instantly was fast asleep also. She slept for perhaps an hour and then woke suddenly with a thrill of fear. But Little Abie was quite all right—still sleeping peacefully. Rachel trembled violently for a moment with the terror of what might have been.

The big clock in the Metropolitan tower chimed three. The baby woke and cried. For a few moments Rachel soothed him, and then gathering him and the coats in her arms and lifting the heavy satchel, again she started onward in her weary, goal-less march.

The sun beat down cruelly. In the streets the city firemen were playing their great hoses on prostrated horses and dogs. A crowd of little children in the gutter were delightedly intercepting the reviving stream.

Rachel by now was faint for food. She must eat somewhere—somehow. But how? She was absolutely penniless. She could get no credit. She could never beg—she would die first.

Her mind grew confused with the awful problem; and then she thought she saw a plan. She would sell her coat. For half an hour she tried diligently but without success. Nearly all the shops were closed on Sunday afternoon, and in the few that were open no one wanted to buy a coat on a sweltering afternoon of Indian Summer in New York.

Westward she still trudged on—sitting now and again upon a doorstep. She was beginning to feel so very ill. And the baby! Rachel noted with alarm his feverishness and lassitude.

She passed a row of substantial looking homes. In some the doors stood wide open and sounds of voices came through them, in tones that suggested happy family groups within. As Rachel stood and listened to them a lump rose in her throat. The tears rushed to her eyes. A sense of terrible loneliness engulfed her.

She knew what she would do! She would enter one of these homes and ask for work. That would not be begging. She would ask if she might wash the dishes for her dinner. That would give her the immediately needed strength. God would take care of supper when the time came. And the night? What of that? What of shelter for herself and Little Abie? Rachel shuddered. And the morrow? . . . And the days ahead? . . . And the long, long, years? . . . A cry broke from her heart: "O God! O loving Heavenly Father, I am so afraid! Take care of us, dear Lord! Take care of us for Jesus' sake!"

A house larger and more pretentious than the others stood on the corner. Through the open window came the sound of children's voices singing a hymn. Rachel listened to the words:

"Jesus give the weary
Calm and sweet repose."

Ah, this was a Christian home! They were singing about the Lord Jesus! And asking Him to give repose to the weary! Oh, how weary she was—and her poor Little Abie! Perhaps God had led them to find their calm and sweet repose right here in this Christian home. How beautiful! This was the very place then where she would ask for work—just enough to pay for her dinner—and then perhaps. . . Well, she would trust the Heavenly Father. He would take care of all the rest.

She climbed the steps and timidly rang the bell. As she did so the music ceased and she could see four beautifully-dressed children leave the room. A neat housemaid answered the ring and looked compassionately at the strange sight before her—a very lovely but bedraggled and weary little mother with a crying baby in her arms. Christina was Scotch and big-hearted. She opened the screen door invitingly.

"Coom in, lassie. What is it? There, there. . . sit ye down a bit. Ye look beat. What wull ye hae, dearie?"

Rachel sank exhausted and grateful into the chair Christina placed for her. Brokenly, shyly, she made her desire known.

"Er—please—I want—do you think I could get—er— some work? Is there anything here that I could do—any kind of work? I'll wash dishes or scrub floors or anything at all—but I must find work, please!"

The hot tears flushed to Christina's eyes. "Ye puir wee lamb," she cried tenderly. "Aye, it's hungry ye air, an' clean worn out! There, there, come into the livin' room an' rest a wee in this nice saft couch an' I'll go upstairs an' tell my mistress."

Christina's voice and her sweet, sympathetic face had a soothing effect upon Rachel. And these soft, lovely cushions. . . and the cool comfort of the beautiful room. . . the electric fans. . . the flowers. . . the bowl of fruit upon the table.

Hope was dawning in her heart, and there is no restorer in the world like hope. Already Rachel felt refreshed and cheered.

Christina had entered Mrs. Pugsley's employ only the day before. She felt, therefore, just a trifle apprehensive as she mounted the broad Colonial stairway and knocked at her mistress' door.

Although the two women were out of view, Rachel could hear their voices clearly. Mrs. Pugsley's, thin and ungracious, rose shrilly.

"Christina, what do you mean by disturbing me? I told you expressly I was not to be called today till five o'clock. Now please understand distinctly, Christina—I told you yesterday— that every afternoon I have my nap from two till four, and I must never be disturbed under any circumstances. Between those hours I want the house kept absolutely quiet. Do not let the children play the piano as they have done today. And any callers whatsoever must wait till four o'clock. Always. And on Sunday until five. Between four and five on Sundays I invariably have my Bible study. That is my undeviating rule. So understand it clearly, Christina, in the future. Now, what do you want?"

Christina took the rebuke with Christian fortitude and meekness. "Please ma'am, I'm sorry but I couldna' help it. There's a wee thing doon stairs—a mither wi' her babe—and' she's a asking for work, ma'am."

"Work! What kind of work?"

Christina grew embarrassed. "Any kind she says she'll do, ma'am—dishes—floors—anything at all. If ye could juist give her a wee bit something, ma'am—she looks. . ."

"Certainly not, Christina!" asserted Mrs. Pugsley emphatically. "I have quite all the help that I can afford at present. I am paying far more than I really should. In any case I would never engage a servant on the Sabbath. It is the Lord's Day, Christina. I am surprised at you that you could have imagined such a thing. I understood that you were a Christian."

"Yes, ma'am, I am," replied the chastened Christina, "but I hae my doubts aboot the wee mither. She looks, ma'am, like a Jew."

"A Jew!" Mrs. Pugsley's voice rose in horror. "You admitted a Jew, Christina, to my house? Never do such a thing again! I have a most intense aversion toward the Jews. Dismiss this one at once. Now go, Christina, and do not disturb me again before five o'clock. I must complete my nap, then have my quiet study of God's Word. I must prepare for my missionary meeting at our church tomorrow."

Rachel, listening below with burning ears, heard poor Christina make one last feeble attempt.

"Please ma'am, would ye mind if I should give the lassie juist a wee bite first to eat? She looks so hungry like-an' the puir wee babe. . .

And then down the handsome ivory and mahogany stairway to Rachel's stricken heart came the reply of a Christian mistress of a Christian home.

"No, Christina, it is against my principles to give food to

129

beggars at the door. It encourages pauperism. And certainly to Jewish beggars—never. We would be over-run with them. . . Stay, Christina. . . If the woman is a Jew, give her one of these tracts as she goes out, 'What Think Ye of The Christ?' And here is a Gospel of St. John. That is the best Gospel to use with Jewish people. It proves to them the Deity of Jesus Christ. . . Here, take this whole package of Gospels with you and keep them in your pantry. Make a practice. Christina, of giving one to everybody who comes to the kitchen door. It is the Word of God and we must never lose an opportunity to send it forth. Now go. Christina, and let me finish my interrupted nap."

Rachel heard Mrs. Pugsley close her door. Then she saw Christina's face at the top of the stairway—angry and ashamed and sad. Heavily Christina started to come down upon her sorrowful errand of turning away from a Christian home of opulence, a homeless, starving mother and her child.

But Rachel spared poor Christina the pain of facing her. Quietly she slipped out through a side door and down the steps. Once more she found herself with her baby upon the hot and terrifying city streets. Her head was hotter than the streets, and her heart was lead. A Christian home! Yes, Max was right: "Jews aren't welcome in the homes of Christians." She would never try another one. But she must get work, somehow, some-where—and very quickly—or they both would die.

Another hopeful plan suggested itself to her. She would try a restaurant. In one of them perhaps they would let her wash dishes for her dinner.

She walked two or three blocks more before she found one. It looked promising. It was clean and white and shining. In the window were tempting mounds of vegetables and slices of iced watermelon. A large sign hung in the doorway:

HELP WANTED

Rachel read it eagerly with renewed hope and courage. And then she read in smaller type the words beneath, and her heart sank and grew sick. For the boycott stood out like scorpions to Rachel.

No Jews Need Apply

She grew confused, bewildered, dizzy. She was ill—very ill. Oh, what could she do? That awful sense of aloneness again.

Would her heart always ache like this?

An unutterable longing for her mother—such as she had not felt in years—swept over her. If only she could go to her and her father's and her brother Ivan's graves. That would be a measure of solace. But Cypress Hills was far away—too far to walk certainly, and she could go no other way.

Then she thought longingly of her dear friends, the Saramoffs, and of Violet Hamilton. Dear Violet Hamilton! She had never seen her since that fatal day. Nor the Saramoffs either. If only she could see them once again. Where were they now, she wondered? Still in Rivington Street? If only she might get there. But Rivington Street; too, was quite too far to reach.

No, there was nothing else to do but just keep on—keep on. God would surely help her. Oh, He couldn't fail her now. But why didn't He do something?

She continued walking westward—one block—two blocks—three. More and more weary she became—more ill—and more heartbroken.

At length she came to one of New York's most fashionable thoroughfares and turned idly into it. In a moment she was caught in the current of the Sunday afternoon society parade. Throngs of richly-apparelled and bejewelled men and women, sauntering with care-free indolence, upon pleasure bent; merry, laughing children with their French or English nurses; brilliant motors; splendid dogs: all surged past the lonely little Jewish mother with her child pressed close against her frightened breast. An occasional cool stare was directed toward the hot, bedraggled, exhausted little figure by the passers-by; the wealthy Epicureans at the sumptuous tables of the fashionable hotels glanced unconcernedly at her through the plate-glass windows; but nothing more. Among the throng, not one eye was there to pity—not one voice to soothe—not one loving hand held out to aid. In the whole vast City of New York there was not one soul that cared.

But God cared surely! Oh, He must, He must! She had confessed His Son. It was all for His dear sake, this suffering. He surely never would forsake her now.

Above the clang of traffic, from a high church tower silvery chimes were pealing forth an evening hymn. The music fell with

131

soothing touch upon Rachel's weary spirit. In its soft tones the Lord Himself spoke words of peace. Rachel felt His presence very near and very precious—very comforting and sweet and strong.

The church—St. X's—was just across the avenue—an imposing Gothic edifice of stone and marble with great bronze doors and leaded stained-glass windows. The worshippers were going slowly up the steps. It was the hour of Choral Evensong.

Rachel felt suddenly a thrill of joy. This was a Christian church! And now it was her church—the church of her Messiah and her Saviour, Jesus Christ. At last she had found a refuge and a home. Those people who were entering were Christians—they were all her brothers and her sisters in the Lord. She would join them for the service; then afterward they all would be so good to her—especially when she showed them Little Abie, and when she told them that she was a Hebrew-Christian. How good the Heavenly Father was that He had led her here to His own House!

Rachel had never been in a Christian church before, but she felt no sense of strangeness. She crossed the avenue and climbed the church steps, merging with the fashionable throng that was entering St. X's portals. She was exultant. She was a Christian in a Christian church! She had come home!

But as the gorgeously apparelled women pressed about her, suddenly Rachel became wretchedly conscious of her own appearance. The white dress, so fresh and crisp in the morning, was now limp and soiled. Her hat was bedraggled. The baby, too, was grimy. She had not noticed this before.

Shyly she hid herself as best she could behind a large, elaborately gowned woman and followed her closely down the center aisle, and slid after her into her elegantly cushioned pew. The woman knelt long and piously in prayer. Then she rose from her knees and took her seat. And then with astonishment she surveyed the apparition beside her. A stranger! Who put her here? She must speak to Mr. Wilkes, the head usher, about this at once. And whoever could the creature be? An untidy mother with a more untidy baby. And—could it be possible? Were these dreadful people Jews?

With shocked amazement Mrs. Stuyvesant-Wilberforce drew forth her bejewelled, gold lorgnette and levelled it suspiciously upon the intruders. With cold, appraising stare she took in all the offending details—the Semitic features, the weather-wilted attire, the baby. Just imagine such a thing! A baby in St. X's. And in Mrs. Stuyvesant-Wilberforce's own pew! And a Jewish baby, what was more! Horrible! She drew herself stiffly into the farthest corner and held up her prayer-book as a barrier.

Rachel crouched miserably into the other corner of the pew and drew Little Abie as far away as possible from his disgusted hostess. Fortunately he was again asleep. What had Rachel done? She felt hurt and grieved.

But soon her spirit was soothed by the glorious organ prelude. It was a Fugue from Bach—one of Rachel's favorites—and never had she heard it played more masterfully. She gave herself up to the exquisite beauty of it, as the harmony swelled and blended with the sunset light shimmering through the richly tinted Gothic windows, and with the fragrance of a thousand flowers banked high before the altar.

And then the Choral Evensong began. From the vestry down the long aisle and toward the altar steps the surpliced procession came—first, little choir boys with their high soprano treble, then older youths and maidens, and at last the deep-voiced men. Rachel sat entranced as all the blended voices, together with the organ and the violins and cellos, re-echoed in her heart in a wondrous symphony of praise.

Then followed the evening prayer, with frequent music interspersed; and next a hymn. Rachel joined in the singing of it with her rich, sweet voice:

> *"The day Thou gavest, Lord, is ended,*
> *The darkness falls at Thy behest;*
> *To Thee our morning hymns ascended,*
> *Thy praise shall sanctify our rest."*

Little Abie stirred and squirmed. And then began to cry! Rachel hugged him close in consternation. His cries increased in lustiness and volume. The gold lorgnette was again turned haughtily upon Mrs. Stuyvesant-Wilberforce's unwelcome guests. That good lady beckoned peremptorily to a pompous usher, elegantly groomed. He understood. Without a word

Rachel and her offending offspring were motioned from the pew. Down the long aisle they were led in full view of five hundred pairs of cold and disapproving eyes, to a secluded pew at the rear of the church. Here, the usher whispered grudgingly to Rachel, she might stay if she could keep her baby quiet—otherwise they would have to get right out.

Chagrined beyond expression and sick and sore at heart, Rachel collapsed within the pew and crouched low behind a mercifully protecting pillar. Fortunately the baby became drowsy and forthwith went off again to sleep. Rachel laid him down upon the cushion and rested her aching arms.

Soon she was comforted by another lovely anthem. And then the curate read the Scripture lesson. He was just a youth, but Rachel admired his earnest, soulful face, and his sympathetic, vibrant voice. His presence had a quieting effect upon her. She wished that after the service she might have an opportunity to talk with him. His lesson was from the twenty-second chapter of Genesis—the story of Abraham's offering up of Isaac. Rachel listened to his reading spellbound. It was one of her favorite chapters—one which she and Violet Hamilton had read together many times—the sublime foreview of the Lamb of Calvary.

One more hymn: "Lead Kindly Light Amid the Encircling Gloom"—which further soothed Rachel's saddened heart—and then the sermon followed.

The Reverend Clarence Cuthbert Clancy, D.D., LL.D., F.R.G.S., pompously ascended the steps to the high canopied pulpit directly facing Rachel. He was fifty-five and eminently aristocratic. His clean-cut features were scholarly and handsome, his ecclesiastical vestments rich and costly. His manner was ingratiating. Leaning well forward over the large open Bible on his pulpit, and extending his uplifted shapely hands benignantly, he began his discourse as Rachel hungrily devoured every word. Here at last would be nourishment. She had not lived that day by bread; but now, she reflected eagerly, she would find food for her famishing—new life and strength and hope—as this man of God would break to her the living Bread of His own Word.

"Dearly beloved," the rector's unctuous voice resounded through the vaulted arches, "our meditation for this twilight hour centers around the narrative we have just been reading from the book of Genesis. This book, now so widely discredited by modern scholarship as to its historical accuracy—particularly in the creation account—nevertheless contains for us much of legendary and of literary value."

Rachel opened wide her astonished ears. What! Genesis! Discredited? Inaccurate? Legendary? Why, Genesis was in the Bible! Whatever could the preacher mean?

"And among the many stories in which Genesis abounds," the rector continued, "none holds greater fascination than this one of the offering up of Isaac by his patriarchal father, Abraham."

"It is a strange tale and, upon the face of it, an altogether revolting one, embodying as it does a father's attempted murder of his son. To understand it aright, however, we must keep the story in its original setting, interpreting it in the light of Abraham's previous life and experience, for the incident demonstrates a survival, in Abraham's mind, of the ancient Chaldaean superstition of a God of vengeance who must be appeased by the offering of human sacrifice."

"Just at the critical moment God mercifully restrained Abraham from this awful contemplated deed; at the same time He graciously afforded him outlet for his truly commendable though mistaken zeal by providing an animal for him to sacrifice in place of a precious human life."

"Oh, how dreadful!" thought Rachel shudderingly. "Why, the man doesn't understand! The story is so wonderful. It speaks of Christ and Calvary. It is all a prophetic picture of His death for us upon the Cross. Why, Abraham is a type of God the Father Who 'so loved the world that He gave His only begotten Son that whosoever believeth in Him should not perish but have everlasting life'—and Isaac represents that Son obedient unto death!"

Exhausted though she was in body, Rachel's mind was stabbed wide awake with pain. She could scarcely contain herself as the Reverend Clarence Cuthbert Clancy, in like modernistic vein, continued for half an hour his eloquent address. Her very blood ran cold as deliberately, complacently, the scholarly rector of St. X's tore God's Holy Word to shreds, insulting Rachel's honor for the ancient Hebrew sacrificial rites, and holding up to ridicule her joyous new-found faith in the

Lord Christ Jesus as the true fulfillment of the paschal lamb. She knew nothing of theology, but she knew her Bible and she knew her Lord; and she recognized this man for what he was—a false prophet—a wolf in sheep's clothing.

But what was he doing here in a Christian church? It was a Christian church, of course—it must be with all the wonderful Christian songs and those Christian prayers. But why did it allow a man like that within its pulpit? So keen was Rachel's Jewish instinct for the things of God, so devoted was her Christian zeal for His inerrant Word, that her spirit was grieved inexpressibly as the sermon kept advancing to its brilliant finish.

"The cross of Jesus has passed through interpretation and re-interpretation in a thousand thought-forms representing a thousand varied complexes. But the concept of the sacrificial lamb belongs only to the Hebrew ritual of the Passover and to the Old Testament economy. In our Christian sybolism it has no place."

"Briefly then, in conclusion, my beloved, what to us is the value of this strange tale? What practical bearing does it have upon our twentieth-century life? For any portion of the Bible is, of course, of worth to us only as it can be interpreted in terms of present-day experience. All other parts of it must go into the discard. What application, then, can we make to ourselves of the story of Abraham and Isaac?"

"Essentially this, it gives to us a larger concept of our God. The God we worship today is the God of love, not the God of vengeful cruelty."

"Let us accept then this challenge to a larger and more noble faith in our Almighty God. And, inspired by the example of Jesus, let us realize more adequately in our own experience. His spirit of self-forgetful love and of devoted sacrificial service toward all His fellow-men. And now my beloved brethren, may grace, mercy, and peace be unto you from God the Father, God the Son, and God the Holy Ghost. Amen."

Rachel's very soul was sick. Oh, the cruel, cruel disappointment! She had come longing for bread and this man had given her a stone.

She felt choked—as if she could not draw another breath. She crouched back in her corner behind the pillar while the choir

136

sang the recessional and marched slowly out, followed by the curate and the rector.

The curate passed quite close to Rachel and as he did so he looked upon her with kind eyes. Hope kindled anew in her heart. Oh, this man was different surely, and he would help her! She must wait and speak with him.

While the last prayer was chanted in the vestry, Rachel gathered up Little Abie, still asleep, and the coats and satchel, and as the final "Amen" was sung in far-off shadowy tones, she slipped out before the congregation rose from their knees.

She crept across the vestibule and there sank almost prostrate upon a bench behind the center door. The worshippers departing through it—aristocratic men with chrysanthemums in their Prince Albert buttonholes, and high silk hats and English walking sticks; women in rich satins and elegant furs and laces; beautifully attired children—all brushed past her and her baby. A few directed toward her a cold, disinterested stare. The majority never looked at her.

At the end of the procession came Mrs. Stuyvesant-Wilberforce, the most lavishly gowned of all. She was laughing and chatting volubly with the Reverend Mr. Clancy, who, divested of his ecclesiastical garments, walked with very evident self-satisfaction beside her. As they paused for a moment before the outer doorway, within a foot of Rachel, the young curate came from within the vestry and approached her. His eyes were still kind, and as he looked at the baby they became tenderly compassionate.

He spoke to Rachel gently, asking her if he might be of service. Brokenly she was trying to reply, when just at that moment Mrs. Stuyvesant-Wilberforce passed out the door, and the rector joined them. He looked frowningly upon Rachel and the baby, then turned to his curate questioningly.

"A lady, Sir, that I believe is in need of help," the curate whispered to him in an aside.

"Very well, Arnold, I will attend to her," replied the Reverend Mr. Clancy coldly. "You may go. Report at my study, please, at ten tomorrow." The hope in Rachel's eyes became despair. She gazed after the curate's retreating figure in an agony of disappointment.

137

"Well, my friend," the rector turned upon Rachel sharply, "so this was the baby, was it, who disturbed my service? Kindly do not bring it here again. Leave it home the next time with its father."

Rachel shrank from him with instinctive aversion; but she was too exhausted in body, too sick in mind and heart to attempt a rebuff. Instead she faltered miserably.

"Oh, Sir, but he hasn't any father now—or any home! We are—you see—I am—"

"Well?" the rector questioned harshly.

"You see—we are Hebrews."

"Yes, I see you are," he replied dryly.

"But now I am a Christian—a Hebrew-Christian."

"Well?" The Reverend Mr. Clancy pulled out his watch impatiently. He had told Mrs. Stuyvesant-Wilberforce that in just five minutes he would be ready. "Well?" he repeated, "what about it?"

"I—you see—I am now a believer—a Christian, I believe in the Lord Christ Jesus and I have confessed Him as my own Messiah, and they—they have—" Rachel's voice trailed off mournfully.

Really this was most extraordinary! Quite too annoying altogether! The Reverend Mr. Clancy was becoming decidedly embarrassed.

"—and my husband's mother," continued poor Rachel miserably, "put us out, and we have walked all day and I could get no food and my baby is so sick and—and—" Rachel's brave spirit broke at last in a flood of wild hysteria.

The rector was distinctly angry. A beggar was it? And a Jew? Really, this was quite too impossible! And today of all days—just when he had at last succeeded in getting what he had been working for for months—an invitation to Mrs. Stuyvesant-Wilberforce's home for tea. And to keep her waiting now for this! Mrs. Stuyvesant-Wilberforce of all people! She was the most important member of St. X's—its very foundation stone in fact. One must treat her with consideration. A salary of twenty thousand isn't picked up every day, you know.

"Oh-h, please, Sir, tell me what to do! I don't know where to go—or what to do!" wailed Rachel wretchedly.

There! Mrs. Stuyvesant-Wilberforce's chauffeur was honking for him. Through the door he could see the handsome limousine, filled with gay and laughing men and women leaning back luxuriously.

"Oh-h-h," moaned Rachel.

The footman was slowly mounting the steps. This was awful, really! Where was the verger anyway? . . . The horn kept honking. . . The footman was standing just outside the door. . . The Reverend Mr. Clancy must go at once. He must never be seen in such a position as this.

Quickly he snatched a card from his pocket, wrote upon it and thrust it into Rachel's hands.

"Here, my good woman, go to this address, and they will help you." He hurried rapidly through the doorway, down the steps and into the waiting motor, and was driven off amid a chorus of merry laughter.

Rachel and her baby were alone in the great empty church! There was a moment of panic. Then from a dim corner the verger approached them. He looked at them wonderingly.

"Sorry, Lady, but I have to lock the doors. I'll have to ask you to be going."

Dazed and mute, Rachel passed out through the portal of St. X's and stood helplessly at the top of the broad stone steps as the verger locked the door behind her. As he did so she glanced miserably at the card the Reverend Clarence Cuthbert Clancy, D.D., LL.D., F.R.G.S., had given her. It read:

> Jewish woman and baby in need
> respectfully referred to
> RABBI MORDECAI MOSES
> No X East First Street
> C. C. Clancy, Rector. St. X's Parish

The last hope died in Rachel's heart. A cry of despair broke from her lips. She was alone with her little baby in New York—hungry and sick and penniless and friendless! Yes, even Christ had failed her! For His sake she had given all—her home, her husband, her friends, her Jewish people—everything. And this was Christianity!

A sense of terror seized her. She was forsaken! Forsaken of man! Forsaken of God! There was nothing left to do. She leaned dizzily against a marble column.

Little Abie was awake now and crying piteously. Rachel soothed him with utmost tenderness, "Mother's precious darling! Mother's own little Baby Boy!"

The lights were now blazing on the Avenue. It was crowded with rushing motors. A thunder-storm was just beginning. Pedestrians were scurrying for shelter. The thought of plunging through the traffic was terrifying—however, that would take but a moment. Then only four or five blocks more—Rachel's strength would last that far—and then—then—just one more final agony—and at last, the black and peaceful River would flow over all their sorrows.

Rachel left the coats and satchel—they would not need them. Grasping Little Abie as firmly as she could in her weak and trembling arms, she started to descend the steps. On the last one her ankle turned. She gave a sharp, quick cry—then fell, a crumpled, unconscious heap, just inside the iron coping at the bottom. There—her baby in her arms—unheeded by the stream of rushing humanity, with its unseeing eyes and its unheeding hearts, she lay—a daughter of Abraham—a child of God by faith in His Son Jesus Christ—before the portals of the Church which bore His Name.

Chapter X.

True Shepherds of Israel

"Go . . . to the lost sheep of the house of Israel."
—*Matthew 10:6.*

"Inasmuch as ye have done it unto one of the least of these my brethren, ye have done it unto me."—*Matthew 25:40.*

Dawn of that same Sunday morning had found Violet Hamilton upon her knees in prayer, on the roof of the little Jewish Mission on Delancey Street in the heart of New York's vast Ghetto.

She had scarcely slept all night, so intense had been the unseasonable heat. In her small, one-windowed room on the top floor of the Mission not a breath of air had stirred. With the first streaks of daylight, therefore, she had climbed the ladder through the skylight to the roof. Here it was slightly better. It was bearable at least.

The gray of the eastern sky was just beginning to brighten with sunrise tints of rose and gold above the East River. One or two pale stars remained, and the thinnest crescent of a moon.

There was a miniature garden on the roof, still blossoming with late Summer flowers; a wicker arm chair stood beside it on a Japanese grass rug. For a few moments Miss Hamilton reclined in it, gazing upon the scene before her as she hummed softly a morning hymn of praise.

In every direction rose the Ghetto tenements. As Miss Hamilton looked over the sea of roofs and realized that thousands of sons and daughters of Abraham were housed wretchedly beneath them, a wave of pity and of longing surged over her. Her heart was heavy with sorrow for them. God's own Chosen People! To whom He had so graciously appointed her, a Gentile, His ambassador!

She felt suddenly a sense of utter futility. Vast flocks of lost sheep of the House of Israel, they were awaiting shepherding—and who was she, Violet Hamilton, helpless and weak, among so many?

But the miracle of the feeding of the five thousand was quickly flashed upon her memory, and its lesson went straight home. She would bring her little loaves and fishes—her love for the Master and her devoted zeal for His service—and He would multiply them by His power to the feeding of this Jewish throng.

And thus with all humility, in the stillness of that early Sabbath morning, the missionary knelt upon the Mission house-top in prayer for Israel.

Long and earnestly she made intercession for the Jews world-wide—for the Jews of Palestine and Russia and the British Isles—for the vast hordes of Jews throughout Central Europe, and all over the United States and Canada—and for the Jews in every other land. And then her prayers focused upon Israel in New York City.

She prayed God's blessing upon their little Mission and its venerable and saintly Hebrew head, and upon who labored with him, both the recognized workers and those countless friends who, by their faithful ministry of prayer and love and gift, were holding up the missionaries' hands.

And then she prayed for the precious Jewish souls God had entrusted to their care—first for the vast multitudes of Jews who were personally unknown; and then for those special ones whom they included in the loving circle of their Mission family.

She prayed for all who had come out boldly in confession of Christ as their personal Saviour, and were in consequence suffering bitter persecution. She prayed next for the many secret believers who, although they had truly received Him into their hearts, yet lacked the courage to proclaim His Name before men. And then she prayed for the scores of Jews among whom she had worked so patiently for years, but who as yet were still in the darkness of Judaism.

And then finally, with intensest longing, Violet Hamilton poured out her heart to God in supplication for the one Hebrew above all others for whose salvation she had day and night been burdened—the beautiful little Roumanian Jewess, Rachel Kalinsky. Where was she now, the missionary wondered? And had she yet found and confessed the Lord Christ Jesus as her own Messiah?

She had never seen her again since that terrible day in her

pretty little flat. Oh, why had she ever gone there? Why had she taken such a dreadful risk? She had suffered agonies of remorse because of it.

But she must have more faith! God had assuredly led her there and obediently she had given Rachel His Word which He himself had promised would not return unto Him void.

Since that fateful December afternoon all trace of Rachel had been completely lost. Miss Hamilton had felt it wiser not to return to the flat for several weeks. And when she did go finally one morning—with the utmost caution—and knocked upon the door, it was opened by a stranger. No, Mrs. KIin-sky not live there. She live there. She Mrs. Zabrowsky. No, she not know Mrs. Klin-sky. She not know where she gone. This her house now. Yes, it looked like her house. The dirty, untidy, altogether unlovely flat quite resembled its new mistress; and was as far removed from Rachel's beautiful little Eden as light from darkness.

And none of the neighbors knew where the little bride in the top flat had gone. She had driven off in a taxi with two big women and her husband the day before the Christian New Year. And when she went she was crying. That was all the gossiping women knew.

All subsequent search through East Second Street and the adjoining thoroughfare had been fruitless. Rachel Kalinsky had passed out of Violet Hamilton's life. But not out of her prayers. Faithfully, day and night they had followed her. And the missionary had the assurance in her heart that one day God would bring Rachel Kalinsky to Himself.

Never had her burden of intercession for Rachel been so intense as on this Sunday morning. With what was a very agony of longing, the missionary pleaded for her at the Throne of Grace.

The sun was two hours high before Miss Hamilton descended to her room and bathed and dressed. She prepared and ate her simple breakfast; and then, as resident missionary, her task it was to prepare the little Mission Hall for the services of the afternoon and evening. She arranged the chairs and hymn books.

And then came the appointment eagerly awaited throughout the week—Sunday morning service in Miss Hamilton's own church up-town—the stately old Fifth Avenue Presbyterian.

Following the reverent, beautiful service, Miss Hamilton, in company with a fellow-missionary, had dinner in the Mission.

And after dinner was the Sunday afternoon Bible Hour for the Jewish children. This was under Miss Hamilton's direction, and no hour of the entire week did she hold more precious, as she gathered around her for the singing of Christian hymns and for instruction in the Word of God, thirty to forty little sons and daughters of Abraham—all keen, eager, beautiful.

Following the meeting tea was served, but Miss Hamilton did not remain for it today. Instead she left the children in charge of her assistants and—despite the burning heat—she hurried forth upon her Sunday visitation.

First she must call upon dear old Granny Blumengarten. Poor old soul! She was seventy-five and sick and lived alone. Up five flights of dark and narrow and malodorous tenement stairs the faithful ambassador of the Gospel labored, gaily humming her "missionary battle hymn":

"They climbed the steep ascent of heaven
Through peril, toil and pain:
0 God, to us may grace be given
To follow in their train."

At the top, in a stuffy, stifling little room she found the aged Jewish woman, quite alone except for a multitude of flies—and with a bowl of chopped cabbage and onion on the table beside her bed, as her sole nourishment for the day.

Tenderly Miss Hamilton ministered to her needs. The flies were driven out, the bed was freshened, the patient was skillfully bathed. Then a nourishing broth, which Miss Hamilton had prepared at home, was heated and served. And finally, to the grateful old soul the Bread of Life was broken as Miss Hamilton read to her from her own Yiddish Bible. After a parting word of prayer and a promise to come back soon, the missionary left her refreshed and comforted.

Next Miss Hamilton visited the Cohen family on East Thirteenth Street. The Cohens consisted of Mr. Solomon Cohen, the father, a tailor by trade, and seven little motherless Cohens. Mrs. Cohen had died the previous winter. Continuous debt and destitution and the cares of her increasing family, all combined

144

finally to break the never-too-rugged constitution, and poor, brave little Mrs. Cohen struggling heroically to the end, went down at last before life's battle.

Jewish family love is strong. At all costs Mr. Cohen must hold his motherless little flock together—hence the several kind offers of neighbors to divide the children among them, adding them to their own large and poverty-stricken families, were appreciatively but resolutely declined by the bereaved Jewish father. His subsequent efforts to be father and mother both to his numerous offspring—tailoring by day and often far into the night, and endeavoring in between to perform a woman's duties—were pathetic in the extreme.

In such a home as this Violet Hamilton was indeed a godsend, with her frequent material assistance, her encouragement of the brave little "big sister" of the family, and her kindly, friendly counsel to the often-times distracted father. There must be something in this English Religion after all, Mr. Cohen reflected thoughtfully after each one of the missionary's visits. If believing in Jesus Christ makes the people as kind as Miss Hamilton, He might be the Messiah for a fact. He guessed perhaps he'd just study into it a bit—from that New Testament Miss Hamilton had brought him—and try to figure it all out for himself.

My, how fearfully hot it was! Miss Hamilton felt nearly wilted. How she would love to go home and have a cool bath and some iced lemonade and then a nap till time for evening service. But no, she must see Zelma. She was so troubled about her. Zelma was such a dear girl and so full of promise. Her confession of the Lord a year ago had been so sincere, and her testimony since so full of zeal. But something had happened. No one seemed to know just what. Lately there had been the saddest change. She had given them untold anxiety. She never came near the Mission any more, and when anyone went to see her she was evasive and deceitful. Yes, Miss Hamilton must have it out with her today. She must get to the bottom of the trouble. It would be a difficult call but one that was most urgent.

Zelma was at home and fortunately alone. So Miss Hamilton, after prayerfully paving the way, with much love and tact drew forth the story from the seventeen-year old Jewess. It was the usual one. Neglect, first, of prayer and Bible study—then companions whose influence was none too helpful—and gradually a slipping from the moorings.

For half an hour following the sorrowful confession there was an earnest heart-to-heart talk between the older and the younger girl, with wise and loving counsel given and received; and when Miss Hamilton left it was with Zelma's penitent promise that she would come back to Christ and yield the guidance of her life to Him.

Time for just one more call before the evening service. Which one of a hundred possible homes should the missionary visit? Here, as in every smallest detail of her life, she prayed for the Spirit's leading. The Goldfinkles! Yes, surely, she must go there. It was three months since she had seen them. They lived quite far. Away up on Forty-ninth Street, But she would take the Subway and there would be time for a short call anyway.

She arrived just as the Goldfinkles—a cultured Jewish family of the more prosperous class—were having tea in their library. Mrs. Goldfinkle, a rotund, motherly soul with beaming countenance, was presiding at the samovar. Her two attractive older daughters were passing the glasses of fragrant Russian tea, while the little sisters were following with plates of honey cakes and nuts. The entire numerous family were present. Besides Mr. and Mrs. Goldfinkle and the four daughters there were the two married sons with their wives and children, the three little boys, and dear old Grandfather Goldfinkle with his snowy head and patriarchal beard. Half a dozen Jewish guests were present also.

Miss Hamilton was greeted eagerly. She was a favorite with all the family. Where had she been? Why didn't she come to see them any more? Too busy? What with was she too busy to come to see her friends? Well, anyway, she must stay now for tea with them. . . Certainly she had time! She must take time. Why not? . . . What? A meeting? . . . What kind of a meeting? . . . Oh, a meeting by the Mission, was it? Did she belong to that same Mission still? . . . Well, what did they do at those Missions anyway? This last question from one of Mrs. Goldfinkle's sons-in-law.

Miss Hamilton was always quick to see an opportunity. Here was one that was exceptional. A cultured Jewish home; a large and influential family; attractive guests; herself most welcome;

and inquiries before her, eager and intelligent: a perfect setting for some keen and effective work of testimony. Quickly sending up a prayer that every word she uttered might be directed by the Spirit, she graciously accepted the proffered tea, and as she sipped it from the china cups and ate the delicate honey cakes, she gradually and tactfully directed the conversation of the whole company into a discussion of the New Testament Scriptures and the Messianic claims of Christ. So vividly did she present her argument, and with such convincing radiance of voice and countenance, that no less than seven of the Hebrew people present were constrained to take the New Testaments she offered them with the promise that they would read and study them with open mind and heart.

Miss Hamilton invited any of them who might care to go, to return with her to the Mission for the evening service. But at this point they all with one consent began to make excuse. The married couples must take their children home. The older Goldfinkle daughters were going to a wedding. The boys were going to a concert. Grandfather was, of course, too old and Mother and Father Goldfinkle must stay home with him. Perhaps next Sunday some of them would come. Miss Hamilton smiled inwardly. She knew all about these "next Sunday" promises, and every other variety of evasion and postponement on the part of her many Hebrew friends. But patience is the watchword of the missionary to the Jews; "undiscourageable" her undeviating motto.

In this visit, however, there was much that was distinctly heartening. For nearly an hour twenty people had listened attentively and reverently to the Gospel. The most thoughtful among them were taking away with them the New Testament. And the bond of sympathetic friendship between the missionary and this delightful Hebrew family had been yet more deeply cemented by this happy fellowship together over their glasses of Russian tea, and over the open Word of God.

But now Miss Hamilton must surely hurry. In half an hour the evening service at the Mission would begin. The hospitable family tried hard to detain her and most happily would she have stayed, but many other Hebrew friends were, she knew, eagerly awaiting her on Delancey Street. And so, amid many expressions of regret, with a grateful and cordial promise to return, she took her departure homeward.

As she came out of the Goldfinkle's house, she had a direct impulse to turn westward toward the Avenue, rather than eastward to the downtown Subway. She could not at all understand why, but so sensitively was her heart attuned to God that she recognized immediately a leading of the Spirit. Quietly she yielded all her will to Him and prayed that He would guide her steps aright.

As she turned into the brilliantly illuminated thoroughfare, her heart was full of praise to God for all the way that He had led that day. God had surely used her. Her heart was overflowing with thankfulness and joy.

And still there was work ahead—she knew it—even now before she should reach the Mission. What might it be, she wondered? Frankly she was puzzled. This leading hither to the Avenue—it all seemed so very strange. The Avenue and Delancey Street were as far removed as day and night. But even on the Avenue God had His precious jewels. And her task it was obediently to seek them out as He should guide.

She started hurrying—a thunderstorm was coming. But before she had gone a block great drops were already coming down. Miss Hamilton had no coat and no umbrella. She must seek shelter until the worst was over.

At the corner stood St. X's—New York's most fashionable church. And also, Miss Hamilton understood, its most outstandingly modernistic one. She had never attended it. Somehow she had felt it would imply disloyalty to her Lord and to His inerrant Word to do so. But now God had an errand for her to do there. A sudden heavy clap of thunder and a flash of lightning, accompanied by a cloudburst—and instinctively Miss Hamilton pushed open the iron gate and rushed quickly up the stairway, where, behind one of the large marble columns, she had safe cover.

The storm was fascinating to her. Thunder and lightning always thrilled her. Never did she feel more conscious of the nearness and the wonder of God than when the elements were raging. In rapt adoration of His glory she watched the tempest until its fury was spent and the rain had ceased. Just a few distant rumbles of thunder remained.

But now she must hurry faster. She was late. The service was already on. Perhaps it was just to view this glorious storm that God had brought her to the Avenue. So thoughtful is He always of His children's joy. No other errand certainly was anywhere apparent.

She ran quickly down the steps and started opening the iron gate. But it did not yield to her touch. She tried fumbling with the latch. And then suddenly she dropped it, startled. For close beside her she heard the strangest sound—*a baby's cry!*

In frightened astonishment she looked down at her feet, and there—just inside the iron coping—in the soft glow from the street lamp on the corner—she saw an amazing sight: the form of a young woman in white, storm-beaten garments, lying apparently lifeless with the crying baby on her breast.

With a sharp exclamation of horror Miss Hamilton bent low over the prostrate form, With quick professional instinct—for she was a nurse as well as a missionary to the Jews—she gently raised the head and felt the pulse. Ah, thank God! Life was still there, but the heart beat was feeble and fluttering. A rapid examination of the baby showed that, despite its exposure to the storm, it was quite all right.

And then the nurse did some rapid, skillful thinking. She must get aid at once. And shelter and care and food. What hospital was nearest?

A deserted little mother and her baby! Whoever could they be, she wondered? Carefully Miss Hamilton turned the mother's head that the light might shine upon her face. And then with a startled cry of mingled joy and anguish, the missionary recognized her—her own beloved Rachel Kalinsky—her most precious God-given trust—the one Jewish soul above all others that she had been longing for heartbrokenly for months.

But oh, how terribly changed! What frightful havoc had been wrought! No longer was the beautiful face rosy and radiant and girlish. It was white and gaunt. On the still lovely features deep suffering was registered. And the suffering was not alone from hunger and prostration. In this face there was tragedy. Whatever could have happened? And had her testimony to Rachel been the cause of it?

Tenderly Violet Hamilton raised her friend, together with the baby, within her arms and tried to bring her back to consciousness with kisses and endearing words. But the only response was a feeble moan which mingled with the baby's cries. With utmost gentleness the nurse again laid her burden upon the hard stone pavement. She must hurry and bring aid.

One of New York's police officers was on the corner within immediate call. In his strong arms he bore Rachel to the nearest drug store while Miss Hamilton followed with the baby. A physician was summoned but before he arrived Rachel, in response to her friends' ministrations, opened her eyes. They were as frightened as a deer's, but the terror quickly changed to peace when Rachel heard, as from a far-off land, the well-loved voice and recognized the well-loved face.

"It's Violet, darling," murmured her friend soothingly. "I'm right here, Rachel, do not be afraid. Here, dear, just sip this milk . . . that's it . . . now close your eyes and go to sleep. Everything will be all right, dear."

The physician came quickly; and gravely, skillfully, he made a rapid diagnosis. Starvation and exhaustion and exposure to the storm. And a grief of some kind. Mental distress very evident. Bed at once and nourishment. And then long and tender care. The baby—nourishment and sleep—quite safe otherwise. Not hurt by the storm at all. Remarkable. A wonderfully healthy child. And handsome, strikingly so. The mother as well. But Jews—h'm. The lady knew them? Indeed! . . . But not their address? . . . Very well, then—a hospital! He had his car.

But firmly and quietly Violet Hamilton interposed. There would be no hospital for her precious Rachel Kalinsky. She would take care of her herself. She would take her and the little one right to the Mission—to her own room—and there she would nurse her back to health and strength and hope with that tender care that none could give as well as she. There was more than physical illness here. There was sickness of the soul. No hospital and mere professional skill could avail for that. Love alone could heal.

"No, Doctor, pardon me," she said with quiet command. "This young woman is a personal friend of mine. I wish to take her home with me and care for her myself. I am a graduate nurse." She showed him her pin.

"Very good," the physician acquiesced. Professional dignity masked his astonishment. Assisted by the police officer he lifted Rachel into his waiting motor. Miss Hamilton followed with the baby. Rapidly they all were driven to Delancey Street.

In the little Mission Hall Jews and Gentiles were gathered for the evening service. The opening hymn had been sung, followed by the Scripture lesson and a prayer in Yiddish. Mr. Joseph Nathan, the elderly and godly Superintendent, was just announcing the second hymn when there suddenly burst upon the meeting a strange commotion.

The street door opened and through it there entered, first, Miss Hamilton. A joyous chorus greeted her. The children had been watching for her eagerly. No service at the Mission was complete without their beloved Miss Violet present. But what was that she was carrying? A baby? Oh, look! Let's see, let's see! The children wriggled and screamed excitedly. Mr. and Mrs. Nathan with greatest difficulty restrained them.

And then to the amazed wonderment of everyone, following after Miss Hamilton there came a great policeman with a lady in his arms. Oh, was she dead? The children buzzed again in wild excitement. And following last there came a doctor. They knew it was a doctor by his satchel.

But they did not know, nor did the physician ever dream it himself, that he was the reason why Miss Hamilton was entering by the main door into the Mission Hall rather than by the side door which led directly to the stairway. She had noted his scornful comment "But Jews—h'm" when he had examined Rachel, and she longed to have a chance to witness to him. And direct verbal appeal would be impossible she knew—but she prayed that God might use this silent testimony of a roomful of Jewish worshippers, to stir his heart toward Israel and toward Israel's God.

Down the Hall, past all the people and the pulpit, the little procession wended its way through the rear door and up the stairway to Miss Hamilton's own room. Good Mrs. Nathan followed while Mr. Nathan, quieting the children, resumed the service. The police officer waited patiently below until Miss

151

Hamilton was at liberty to answer his official questions, after she had received instructions from the doctor.

And then at length, the officer and the doctor both departed, the missionary became the skillful nurse, as she was the tender and devoted friend, to the little Jewish mother and her child. And Rachel's heart at last had rest. She was quite conscious now and happy, though oh, so very weak. She did not know where she was, nor did she care. It was enough that her dearest Violet Hamilton was right beside her whispering tender words of love and comfort. She had eaten. . . and now she would sleep. . . oh, how good God was!

There in that humble little room in the humble Jewish Mission on Delancey Street, Rachel and her Little Abie stayed during many days while Violet Hamilton and dear silver-haired Mrs. Nathan continued their loving ministrations to them. And Mr. Nathan came frequently to minister those spiritual consolations which only one of his ripe and saintly experience could give.

And as Rachel grew stronger, gradually others were permitted to visit her and Little Abie—the other Mission workers and Mission friends, and finally the little Jewish children. They all loved her—and her cunning little baby, what fun it was to play with him. And Rachel's heart, above its inevitable sorrow, rejoiced that God had brought her here among these true Christian friends.

Very wisely Miss Hamilton and the others did not press her for her story. They satisfied themselves on one point only—yes, she was at last a Christian. Miss Hamilton's heart exulted. That was all she needed yet to know—the rest could wait. Very easily much could be inferred.

But gradually it all came out, the entire story. How graciously He had sent her own beloved Violet to find her, and to bring her here to this abode of peace. How exultant was her heart with praise!

But as Rachel's health returned and the weather was cool once more—winter indeed was rapidly approaching—her mind became troubled over the very practical question of ways and means. No one had mentioned money to her, and she had been too weak to think about it. But now she must get it all thought through. Some one must have been providing for her needs. Could it have been the Nathans and dear Violet? Oh, but they must not make such sacrifice! They were not blessed with this world's goods, she knew. She must not be a burden longer.

Rachel above all things, was a girl of independent spirit. Just as soon, therefore, as she was able she must seek means of livelihood—some method of support whereby she could make full provision for herself and Little Abie. She prayed much for wisdom and for guidance; and soon God wonderfully opened up the way.

Ever since her conversion one passion had consumed Rachel—that she might give her life to Christ for testimony among her Hebrew people. She knew for this there must be preparation: definite, systematic Bible study and careful Christian training. But how could she obtain this and at the same time support herself and the baby? The problem was indeed a hard one.

But not in vain had Rachel suffered. One lesson she had learned supremely—that of trust in God's unfailing faithfulness. He would make it all quite plain. And very soon He did.

She had taken Mr. Nathan into her confidence. He was as wise as he was saintly. Prayerfully he consulted with Christian friends of influence and they confirmed his own impression. Mrs. Kalinsky and her son should move to the Peace Mission two blocks away. In this mission house other young women involved in the work resided. While she and little Abie lived there, she could help in the domestic duties which would be remuneration for her living costs. The workers would be delighted to help care for little Abie, while she devoted some of her time to a Bible Study Course.

The plan was an ideal one. And so wonderfully did the Father undertake for Rachel that all arrangements soon were made.

Christmas she spent in the Mission—and the Christmas week. By this time there had come complete return to health and strength under the loving and efficient care of Violet Hamilton and dear Mrs. Nathan. But with Christmas there had come also much heartache, for it was to Rachel the season of sacred memories. Just two Christmases ago she had been married. And last Christmas had seen the wrecking of her and Max's precious home. How much had happened since! In spite of the efforts of her friends to keep her happy, her mind would repeatedly revert to all the stormy pathway.

But beneath her sadness and her longing for her husband, the Christmas joy and peace was in her heart—her first Christmas as a believer in the Christ. And in the little Mission, with Christmas services, with their carols and their praises to the Babe of Bethlehem, Rachel's soul was truly blessed.

And then came once more the last day of the year—the second anniversary of Rachel's wedding—and with it she said good-bye to all the devoted Mission friends, and took up her abode in the Peace Mission.

It was a strange year upon which she entered—a year of intermittent cloud and sunshine, of mingled joy and grief. The heartache was never absent. And yet in all her sorrow there was no bitterness—no rebellion. Rather there was praise. For unto her it was given in the behalf of Christ, not only to believe in Him, but also to suffer for His sake. And she rejoiced that she was counted worthy.

And always there was the battle against her own physical frailty. Never of rugged constitution, the strain of her many duties made heavy inroads on her vitality. Her domestic work was in the dining-room—five hours every day—and the heavy piles of plates and the heavier trays and the constant standing on her feet occasioned many an hour of exhaustion and of pain.

But by all these means God was graciously refining and fashioning and strengthening His child, and leading her gently forward toward the fulfillment of His own great purpose for her life, which had been hidden with Him since the foundation of the world.

Thus as that first year passed, Rachel grew in intellect, in character, in grace. Deeper and ever deeper became her knowledge of God's Word! closer and ever closer her fellowship with Christ; stronger and stronger her faith; and ever richer and more fruitful her Christian testimony among both Jew and Gentile.

More and more, was she daily becoming fashioned into His likeness Whom she adored; more and more was she learning to know Him, and the power of His resurrection, and the fellowship of His sufferings.

But not yet was she fully conformed unto His death. Not yet had she attained, or was she already perfect. Not yet had she fully apprehended that for which she had been apprehended of Christ Jesus. There must be still more refining of the gold—still deeper experience in the seven-times heated furnace of affliction.

And so, just as she was entering upon the second year at Peace Mission, God put Rachel Kalinsky's faith to a yet more fiery test than any she had thus far known. He asked of her, her all.

Chapter XI.

The Underneath Peace

"And the peace of God, which passeth all
understanding, shall keep your hearts and minds
through Christ Jesus." —Philippians 4:7.

God asked of her her all—even her one ewe lamb—her
Isaac sacrificed upon the altar. The blow fell with terrific
suddenness—all unexpectedly and without a moment's warning.

It was on a Sunday afternoon. Rachel was enjoying a day of
rest after a heavy week of work. As a special treat she was
taking Little Abie to see Mr. and Mrs. Saramoff in Rivington
Street. These dear old friends had welcomed her back with joy
when first she had sought them, and many an afternoon since
her heart had been refreshed by a visit to their humble tenement and by kind Mrs. Saramoff's motherly hospitality.

Little Abie, dressed in his best, was in his most winsome
mood as Rachel carried him through the hall past many friends.
He had won the hearts of all. She was just going out the front
door with him when one of the housemaids detained her.

"Mrs. Kalinsky, I was looking for you! There are four gentlemen waiting to see you. Jewish gentlemen they are, ma'am—in
the reception room."

Four gentlemen! And Jewish! Whoever could they be, Rachel
wondered? Her heart began to pound heavily. Instinctively holding Little Abie tighter, she entered the small room at the right of
the street doorway. For an instant her breath nearly left her
body. Seated stiffly on straight chairs around the room the dele-
gation was awaiting her—Jacob, Joseph, Otto and—pompously
eclipsing them all—Rabbi Mordecai Moses.

They wasted no time on preliminaries or amenities. Swiftly
they came to the issue—Rabbi Moses acting, ex-officio, as chair-
man of the committee.

"Rachel Mendelssohn, have you yet repented and recanted?"

After the first shock Rachel immediately regained her innate poise. Drawing herself up, her grasp upon little Abie becoming yet more firm, she replied:

"Repented of what, Sir? Recanted what?"

"Repented of your awful sin of apostasy and idolatry in your worship of another God. Recanted your confession of that blasphemous Jesus Christ."

Rachel's eyes flashed gloriously. "The Lord Christ Jesus is the Son of God and Israel's Messiah! I adore Him with my whole heart and I purpose to serve Him with my whole being throughout my entire life!"

The Rabbi nodded his head contemplatively, affirmatively. The other men exchanged significant glances of satisfaction. Jacob smiled with malicious cunning.

"Doubtless, however," the Rabbi continued, "you would sell Him for your price—a trip to California, perhaps—this check for five thousand made to your order by your former husband, Max Kalinsky—your reinstatement in his home and heart. These are the terms he authorizes us to offer you for your renunciation of the heretic Christian faith. Here, do you accept them?" He extended the check towards Rachel.

Deliberately she took it from his hand, and with the bearing of a queen she tore it into fragments before his face. "That is my answer," she said quietly.

"Oh, it is, is it?" snarled Jacob wrathfully. "Very well then, this is our answer."

With a fearful oath he snatched Little Abie from Rachel's arms while Otto, upon a prearranged signal, quickly seized Rachel and gagging her to prevent outcry, tied her securely to a chair. Then while Joseph stood on guard in the doorway and motioned that the coast was clear, Jacob carrying the baby, followed by Rabbi Moses and Otto, walked quickly out of the room and out of the building into a waiting taxi. Joseph flung a parting shot at Rachel.

"All right, my girl, stay a Meshumed. Stay an accursed Christian if you want to be one. But your child is a Kalinsky and a Jew."

Calmly he followed the others into the taxi; the door was slammed shut; and the car drove off at a furious pace, leaving Rachel captive and dumb, and prostrated with terror and grief.

157

Thus, an hour later, they found her. It was still another hour before they were able, from Rachel's incoherent, hysterical utterance, to piece together the tragic story. And by that time it was too late.

While tender hands and hearts ministered to Rachel's grief, three of the Mission personnel, under police escort, hastened to the Kalinsky home on East Eleventh Street. It was closed and boarded up. The family had left, so their neighbors told them, just that morning for California. No, they had left no address. The other Kalinsky homes too—Joseph's and Otto-were closed, as well as Max's shop.

A subsequent visit to Rabbi Moses gave but small satisfaction. What! The Kalinsky baby kidnapped! Not Mrs. Deborah Kalinsky's grandson, surely? Shocking—inexpressibly so! No, he had heard nothing of it whatever. He had just returned that morning from a week's trip to Boston. Yes, he knew the Kalinsky family well—a wonderful family. He had married all of them—Max and Rachel not three years ago. A terrible tragedy, their separation. He himself had done everything in his power to avert it. But the woman had proven false. Too bad though about the baby—quite too bad. He would be glad to lend his services in any way possible for its recovery.

And then followed long and dreadful days for Rachel. It was as if all the beauty of life had turned to ashes—all its joy to dust. With empty arms and dull, unseeing eyes she went mechanically about her duties, performing each one of them with conscientious faithfulness, but with a heart of stone. There seemed to be a paralysis of all ambition and initiative—an utter deadness of spirit. Days there were when she could not even shed a tear, so awful was her grief. She had drunk the cup of sorrows to the dregs.

All efforts to find the baby through many months proved unavailing, so carefully were the Kalinsky's movements covered and their whereabouts concealed.

But with early Spring word came suddenly from them in a letter to Rachel post-marked Pasadena. The handwriting was Max's. Trembling Rachel tore it open. She read it breathlessly:

Villa Buena Vista, Pasadena, California,
March 16, 19—

My dearest Rachel,

You will be glad to learn that nearly all of us are settled here in California—Mamma and Little Abie and I, and Jacob and Sarah and their children, Joseph and Rose and their family, and Otto and Goldie and theirs. We all like it fine. You will too when you get here.

We boys have taken an orange ranch together and it's going great. There's heaps of money in California in oranges. We're getting rich quick.

We have our three houses just like New York. Now it's up to you when we are to get the fourth house for you and me and Little Abie. I tell you it's all up to you. All you have got to do is to telegraph and promise me you'll throw all this Christian business overboard, and I'll sign up for the house tomorrow. I'll wire you the money and you can be here in a week.

The house is a swell one—a bungalow—right in the middle of the orange ranch, facing the snow-capped mountains. It has seven rooms and three baths, and all modern improvements. Electrical equipment for everything. You won't know yourself, your housework will be so easy.

There's a fine garage, and inside of it there's going to be a big surprise I've bought for you. I won't tell you what it is, but believe me, she's a beauty, and all your very own.

Everything is yours—within one week—for just your promise to give up your faith in Jesus Christ. So it's up to you.

Now do be sensible, Rachel, and think it over. You know, how much I love you and how I want you with me. So wire quick and tell me that you're coming home.

With much love. Faithfully, your husband, MAX.

P.S.—Every night Little Abie cries for his mamma.—M.

This was the first of many similar letters. They began coming thick and fast, and each one was more insistent, more pleading, more full of enderd endearments than the last. The battle every time was fearful. With each letter Rachel's heart was torn. The temptation to yield to natural love and longing was terrific.

But God kept Rachel Kalinsky strong. Prostrated though she was during every conflict, she came out of all of them more than conqueror through Him Who loved her. Christ was her choice above every earthly tie however dear. Christ was her portion.

Christ was her stronghold in the day of trouble. Christ was her all in all.

Thus she replied invariably to Max. She assured him of her unchanging love. He and Little Abie were dearer to her than her life. But her Lord Christ Jesus must always hold first place. Oh, if only Max would confess Him too, she would start for California in a moment. And then they all would be so happy together—just she and Max and Little Abie in their own dear Christian home.

Then letters of another sort began to come. These were from Mrs. Kalinsky or Sarah. Little Abie was sick, awfully sick. Last night they thought he was going to die. They had to have three doctors for him and two trained nurses. They all said they had never seen a worse case. Next week he had to have a terrible operation. What kind of a mother was she anyway, to stay away from her dying, only child?

These letters shattered Rachel's nerves completely. Each one brought on a fit of hysterical weeping followed always by prostration. She could neither eat nor sleep. Her work and study fell to pieces. Her friends in the Institute and elsewhere watched her with alarm. They feared her mind would finally give way beneath the awful strain.

But One had promised: "When thou passest through the waters, I will be with thee; and through the rivers, they shall not overflow thee; when thou walkest through the fire, thou shalt not be burned; neither shall the flame kindle upon thee." And God held Rachel fast. He Who was refining the gold in the fires of His own all-wise design would never allow one degree of heat too much. The fires, the crucible, and the precious gold within the crucible were all held secure within the pierced Hand.

And through that mysterious alchemy of suffering, very gradually, very gently, God's blessed gift of peace began to fill Rachel's being. Like a river it flooded her inmost soul. She entered upon an altogether new and wonderful spiritual experience—a realization of the depths of that mysterious joy that goes deeper down than any pain. She remembered how once, when she was a little child she had been very ill. And one night the suffering had been intense, but beneath it she was conscious

160

of the warmth and soothing of her mother's arms, and in a strange, mysterious way the pain itself grew sweet. So even now, the agony of heart was sanctified by God's own peace the—deep underneath peace—that peace of God, which passeth all understanding.

This peace enfolded Rachel as with a softest mantle until the pain was soothed and until her heart seemed even like the poet's "burnt out craters healed with snow."

Rachel herself marvelled at it. It was a paradox, how she could suffer to the last ounce almost of her very life blood, and yet at the same time experience as an actual and vivid reality, the restfulness of God—that perfect calm that abides at the center of a storm.

She marvelled—until she realized that her peace was born of faith—faith in her all-conquering Christ. She was His and He would guard His own.

Her loved ones, too, were in His tender keeping. One day, in His all-gracious love, He would bring them to Himself and He would give them back to her. She did not know how, she did not know when. But she knew that He was faithful Who had promised. And He had promised: "Ask and ye shall receive." So Rachel asked for Max and Little Abie. And with the simplicity of a child she claimed the answer to her prayer.

Out of this wonderful trust there came new strength. Not only did Rachel become sufficiently strong in herself—strong of body and of spirit—to resume her duties, but she received that overflowing strength which blesses other lives. Consciously she realized that she was being used of God with spiritual power. This caused her deep thanksgiving. Somewhere she had read: "When we cease to bleed, we cease to bless." And her prayer thenceforth had been that according to the measure of her bleeding might be the measure of her blessing unto other lives.

When, therefore, she had tokens that out of her suffering, streams of healing were flowing into many other hearts, she accepted with sweet content her bitter cross. Nay more, she rejoiced with joy unspeakable and full of glory that God had thus honored her, in entrusting her with such a sacred sorrow which He Himself would sanctify and bless. When with the close of each day she knelt in prayer, she smiled through her tears as she whispered to Him: "My Father—my Lord—with all my heart I thank Thee!"

Day by day as the missionary vision became clearer, the conviction deepened in Rachel's heart that God had called her as a chosen witness for Himself. And as, in obedience to His call, she yielded her life to Him in joyous consecration, she prayed in all sincerity of Christian purpose the prayer of every true missionary of the cross of Jesus Christ:

"Lord, speak to me, that I may speak
In living echoes of Thy tone;
As Thou hast sought, so let me seek
Thy erring children lost and lone.

Oh, teach me, Lord, teach even me
The precious truths Thou dost impart;
And wing my words that they may reach
The hidden depths of many a heart.

Oh, strengthen me that while I stand
Firm on the Rock, and strong in Thee,
I may stretch out a loving hand
To wrestlers with the troubled sea.

Oh, use me, Lord, use even me
Just as Thou wilt, and when and where,
Until Thy blessed face I see,
Thy rest, Thy joy, Thy glory share."

And God answered this prayer in a wonderful degree in Rachel Kalinsky's life. Through her, His Spirit breathed comfort and peace to many a weary heart; through her, He imparted to many a storm-tossed mind the wisdom that cometh only from above; through her He graciously gave the Word of Life unto the salvation of many precious souls.

Ere long Rachel became a recognized spiritual power in the life of the Peace Mission. Her room became a sanctuary for her many friends. Problems and sorrows of every kind were brought for her unfailing sympathy and prayer.

Steadily her missionary witness among her own Jewish people broadened. Whether it were in the quiet visits in the Ghetto homes and in the hospitals, or in the bolder witness upon the New York streets, in connection with the frequent open-air meetings of the Peace Mission, her testimony was always with conviction.

More and more, "the little Jewess who has suffered so much for Christ" became well known.

In the Jewish Mission on Delancey Street as well, Rachel was greatly used of God. Every Saturday afternoon she went there, and as many evenings through the week as she was able, assisting her good friends, Mr. and Mrs. Nathan and Miss Hamilton, in whatever way she might. Her loving ministry among the children and the mothers, and her clear testimony for Israel's Messiah in the Gospel meetings at every opportunity—all contributed in no small degree to the life and the effective service of the Mission.

Thus with her spiritual growth and witness advancing rapidly, and with God's peace prevailing underneath her constant sorrow, she became a gem of faithfulness and fruitfulness for Christ.

Rachel was taking a brief holiday previous to moving back to Mr. Nathan's Mission where, in the absence of Miss Hamilton, she was to assist for the summer in the children's work. Miss Hamilton was at present in the West, combining a study of the Jewish missions there, with a much needed rest in her California home.

Rachel was packing her trunk, amid many interruptions from friends who dropped in for a fond good-bye, when the fateful Pasadena letter came!

It was the first California letter she had had in many months. In her excitement she did not notice that the handwriting was not in Max's usual style. She tore it open with controlled excitement; but the control gave way to screams of joy as she grasped the import of the words:

Pasadena, California, June 7, 19—.

Rachel:

You have won at last!

I have decided to join you in your Christian religion.

I promise you that I, too, will believe in Jesus Christ and will confess Him publicly as our Messiah, if only you will come home.

I can't stand it without you any longer. Come soon. Take the first train possible. Wire me what time you will arrive.

With love, MAX.

P.S.—Enclosed is a check for $300 for your trip. Lots more money when you get here. MAX.

P.S. 2—Little Abie is fine. He says: "Tell Mamma to hurry up and come. I want my Mamma." MAX.

P.S. 3—Get here by a week from Sunday so we can have a drive in your new car. Just wait till you see it.

Much love, MAX.

Rachel was wildly, deliriously happy. She rushed from one to another of the girls in her room hugging them, while she laughed and sobbed hysterically. Then she ran through the corridors with the letter in her hand, knocking on doors and talking excitedly at her astonished friends who opened them: "Max is saved! Max is saved! I'm going tonight to California!"

Like wildfire the news spread through the Peace Mission, "Rachel Kalinsky's husband is converted. He has sent for her to come to him in Pasadena." All of Rachel's younger friends exulted with her in loud exclamations of praise and jubilation.

Her older friends, however, and those of the faculty who were yet remaining in the building, were more reserved in their expression of congratulation and joy. Their satisfaction was tempered with the caution born of longer experience. Would not Rachel sit down and talk things over with them quietly before she made preparation for her distant journey?

But Rachel had no time. She must get her money. She must wire Max. She must tell Mr. Nathan. She must go shopping. She would have to buy new clothes. Then she must get her ticket and see about her trunk. It was eleven o'clock already and the Western Limited left at seven-thirty.

So off she flew at once. She went to the telegraph office first of all, and then to the Mission in Dalancey Street. There, in a

164

manner utterly foreign to her usual reserve, she burst suddenly upon good Mr. and Mrs. Nathan with the startling tidings, "Oh Mr. Nathan! Mrs. Nathan! Max is converted! My husband is a Christian! And he has sent for me to come to him at once! I am leaving to-night for California!"

While gentle Mrs. Nathan drew the excited girl to a seat beside her, Mr. Nathan took the letter Rachel extended to him and read it gravely. And then his face grew sad, for it grieved him exceedingly to dash the hopes of this happy, trustful child. But well he understood the duplicity of the unregenerate Jacobs of his race. And clearly this letter was spurious.

As gently, therefore, and as kindly as it was possible for him to do so, Mr. Nathan, assisted by his motherly wife, endeavored to enlighten Rachel and to restrain her from her purpose of going to Max—at least until she should receive evidence of the genuineness of his conversion.

But Rachel was deaf to every argument. Of course Max was converted. Why else would he have written her? And had she not prayed? Had not they all prayed for this very thing? Where was Mr. Nathan's faith? No, she couldn't possibly wait, not another day. She was so sorry to disappoint these dear friends about the summer's work among the children, and after all they had done for her too. She owed them a debt of gratitude and of love that she could never repay. But Max was her husband and he needed her. She must go to him at once. No, nothing would stop her, nothing. She was going to California tonight.

And so, realizing that further remonstrance was vain, sadly and with deep misgivings of heart, her kind Hebrew-Christian friends could only bid her a loving farewell, as they committed her with earnest prayer to the Lord for His grace and guidance upon all the future pathway.

When she returned to the Peace Mission, the friends there—with whom Mr. Nathan meanwhile had been in anxious consultation on the phone—also tried to restrain her from her hasty departure. But they, too, saw that all their efforts would be useless. She was adamant against every entreaty. Her husband was converted. He needed her. God had sent her the money. This was proof surely that it was His will that she should go.

She spent a feverish afternoon completing her preparations.

She had no time for visiting with even her closest and dearest friends. She had no time for prayer—and no inclination. One thought alone obsessed her. She was going to California! She was going to Max and Little Abie!

Not until she was actually aboard the overland express, with the last good-byes said to the large group of Mission friends who had gathered at the Pennsylvania Station—not until the wheels were actually turning westward—did she pause to question the wisdom of her going.

And then doubts assailed. Like a flood the enemy came in. What was she doing? Could those dreadful things be true that Mr. Nathan and some of the others had suggested? Could it be possible that her husband was deceiving her? But no! She had prayed! She had pleaded earnestly for Max for over three years. And God had answered at last. She must not doubt. It was lack of faith. She would believe.

But still the uneasy questionings persisted. Added to them was intense nervousness and not a little fear. It was the first time in her life that she had travelled so far alone. And the first time, too, that she had been on a train overnight. She felt suddenly very lonely. The good friends in New York were now all left behind—and what lay before her? She scarcely slept all night, so frightened did she become.

But with the morning she felt better. After breakfast she made friends with a lady and her little children in the opposite seat. Some other passengers also were friendly, and the conductor and the porter both were very kind. The scenery, too, was keenly interesting. It was not long before her calm was restored, and she gave herself up to real enjoyment of the trip. Before she reached Chicago she had made many new acquaintances, and the rest of the journey was full of delightful diversion.

One thing she found difficult. That was prayer and Bible study. She would have it later, she argued. Just now there were too many interruptions. Besides, it hurt her eyes to read upon the train. There was brief prayer each night and morning, especially for Max and Little Abie, but her usual seasons of deep communion were suspended. And of course in consequence there was a diminution—of which at the time she was unconscious—in her spiritual power.

166

Along the entire way she telegraphed each morning to Max. Now she was in Kansas—now Colorado—now Arizona—now only twenty-four hours more and she would be home.

At last the prairies and the Rockies and the desert all were left behind, and Rachel was in the Golden State, within three hours of her destination. As the train neared Pasadena she was in a vortex of excitement. Joy and terror alternated. Five minutes more and she would be with her husband and her child! They would be there to meet her, surely. But oh, what lay before them in the future?

The train pulled slowly into the station. The long journey was ended. The new life was about to start. The porter gathered up the coats and handbags. Rachel followed him, her heart beating wildly. She peered half-fearfully, half-joyfully through the windows. With a terrible shock she saw them—Mrs. Kalinsky, Sarah, Jacob, Otto!

But where was Max? Rachel scanned the platform anxiously as she descended the steps. Max! O Max! Where was he?

But Max was certainly not there. And for the best of reasons. At that very moment Max Kalinsky was a thousand miles away. So Mrs. Deborah assured her with malicious triumph when Rachel, after greeting her and the others with forced cordiality, immediately asked for him and Little Abie. Sarah and Jacob and Otto with one voice and one accord echoed their mother's triumph. Yes, Max was a thousand miles away—in Seattle, Washington. On important business. He left ten days ago. He would be gone a month. Little Abie? Oh, she needn't worry about Little Abie. He was all right enough. He is in a place where he wouldn't bother anybody. When his father left for Seattle his grandmother and his uncles had put him in an orphanage. That was the place for that boy. They wouldn't stand for any of his nonsense there. Thus they greeted the stricken wife and mother. Thus they told her of her loved ones.

But they did not tell her that Max Kalinsky knew nothing whatever of any of this—that he was innocent and ignorant of his mother's and his brother Jacob's treachery. For treacherous they had been indeed in thus bringing Rachel—through forged letters and telegrams—across the continent to the cruel net which they had spread for her unwary feet in California.

167

From that moment forward the bitter orthodox Jewish hatred toward one of their own who had dared to confess faith in Jesus Christ, developed rapidly in its expressions, until within one week it had reached its fearful climax.

They all drove away from the station in the elegant limousine which Max had bought for Rachel. Mrs. Kalinsky did the driving. And she drove as she did everything else—determinedly, defiantly. Traffic regulations were flouted with scorn wherever possible. When, by force of necessity—other cars or an officer of the law blocking progress—they were obeyed, it was with an air of sullenness and resentment.

Terror now held full sway in Rachel's heart—terror of the reckless driving, but far greater terror of approaching nameless danger. Deadly fear kept her dumb. All the others, too were silent—grimly silent with wicked satisfaction.

The car at last bowled through a stately-spruce-bordered driveway, extending beyond which on either side were acres of orange trees, their branches laden alike with golden fruit and with fragrant orange blossoms. All were encircled by the snow-capped mountains.

After many windings the driveway led finally to a pretentious, rose-embowered bungalow—the California home of Mrs. Deborah Kalinsky.

And here in this beautiful abode, amid its lovely setting, the last fearful act in the tragedy of Satan's fury against a Jew who had become a Christian, was wrought out to its horrible conclusion.

Within five minutes of her entrance to the house, Rachel found herself in a small basement room, securely imprisoned behind barred windows and a bolted door. Here she would remain, she was angrily informed, on bread and water fare and all alone, until she recanted her belief in the despised and hated Jesus.

For seven days and nights Rachel held her ground unflinchingly. Anguished in heart, almost prostrate in body, faint for grief and for want of food, she yet was strengthened with might by His Spirit in the inner man to continue bold in her confession of her Lord. Morning and evening her tormentors came to her with their sinister question, "Rachel Mendelssohn, do you renounce your faith in that blasphemer, Jesus Christ?" And always with quiet strength and with radiant countenance, she replied, "The Lord Christ Jesus is my Saviour and my King. He is the Messiah of our people Israel."

Day after day they grieved her gentle heart with cruel mockings. So Jesus Christ was the Messiah, was He? A fine Messiah He had been to her. What had He ever done for Rachel? Come now, be honest with her own heart about it. She had been a Christian for three years. What had she gotten out of it? What one thing had Jesus ever done for her? Was she rich? Was she happy? Did she have her husband and her child? Did she have her home? Did her friends have any further use for her? If Jesus Christ were the Messiah, and she were His disciple, what was He doing for her now? If He were the Son of God wouldn't He be strong enough to deliver her from this? If He's the Messiah, here's His opportunity to prove it. Let Him break these bars for Rachel if He's the Almighty God!

With undaunted courage and with undeviating loyalty to Him Whom her soul adored, through those seven awful days and nights she remained the victor against her enemies—and His.

But with the eighth day the brave spirit broke. Not in her devotion and her loyalty to Christ—with her last breath she would be true to Him—but in her self-control. For her enemies, infuriated by her strength of purpose, at last had resorted to the Inquisition. And their torture was excruciating to the last degree. For the rack they chose to use was Little Abie.

He had not been placed in an orphanage. That was a lie, pure and simple, forged in the furnace of their malice. He had been right there in the bungalow. And day by day Rachel had heard his sweet baby prattle and his merry laugh, without being able to see his face or to clasp him to her heart. That had been torture enough. But it was not the rack. The rack had been fiendishly planned and held in secret reserve as a last resort. And now the hour of Rachel's anguish thereupon had come.

Early in the morning of the eighth day they came to her—Mrs. Kalinsky, Sarah, Jacob—and with them a Jewish rabbi and a Jewish physician. The rabbi put the usual question: "Rachel Mendelssohn, do you yet recant?" And Rachel gave the unfailing answer: "I do not." Jacob left the prison room quickly. Five minutes later Rachel's anguished ear heard fearful sounds just outside her closed and bolted door-sounds of Jacob's cruelty to Little Abie and her darling's sudden, piercing shrieks. For a moment only was she able to endure it. Then with the ferocity of an animal from whom a wolf has torn her young, she struck at Mrs. Deborah Kalinsky.

It was exactly what they had designed. Their case was complete. Witnesses were present. The evidence stood out in angry red marks on Mrs. Kalinsky's face.

The plot concluded with amazing speed. Rachel's limousine was waiting. Inside of three minutes she was seated within it, the rabbi on one side of her, the Jewish physician on the other. Jacob was in the front seat beside his mother. She, of course, was at the wheel.

And never did she drive more ruthlessly. Northward toward the mountains they sped, then miles and miles beyond them. All day they drove. The shadows lengthened. Night began to fall. The air grew chill.

But Rachel did not feel the chill of the atmosphere, for already she was frozen—frozen with terror and grief. She closed her eyes as they drove yet more wildly through the darkness toward—she dared not imagine what.

At last the car slowed down—then stopped. It was now quite dark—and starless. Rachel opened her eyes—then instantly closed them again to shut out all the horror. For in that instant she had seen—and comprehended.

Before them stood a grim stone building, with lights in occasional windows. Above the entrance, on an illuminated sign, the letters stood out boldly:

SANTA X—HEBREW HOSPITAL

The end came swiftly. Rachel herself precipitated it by her convulsive outcry and her struggles as Jacob and the rabbi and the doctor seized her rudely and dragged her from the car. The Jewish house physician and an orderly advanced to meet them. The patient was violent, assuredly. No possible doubt of her condition. The testimony of the family and of the rabbi and the visiting physician was undisputed. Dr. Aaron, the house physician—and the rabbi's old-time friend—could discern the situation perfectly. Of course—of course. He had the evidence

170

himself—right there.

God is merciful—full of compassion and of tender mercies. Had He been otherwise, that one night of horror in the psychopathic ward of that Hebrew Hospital in California would have sealed Rachel Kalinsky's doom. Another hour of it even, and she would have been in fact what the Kalinskys and their companions-in-evil declared her—insane.

But even there in that house of worse than death, His hand was not shortened that it could not save, neither His ear heavy that it could not hear. He himself had promised: "Before they call, I will answer; and while they are yet speaking, I will hear." And long before Rachel, during that whole ghastly night implored His mercy, His ear had been bending toward His child. He knew all the way that she had taken as, off-guard, she had departed from the pathway of His will. And already before she was half-way across the continent, He had His angels of deliverance in waiting.

Far more rapidly than the overland express had carried its precious cargo westward, had the wires flashed to California the warning of Rachel's danger. Wise Mr. Nathan, after prayerful consultation with friends at the Peace Mission equally concerned for Rachel's safety, had immediately established telegraphic communication with Violet Hamilton who was then in San Francisco.

And Miss Hamilton, experienced as she was in the Jewish work, and skilled in her knowledge of the Jewish hate of Christ—and the desperate lengths to which this hate would go—knew how to act. Under Mr. Nathan's instructions, as he kept in close touch with her by wire, she acted swiftly and prudently and well.

She drew to her aid influential Hebrew-Christian friends throughout the Golden State—And these, by rapid, concerted action were able to notify the detective forces. Before ever Rachel arrived in California the Kalinsky home was located and all the movements of the family shadowed. During the week of Rachel's persecution, all unsuspected, watchful eyes were upon the dwelling, and protecting arms were near her. Her exit between her captors was watchfully observed, and the wildly driven car was closely followed all the way to Santa X—and to the Hospital. And within twelve hours of Rachel's fearful incarceration, she was released and borne away in safety.

At her own entreaty, no arrests were made. Even to secure her child she would not resort to legal measures. She preferred the longer but the more peaceful and God-honoring method of prayer. For her husband must not be irreparably estranged. Her Heavenly Father, too, must work His will in His own time and way.

Straight to Violet Hamilton's beautiful home they took her—among the pines, high on the flowered cliff above the breakers—at lovely Carmel-by-the-Sea. There, amid the charms of this picturesque setting, soothed by the distant booming of the ocean strengthened by renewed communion with her Lord, Rachel ere long recovered from that last terrible shock in the long history of her sorrows as a Hebrew believer in the Christ.

Under the fragrant pines she spent many hours of happy fellowship with her devoted Violet. Humbly and contritely she listened as her friend gently revealed to her the points at which the closeness of her walk with God had been allowed to lapse.

There had been at first, perhaps, all unconscious to herself, a measure of pride in the prominence that she had been given as a Hebrew-Christian. Then when the fatal letter had come she had failed to spread it, as Hezekiah had spread his letter of old, before the Lord. She sought not the counsel of the Lord, and failed to try the spirits, inwardly prompting her hasty action, whether or not they were of God. She did not trust in the Lord with all her heart, but leaned unto her own understanding. And then neglect of prayer, carelessness concerning her fellowship with Christ—all these had made Rachel an easy prey to Satan's wiles, always directed with malignant fury against any Jew who dares to become a follower of the Lord Jesus Christ.

In deepest penitence Rachel sought and received the Father's forgiveness, and again she knew the favor of His smile. Out of her grievous chastening a wiser and a fuller trust was born. And once again she realized the deep underneath peace, in all its blessedness and sweetness.

Rachel's disappointment in the results of her trip was keen, and her grief for Max and Little Abie was poignant; but the Father's consolations were infinitely tender. And with all His spiritual gifts to His trusting child at this time of renewal of her fellowship with Himself, none was more precious than the assurance—more firm than it had ever been before—which He gave to her, that one day the dearest treasures of her heart would be restored. It might perhaps be years, but the answer to her prayers was sure.

And so in September, when Miss Hamilton had to return to New York, Rachel, knowing that it was the Father's will, quietly went with her. It was hard to leave Max and Little Abie so far behind—hard to put the continent once more between them. But the vision was assured. One day her husband and her child would be His own—and Rachel's own. Meanwhile she could safely leave them in His all-wise and loving care.

She too was safe within the Father's keeping. Again placing her hand in His in perfect trust—with her faithful Violet beside her—she started back upon the eastward journey. Friends of Miss Hamilton were visited along the way; and Rachel also gave her testimony; the last wonderful day was spent together by the two close friends at Niagara Falls—their Best Friend vividly present with them in consciously realized joy and power. And then finally by the first of October, Rachel Kalinsky was back in the greatest Jewish center of the world—the Ghetto in the City of New York.

Chapter XII.

Eden Restored

"Weeping may endure for a night, but joy cometh in themorning." —Psalm 30:5.

Back again in New York City—a chastened Rachel! Back in her dear New York! But no longer in the magnificent building of the Peace Mission on the refined and quiet street uptown. No longer even in the comfortable Mission on Delancey Street. Rachel's abode now was one small room on the top floor of a wretched tenement in Rivington Street—the same tenement in which, in the basement, dwelt her good old friends, the Saramoffs.

For that was all that she could now afford. Independent as she had been always, Rachel was unwilling to accept further bounty from any of her friends, especially those in the Mission or the Peace Mission whose counsel in June concerning her California venture she had so willfully ignored.

Gladly would Mr. Nathan have found a place for her upon his staff, but with Miss Hamilton returned, his ranks of missionaries were full.

Salaried positions anywhere were hard to find. For never had New York City experienced an unemployment situation so acute. Bread lines extended for blocks; every mission and social agency in the city was taxed to the utmost limit of its relief resources. For days Rachel literally walked the streets in search of work. And all she could find, at last, was a menial position in a laundry on First Avenue. Here, at almost starvation wages, she must stand at an ironing board for eight hours every day.

On her return from California Rachel had once more accepted gratefully—for just a little while, until she could be financially independent—the Mission's generous and willing hospitality. But just as soon as she found work and saved a little bit ahead, she quietly sought quarters of her own.

One day when she was visiting the Saramoffs she noticed a sign outside the tenement: "Flat to let." At once she made enquiries. And because the one miserable little room on the top floor was within the compass of her slender purse, and especially because it was in the same building with dear old Mr. and Mrs. Saramoff and Little Jessie, she engaged it on the spot.

A couple of visits to second-hand furniture shops, a few hours with a scrubbing brush and her paints and stencils and her clever needle—and the poor little abode was ready for Rachel's lonely occupancy. A cot, a dresser, a small round table and four cheap chairs constituted at the start the sum total of her household goods.

But even here the stamp of Rachel's artistic individuality was impressed. The rugless floor was stained, the walls were tinted a soft rose, the furniture was soon transformed from battered ugliness to actual beauty; and the bareness of the room was relieved by inexpensive bright chintz hangings for her one small polished window, with a cover for her cot to match. The erstwhile rusty stove was also miraculously rejuvenated, and with its now gleaming metal and the glowing fire within, it gave to the humble dwelling at least a semblance of the atmosphere of home.

The fires would mean less food and scantier clothing for Rachel, and also the added strain of carrying the wood and coal herself up six steep flights of stairs. But fires Rachel had to have, not only for their necessary warmth in the otherwise unheated room, but especially for cheer and comfort to her lonely heart.

Above the stove Rachel hung a row of shining saucepans, and she adorned the dresser with half-a-dozen old blue plates and cups and saucers. And then, as her one extravagance, she bought for herself a small brass tea-kettle and one brass candlestick. These would be faintly reminiscent of the lovely heirloom brasses she had lost. The kettle would be singing on the stove to greet her after each day's work. The candle she placed within the window and lighted every night—for Max. This was his beacon, to guide his and Little Abie's footsteps home.

Such now was Rachel's life—the sordid laundry every day with its weary and oft-times painful hours; and then at night the tenement. But she was uncomplaining. Never a murmur passed her lips. For she had learned the blessed lesson of homing herself within the will of God. In the center of His will was perfect peace. Outward circumstances were temporal and transient only. They were but the scaffolding of the inner spiritual temple—that unseen building of God, the house not made with hands, eternal in the heavens. And realizing this, God's will to Rachel grew infinitely sweet.

It was the place of perfect rest—the King's chariot of the Song of Songs "with its pillars of silver, the bottom thereof of gold, the covering of it of purple, the midst thereof being paved with love." And when the weariness became too great and the heartache all too heavy, Rachel loved to repose within its mighty strength, and have it carry her and all her burden through the day. Safe ensphered within this fortress—the Father's will—His perfect wisdom united with His perfect love—straightforward she would go on His appointed pathway for her life, untouched by any danger, undisturbed by any storm. And from the chariot as onward she was borne, she would proclaim to the daughters of Jerusalem the glories of her King.

To them at every opportunity she gave His Word—within their homes, upon the street as she went to and from her work, among the other lodgers in the tenement, and especially among her fellow-workers in the laundry.

Each day at the noon hour she would gather around her a group of Jewish girls—girls whom first she had won to herself by little acts of kindness—and these she would tactfully and lovingly instruct out of the New Testament Scriptures, in those things concerning their Messiah.

Always on Sundays she visited the Mission. She would help Miss Hamilton with the children's meeting in the afternoon, and then at the evening Gospel service her witness for the Lord— whether in word or in song—would invariably be given. Seldom was there a Sunday when one Jew at least did not find, through Rachel's radiant testimony, his true Messiah.

She became greatly beloved by all her new associates, because love begets love, and she loved them. She loved the Jewish mothers, for she too was a Jewish mother. She loved the babies, for she had lost a little baby of her own; and she loved the children for the little child that her baby had by now become. She loved the dear old Jewish grandmothers, for the sake of dear old

Grandmother Kalinsky of still precious memory, and Mrs. Saramoff and her own sweet little grandmother in far-off Roumania. And the long-bearded, patriarchal grandfathers, too, she loved.

Yes, she loved them all—her dear, dear Jewish people. Love was the key in all her Christian testimony among them. For love alone is the key that will open Jewish hearts. Once opened, Rachel knew, the Gospel would gain welcome entrance.

Always when Rachel came home from work at night she would stop for a few moments in the basement to chat with the Saramoffs. Dear Mrs. Saramoff would usually have some little treat awaiting her—a plate of cakes, perhaps, or a bowl of steaming noodle soup. Not much could the elderly couple do by way of material gift for their "poor, dear little girl," but out of the abundance of their deep poverty they enriched her lonely heart by the abundance of their love.

They always tried to keep her for supper. Sometimes she would stay, but more often she preferred to be alone in her own quiet little room upstairs. She would carry up her hod of coal which she had left in the basement in the morning, and before she did anything else she would repair the fire and put the freshly filled kettle on to boil.

Then she must lie down and rest, for always she was so very, very tired and her feet and back were aching. Usually she would fall asleep—and wake to see the ruddy glow from the stove filling the room with soft, tranquil light, while the little kettle hummed and bubbled soothingly. Sometimes she would lie there for another hour in the rich warm glow, perfectly quiet as she held communion with her Lord.

Still in the spirit of prayer, she would get up and light Max's candle in the window. Then she would spread the table with a snowy cloth and arrange tastefully upon it the blue dishes from the dresser. And always she would set three places—one for herself, one for Max, and one for Little Abie. Before them she would draw up three chairs. And opposite her own place she invariably drew up the fourth chair—for the Heavenly Guest. Of His Presence she was always vividly, joyously conscious as she prepared and ate her all-too-frugal evening meal.

Supper ended, she would bring the candle to the table and in its light she would read from her beloved Bible—one that dear Violet had given her. It was worn almost to ribbons now, but each day it grew more precious to her. Over its pages while still she lingered at the table, she would have with her Lord the deepest fellowship of the entire day. This had been hers and Max's "cozy hour"—the hour after supper—in their beloved ingle-nook. Ah, how tenderly did she remember it! But now this quiet hour here was even yet more sweet, for it was her time alone with Him.

And then, nearly every evening, Rachel would hear coming down the hall the click-click-click of tiny crutches. Soon there would be the familiar rap at the door, and Rachel would open it upon the happy face of Little Jessie The crippled child was nearly fifteen now, but she seemed no more than ten, so very small she was and delicate. But within the fragile little body there was a heart that beat strong and true for Rachel and for Rachel's and her own Messiah. And tired though Rachel always was at night, she was never too tired to draw Little Jessie to her lap and read with her, by the candle light, their evening story from the Word.

Then Little Jessie gone downstairs again, Rachel would wash her dishes and set her tiny home in order, and arrange her clothing in readiness for her early departure in the morning.

The long day ended, before she slept Rachel would kneel beside her little window for her good-night prayer for Israel. She would look out over the sea of Ghetto roofs and intercede for all the Jewish people underneath them. For the million-and-three-quarters of Jews throughout the whole vast city, and then for Israel world-wide she entreated—that God would speedily send forth His Spirit upon them in reviving power.

Then last of all, before she extinguished Max's candle, she poured out her soul in fervent intercession for him and Little Abie. She prayed that the time of their homecoming might now be very soon. As she believed with all her heart that the time was growing short ere the coming of the King; and as she knew that Israel was to be His great Millennial witness to the nations; so did she plead that she and Max, united in their Christian faith and testimony, might yet have the joy of winning many Jewish souls before Messiah should appear.

The yearning of Rachel's heart for Max grew more and more intense, for the time of waiting seemed so long. One year—two years—three years—four. Slowly they wore away, each one longer than the last. It was seven years since her conversion—nine years nearly, since her marriage. And already she had drunk life's sorrows to the dregs. Already her hair, once as black as a raven's wing, now was thickly streaked with gray. The one-time happy, rosy face was white and thin and sad. And on tired days—and nearly all the days were tired now—the brave little shoulders drooped heavily. But the wonderful eyes were still the same—dark and luminous and soulful. Only there was in them now, unfathomable depths of suffering.

As Rachel went about the Ghetto streets, she frequently met old-time acquaintances and friends. But they never recognized her. Three or four times when she tried to speak with them she was rudely rebuffed. On several occasions children, who formerly had begged "Auntie Ray" to come and play with them, now threw missiles after her with jeers and curses. More than once a Jewish boy—instigated by his parents—spat in her face and hissed "Meshumed."

But she met these insults always in the same sweet spirit of forgiving love, and with a fervent prayer upon her heart for the conversion of these little sisters and brothers of her beloved Hebrew race.

Ever since Rachel's return from the West, the longing to see Esther, her old-time chum, had been intense. Esther and Ben had remained in New York after the other Kalinskys had gone to California; but now that the family were all away, Esther seldom came down town. And Rachel had always lacked either the opportunity or the courage to go up and visit her.

But seven years had elapsed since Rachel had seen her dearest friend, and the yearning for her had become unbearable. And so, one Saturday afternoon when Rachel had a half-holiday from the laundry, she journeyed northward to the Bronx and found her.

Ben was away—fortunately for Rachel. Had he been home her reception would have been vastly different. But Esther was lonely. She was also sad of heart that day and very tender, for her little child was ill. When, therefore, she opened the door and saw before her the girlhood friend whom she had never ceased to mourn, there was a sudden rush of tears and a sudden melting of the wall of ice which she herself had raised between them for seven lonely years.

Half shyly, but altogether joyously, Esther drew Rachel inside the door and in an instant the two dear friends were weeping in each other's arms. The long Winter of their sad estrangement was at an end; the joy in their reunion gushed forth like freshets in the Spring.

A happy hour followed—one of their dear old-time cozy hours in Esther's attractive kitchen. While the samovar bubbled and steamed between them, very gently each drew out the other's confidence. Rachel entered sympathetically, and without a tinge of envy, into Esther's joys and sorrows, as Esther told of her happiness in her pretty little home, but also of her present anxiety in the illness of her child and in Ben's business difficulties.

Then Esther, as the older friend, tactfully learned all about the laundry and the lonely tenement. And then with greatest tenderness—for she could clearly see that Rachel's wound was deep—she told her all she knew of Max and Little Abie from the frequent California letters. Both were well. Little Abie was seven now and was going to public school. The Kalinskys all were well and happy. They loved California and were going to stay there always. They wanted Ben and Esther to join them as soon as possible. The orange ranch had prospered beyond their most avaricious dreams. They were living—all of them—in luxury.

But on the one subject uppermost above every other in Rachel's heart—her faith in the Lord Jesus Christ—there was mutual reticence. Between Rachel and her dearest earthly friend, the Name of her Heavenly Friend was not once spoken. Wisely Rachel perceived that the time was inopportune. But she could wait quite patiently now. It was much that she had won back Esther to herself. That must be the first step always. In time—the assurance was strong in Rachel's heart—with continued believing prayer she would win her also for her Lord.

Warmly Esther invited Rachel to come back again. She could not come down town until Ben returned, and he would be away six weeks. But Rachel must come up—and very soon. And Rachel gladly promised.

But it was a full month before she was able to get up to the Bronx again. At last on a Jewish holiday, when the laundry was closed all day, she went.

When she arrived at Esther's house she noticed that the shades were down. Was the family away, she wondered? But no, the front door was ajar and a milk bottle stood outside. A stranger responded to her ring—an elderly Jewish woman with a shawl about her head, and with her apron at her streaming eyes. Silently she motioned Rachel to come in.

Rachel was conscious at once, as she stepped inside the doorway, of a tenseness in the atmosphere. There seemed to be a weird hush over everything—a surcharged electric silence.

And then suddenly and piercingly the silence was broken by the wailing intonation, from an inner room, of the *Kaddish*— the Hebrew prayer for the departed.

As Rachel, strangely bewildered, was pushed inside this room by the muttering old woman, she saw a sight that made her draw back startled. The shades were tightly drawn. Every ray of daylight was excluded, replaced only by seven dimly burning candles. Around the room on chairs and boxes were seated several Jewish neighbors—the shawl-hooded women rocking violently back and forth and sobbing; the men sitting silently upright with their fingers interlaced upon their knees. Some of them were sitting on the floor, commencing to wail the *Kaddish*.

At the farthest end of the room Rachel recognized Ben, crumpled in a chesterfield with his head buried in his arms, as brokenly he sobbed aloud. Esther sat on a footstool at his feet, gently trying to soothe and comfort him. But all her efforts were in vain.

Rachel slipped silently into a chair behind the door, and out of Ben and Esther's view. Ben, she was sure, would resent her intrusion bitterly. He was in terrible grief of some kind, very evidently—and the friends and neighbors had come to mourn with him. But whatever could it be, Rachel wondered? Whatever could have happened? And then suddenly, with a fearful shock, she heard. An old Jewish grandmother sitting next to her told her the paralyzing news.

Deborah Kalinsky was dead. A week ago a telegram had come from California. And just this morning Ben had received a letter with the details of the tragedy. It was written to him by his brother Max. Here it was—they were passing it around for everyone to read. Would she care to look at it?

Trembling at the news, Rachel trembled yet more violently at the sight of Max's handwriting. Concealing herself from observation as closely as was possible, quickly and tensely she scanned the pages of the letter.

Her mother-in-law had been killed by an auto crash. It was Rachel's own limousine that she was driving. And, as might have been expected, with her usual wild speed. And also—so Rachel was able to infer as she read between the lines—with her usual defiant disregard of traffic regulations. Red lights were always quite inconsequential to her if the coast looked clear and she chose to ignore their warning.

But this time the red lights had meant danger. Unsuspected by Mrs. Kalinsky, a large motor truck was rounding the sudden curve ahead. Too late Mrs. Kalinsky saw it. Instantly there came a terrific crash as truck and limousine met in head-on collision.

From underneath the wreckage of the expensive car they extricated her, mangled and bleeding. But life was not yet extinct and they bore her to the nearest hospital—with a shudder Rachel read the name—the Hebrew Hospital of Santa X—.

There, through a night of terrible agony, Deborah Kalinsky lingered. But with the dawning of the new day—a day of golden California sunshine—her spirit fled.

Rachel suddenly felt sick and stunned. She was shaken to the very foundations. She must get away at once—before Ben or Esther saw her. Quietly she slipped out the door, and walked the short distance to beautiful Bronx Park and sat weakly down upon a bench beside the lake. The whole fearful scene flashed vividly before her eyes—the angry blaze of the red lights—the sudden crash—the mangled form of Deborah Kalinsky. And then the hospital—The Hebrew Hospital of Santa X—!

For a full hour Rachel experienced a raging tumult of emotion within her breast. But at last, beside the quiet lake, her spirit gradually became soothed, as she held communion with her Lord and prayed the whole thing through. When finally she started home her heart was entirely at peace. She could thank God in all sincerity that it held no bitterness—no hatred. Rather there was entire forgiveness of the one person on earth who, above all others, had been her cruel enemy. Nay more, Rachel felt toward Deborah Kalinsky even the compassionate love of Christ.

For in the peaceful quiet of the Park, God had revealed her mother-in-law to her in an entirely new light. No longer did she appear as an agency of Satanic opposition against a Hebrew believer in the Lord Jesus Christ, but she was the instrument of Rachel's chastening in the Father's hand. All that she had practised of cruelty and vicious malice toward her had been over-ruled of God and directed by Him to the refining of the gold in Rachel's character and faith. Like Joseph of his brothers, Rachel could truly say of Deborah Kalinsky; she thought evil against her; but God meant it unto good.

Then too, Rachel must never forget—she owed her much. Deborah Kalinsky had been her mother's life-long, dearest friend. Faithfully she had ministered to her in her darkest hour. Faithfully, too, she had befriended Rachel as her mother's orphaned child, and had given her a home.

And—above everything else—to this woman Rachel owed her husband. She was Max's mother. And Max had loved her devotedly and so had she loved him. Her love had been thoroughly selfish and unwise, it was quite true; but nevertheless Deborah Kalinsky had loved her son, and for his sake Rachel must love her.

But her soul! What of Deborah Kalinsky's soul? Rachel shuddered. But there, too, God gave peace. Who could tell what dealings He might not have had with her during those last terrible moments of her life? In the eleventh hour the dying thief upon the cross beheld the Christ, and confessing Him was granted full forgiveness, and a joyous entrance into Paradise. Who dared say that it might not be the same with Deborah Kalinsky?

One thing at least Rachel knew, and in this she rejoiced with deep thanksgiving. She had unfailingly borne to her mother-in-law a true witness for her Lord, even at such fearful consequences to herself. Faithfully she had given her God's Word. And she had His own promise: My Word shall not return unto me void.

Yes, Rachel could quite peacefully entrust the immortal destiny of Deborah Kalinsky to her Creator. Her soul was in the loving hands of Him Who gave it. Rachel's concern now was for the souls of the Kalinskys who yet were living.

Of Max's and Esther's salvation she now had full hope. God had given her entire faith to claim them both. If Max and Esther could be won, it would be an easy matter to win Ben. For they three—Max and Esther and herself—would unite their hearts in intercession for him, not to be denied.

And then the others—what of them? Otto? Goldie? Joseph? Rose? The children? Yes, she even dared to hope for all of them. With each new convert added to their Christian ranks, the praying force would be to that degree augmented, and the opposition weakened to the same degree.

But Jacob? Sarah? Had she faith enough for these? And then she reflected: Is anything too hard for the Lord? And trustfully her heart responded: With God nothing shall be impossible. Even Jacob. Even Sarah. Yes, she dared to believe even for Rabbi Mordecai Moses.

Twilight was falling as Rachel reached her home. She was thinking now of Max. Ah, her precious Max! Her own beloved husband! A sudden thrill of joy filled Rachel's heart, All things work together for good to them that love God. This was one of the all things. His mother's death would work for Max's highest good; with Deborah Kalinsky gone, there now would be new life and hope for her idolized youngest son. For at last the cords that had fettered him so long were broken.

Those silken shackles of jealous and unwise maternal love which all his life had held his spirit bound were now released, and at last the true Max Kalinsky—the manly, upright, noble Max Kalinsky that Rachel knew her husband to be, beneath the exterior of selfishness and dominated, flabby will—would now emerge in all his essential fineness.

And it would be under Rachel's influence. She would have *her* chance with him at last. Two golden keys to Max's heart she held—the keys of love and prayer. These must inevitably win. Max Kalinsky's life would grow strong for God and man.

The summer dragged heavily. The days were hot and sultry.

Rachel's courage and endurance were tested to the utmost. The laundry work became more and more difficult. The hours were lengthened, while at the same time wages were decreased. That meant for Rachel insufficient food. Her slender strength grew less and less in consequence. There were frequent days of illness. But still she never murmured. It was all within the Father's will.

Each day she looked longingly for a California letter. Max would surely write her now. But no letter came. She wrote to him—a letter full of tender sympathy and love and longing. But there was no reply.

But still Rachel kept unfaltering on, sustained by His unfailing, all-sufficient grace—with faith undaunted that Max would even yet be won.

At last the summer days were ended, and the nights were cool once more. Once more the stove was lighted every morning. And every evening without fail—Max's candle was lighted in the little window.

Again it was October, and the season of the Jewish holidays. *Rosh Hashanah* came—the Jewish New Year—and with it the procession to the River. The streets were thronged with Jews—men, women, children, babies, grandmothers, grandfathers, rabbis and even an occasional *Rav*—all were marching on the sidewalks and through the middle of the streets; and every one except the babies and the very tiniest children was carrying a Hebrew Prayer Book. And all were going in the one direction—to the embankment, or to the Williamsburg Bridge which spans the East River connecting Brooklyn with Manhattan. On the Bridge, high above the water—hundreds of feet aloft—there was a solid black line of Jews. Thousands and ten-thousands of them, and every one doing the same thing. With their Hebrew Prayer Book open before them, the Jewish multitudes there, like the multitudes along the River's bank, were reciting the *Rosh Hashanah* prayer; and as they did so they emptied out all their pockets, scattering into the dark waters below—*their sins*. Then, the ceremony performed, gravely they wended their way westward and homeward, complacently self-satisfied that they now were wholly righteous.

Following *Rosh Hashanah* the intervening seven days passed, and at last it was once more the eve of the great *Yom Kippur.*

As Rachel came home late in the afternoon from her laundry, the streets again were thronged with Jews, in anticipation of the day of penitential prayer and fasting on the morrow.

It had poured all day, and though the rain had stopped, it still was damp and dismal. Rachel's coat was thin and her shoes were sadly worn, and the dampness penetrated keenly. When she reached the tenement, without stopping to-night to see the Saramoffs for she was too tired, she climbed once more the long, steep flights of stairs, dragging the heavy hod of coal behind her. She was chilled to the very heart and almost fainting with fatigue.

At last she reached the top, quite breathless. She entered her little room and locked the door, then dropped upon her couch exhausted. A paroxysm of coughing seized her and then a fit of uncontrollable sobbing. She ached in every nerve. Her head was hot and burning, but at the same time she was trembling violently with a chill. Was she going to be sick, she wondered? Oh, but she *must* not be! She could not afford it. She could not miss even one day of work. Her rent was due next week. And certainly she had no money for a doctor.

For a moment a sense of terror seized her. Oh, when was this ever going to end? How could she still keep on? How long would her slender strength hold out? And when it failed, what then? Was she going to die, forsaken and alone, here in this wretched tenement? And Max and Little Abie! Had her faith for them been all in vain? The poor, distracted child cried miserably, as she crept for warmth and comfort underneath the blankets.

He giveth His beloved sleep. Within five minutes Rachel was enfolded in deep and sweet oblivion. When she awoke an hour later she was much refreshed. The pain was eased and there was a sense of delicious warmth and peace. She still felt ill—too ill, she feared, to go tomorrow to the laundry—which would operate as usual on the great *Yom Kippur*, because the Gentile management would not recognize the Jewish holiday. Yes, she was much too ill to work tomorrow. And that was serious, for funds and food were dangerously low. And yet despite it all, her heart was filled with peace.

For He giveth His beloved sleep. And during sleep He gave to

186

His dear child full restoration of spirit. Everything to Rachel now was quite all right. If, really, she were going to be sick, it did not matter. Nothing mattered save the Father's will. If she could no longer work, why then by some means otherwise, the Father would provide.

If it should be His will even to take Rachel Home unto Himself—ah! that would be joy unspeakable and full of glory. Perhaps it might be only by her dying that Max and Little Abie could be brought to Christ. If so, then gladly would she lay down a thousand lives. While she was absent from them in the Better Land, quite safely she could entrust her loved ones to the Heavenly Father's care.

The deep underneath peace once more enfolded Rachel. And with the spiritual peace there was entire physical repose and relaxation. She lay quite still for almost another hour, yielding herself completely to its delicious, soothing influence. The room was now quite dark save for the ruddy firelight and the reflection from the lights outside. It had commenced to rain once more and the drops were pattering softly on the window. Peace—perfect peace—and wondrous heavenly joy—was flooding Rachel's being.

Feeling deeply strengthened, she soon got up. No, she was not going to die—not yet. God still had work for her to do on earth. And as long as she lived He still would be her unfailing portion. As her days, so would her strength be. So, too, would be His all-sufficient grace.

She mended the fire and filled the brass kettle for her tea. Then she lighted Max's candle. And then she prepared her meagre supper—ah, all too meagre now! But pitiful though it was, still Rachel spread the snowy cloth and still she set the three places with the blue dishes from the dresser, and drew up the three chairs—with the fourth, as always, for the Heavenly Guest.

Soon the little kettle was bubbling and the roast was delicately browned, when down the hall there sounded the click-click of Little Jessie's crutches. But tonight even dear Little Jessie was not welcome. Rachel yearned to be quite alone—alone with Him. Each moment of this peaceful, restful evening she was treasuring so jealously. So, although the child knocked insistently, Rachel remained absolutely noiseless—until Little Jessie, disappointed that Rachel must have gone outdoors again, went clicking off downstairs.

As Rachel ate her supper, that wonderful sense of peace which it seemed she had never realized as vividly as tonight, deepened into infinitely tender sweetness. The Heavenly Guest was very near and very real. His Presence seemed visible and tangible. The humble room became suffused with glory.

Her supper finished, once again Rachel drew forth her precious Bible, and together with Him she tarried over it in closest fellowship. The promise stood out to-night with more convincing power than she had ever experienced before: "I will never leave thee, nor forsake thee. . . Come unto me, all ye that labour and are heavy laden, and I will give you rest. . . And God shall wipe away all tears from their eyes."

And for Max, as *never* before, the promises fairly flamed from the page, blazoned in richest gold: "I have seen his ways, and will heal him. . . Out of weakness were made strong. . . Hath He not promised, and shall He not perform? . . . Ask, and it shall be given you. . . According to your faith be it unto you."

She went to the window and trimmed Max's candle—until it burned with glowing, steady light. Could his life soon glow for Christ? Of this she had no doubt whatever. God had promised. And He would perform.

And something—some thrilling joy within her heart—told her the waiting would not now be long. As Rachel knelt at the window she gazed once more upon the Ghetto housetops praying for her beloved Israel beneath them. Ah! the time was surely near when she and Max, joined together in their love for one another and for Christ, would be led out by His Spirit for extensive witness to their people.

And Little Abie also! As he grew up they would prayerfully nurture him in the Christian faith and life, as they prepared him for the Christian ministry. And then together—should the Messiah longer tarry—their little trinity, united in perfect oneness with the divine Trinity of Father, Son and Holy Spirit, would go forth among Israel to do mighty battle for the King of kings.

From the little window, in the distance, Rachel could see the great Metropolitan light—fraught with so many precious memories of her Eden in East Second Street. Towering above all other lights it shone with luminous, far-reaching power. Within the circle of its rays, tens of thousands of Hebrew souls were dwelling. As the great light, high and lifted up, was a beacon to their physical eyes, so Rachel prayed that the Light of Life would become the Heavenly Beacon unto Israel in its spiritual blindness.

Through their three devoted, consecrated lives might He shine forth to their dear Jewish people, first, in New York City—America's Jerusalem—and then to still other Jews beyond—withersoever the Spirit willed to lead them. To Roumania, might it be—the beloved land of Rachel's birth? To Russia—among whose vast hordes of Jews her own and Max's forbears had been numbered? To Poland possibly? Or even Palestine—the divinely promised Homeland of the Jew? Ah, well! it mattered not. It was all one field—vast and world-wide. The sheep of Israel's fold were found upon a thousand hills. God knew where He would have His servants witness. Step by step, as He had led them to this hour, so would He lead them forward all the journey through. This Jehovah was their Jehovah, for ever and ever: He would be their Guide even unto death.

Rachel heard footsteps coming toward her door. Was it Little Jessie back again? But no, it was a firmer tread. She listened. . . . then she *knew*.

Very quietly she smiled. And then she left him standing there—knocking . . . knocking . . . while for a moment, Spirit-filled, she paused and lifted up her heart in thanksgiving and adoring praise to God. And then—she flung the door wide open.

He stood there, broken and contrite, with Little Abie—*Big* Abie now, the "big, big boy"—fast asleep within his arms, quite tired out, poor little laddie, after the long, long day of searching for his mother through the Ghetto of New York.

Silently, tenderly, Rachel drew them both inside. And then she closed the door. Still without a word save those fathomless words Max read within her eyes—she took Little Abie from his father's arms and clasped him in one long and convulsive embrace to her hungry heart.

Then, while Max sank upon a chair beside the stove and buried his face in his hands with bitter, penitential weeping, she carried Little Abie to her cot, and gently laid him down, tucking him tenderly within her blankets as she gave him a mother's good-night kiss for the first time in six, long, lonely years.

And then—she turned to Max. . . .

Love suffereth long and is kind . . . beareth all things, believeth all things, hopeth all things, endureth all things. . . . Love never faileth.

Nor did Rachel's love for Max fail now when, sobbing in heartbroken shame and sorrow, with utter self-abasement he made confession of his sins—of all his contemptible cowardice and selfishness and greed; of his awful cruelty to Rachel and their little son; and of his base disloyalty to Christ—in Whom as a child he had believed, but Whom he had never manfully acknowledged as his own Messiah.

Cringing fear—fear of the consequences of confession; unwillingness to pay the price demanded of every Jewish believer in Jesus Christ—these had occasioned Max Kalinsky's downfall. And back of them all had been his lust for gold. For filthy lucre he had almost lost his soul.

But now all the wealth of gold that he had gathered—all was poured out in fulness of surrender at the Master's feet. His wealth and his life alike—together with Rachel's life now were wholly consecrated to the King—for whatsoever service He desired—among his own beloved Jewish people.

Of his mother, Max said little. His loyalty to her was very manly, very fine—and his filial grief was deep. But Rachel's quick perception sensed aright that Max realized now how baleful, by reason of her dominating will, his mother's influence over him had been. As a devoted Jewish son he would never cease to mourn her; but at the same time he gloried in the new-found freedom of his manhood.

Gently, patiently, tenderly, Rachel listened to it all—the whole heartbroken story of his wasted years—and as she listened, she forgave. Soothing him in his deep remorse and grief, even as she would have soothed their little child. And doing so, her heart had perfect peace. For in her husband she had faith and hope and love. And the greatest of these is—LOVE.

The red coals in the stove cast a warm glow over the humble room and over the face of the sleeping child, and over the two radiant faces at the little supper table. The brass tea-kettle was bubbling and singing joyously in welcome. The toast was a delicious brown. Peace was flowing like a river—the deep underneath peace—the peace of God that passeth all understanding.

In the window Max's candle had burned down to its socket. Only a feeble, fluttering flame remained. But the candle light was no longer needed now. Henceforth Max Kalinsky's footsteps would be guided by the Light of Life. For the wanderer had at last come home—home to Rachel—and home to his Messiah.

THE END.

Read these other inspirational, character-building books:

The Bishop's Shadow
– the story of a street boy and his beloved Bishop.

Theo, The Big Brother
– a sequel to "The Bishop's Shadow" continuing the story of Theodore Bryan.

A Charge to Keep
– the story of a lad who trusted God when misunderstood and falsely accused.

Available from:
Joyce E. Nolt
1593 Lancaster Rd.
Manheim, PA 17545